THE DANGERS OF SLEUTHING

A *bing* drew Hope's attention from her notebook to her phone.

A message appeared from an unknown number.

Leave the past in the past or you'll have no future.

Hope dropped her pen and grabbed her phone. Her heart raced. She stared at the message. She shot up from her chair and rushed to the windows that overlooked her property.

All she saw was a dark and snowy night.

Was the person out there watching her house? A lump caught in her throat. She tapped on the app for her smart doorbell. The video included with the doorbell gave her a fairly good view in the front of her house and at the back of her house, where the second doorbell was located. She didn't see anyone in the area.

Irritated by the anonymous threats and by feeling like a victim, she took the bold, but probably not smart move and texted back.

Who is this?

She waited for a reply.

Someone who is giving you one more chance. Choose wisely . . .

Books by Debra Sennefelder

Food Blogger Mysteries
THE UNINVITED CORPSE
THE HIDDEN CORPSE
THREE WIDOWS AND A CORPSE
THE CORPSE WHO KNEW TOO MUCH

Resale Boutique Mysteries
MURDER WEARS A LITTLE BLACK DRESS
SILENCED IN SEQUINS
WHAT NOT TO WEAR TO A GRAVEYARD

Published by Kensington Publishing Corporation

The Corpse Who Knew Too Much

Debra Sennefelder

KENSINGTON BOOKS
www.kensingtonbooks.com

KENSINGTON BOOKS are published by

Kensington Publishing Corp.
119 West 40th Street
New York, NY 10018

All Kensington titles, imprints, and distributed lines are available at special quantity discounts for bulk purchases for sales promotion, premiums, fund-raising, and educational or institutional use.

Special book excerpts or customized printings can also be created to fit specific needs. For details, write or phone the office of the Kensington Sales Manager: Kensington Publishing Corp., 119 West 40th Street, New York, NY 10018. Attn. Sales Department. Phone: 1-800-221-2647.

Kensington and the K logo Reg. U.S. Pat. & TM Off.

First Kensington Books Mass Market Paperback Printing: October 2020
ISBN-13: 978-1-4967-2891-3
ISBN-10: 1-4967-2891-2

ISBN-13: 978-1-4967-2892-0 (ebook)
ISBN-10: 1-4967-2892-0 (ebook)

10 9 8 7 6 5 4 3 2 1

Printed in the United States of America

This book is dedicated to my sisters,
Alice and Cathy

Chapter One

Hope Early pulled the mudroom door closed behind her before the bitter cold air infiltrated her home. Fighting against the harsh wind, she juggled a container of cookies in her other hand and braced herself for the short dash to Oliver Marchant's plow truck. The truck rumbled onto her property fifteen minutes earlier. Its mission was to clear the newly fallen six inches of snow. Thanks to the storm cycle the Northeast was caught up in, Oliver was a regular visitor.

The season began with light snow showers that quickly turned into angry snow events, pounding Connecticut day after day. Well, at least it felt that way. Last night's storm was just another hit to the region, and to her checking account.

The clang of the plow dropping to the paved driveway

jolted Hope, and she winced at the loud noise. She prayed the sharp edge of the plow wasn't damaging the newly paved driveway. Replacing the gravel with a paved surface wasn't an inexpensive project. In fact, not much involving the old farmhouse was cheap. She exhaled a chilled breath and carefully maneuvered toward Oliver's truck. By the time she reached the driveway, he'd put his vehicle in reverse and was backing up so he could position the truck to push another stretch of snow off to the side.

Hope made her way to the driver's side of the truck and lifted the reusable container to the window. She'd baked a batch of Double Chocolate Oatmeal cookies. The name was a mouthful. When she was developing the recipe, it felt like she'd added in everything but the kitchen sink. Lesson learned: don't create recipes when hungry. Her standard practice was to make the recipe three times before she published it on her blog, and that morning was her fourth time making the cookie. Yes, she loved it that much. So after she finished the morning chores, which included feeding her flock of chickens, her energetic dog, and her diva of a cat, she pulled out the ingredients and began mixing. By the time the first baking sheet of cookies had come out of the oven, she was starving. She'd been so busy, she hadn't made breakfast. Again, another lesson learned: don't bake on an empty stomach. With all the cookies cooling on a rack, she'd helped herself to three cookies after pouring a large cup of coffee. Not exactly the breakfast of champions, but for a food blogger short on time it was the perfect meal.

Oliver shifted the truck into Park and rolled down the window. The sound of a woman's voice caught Hope's attention, surprising her because he was alone in the truck.

"That's all we have time for today. Be sure to check out the show notes for more information. Join me next week as we continue the *Search for the Missing*."

Oliver fumbled with his phone and the voice disappeared.

"Sorry about that. Listening to podcasts helps the time go by. There's only so many times I can listen to the weather forecast on the radio. What do you have there?" His face was lit up with anticipation as he eyed the container.

"Double Chocolate Oatmeal cookies. Fresh out of the oven this morning. I thought you could use a little treat." She handed him the container.

"Wow. They sound delicious. Thanks, Hope. I didn't have time for breakfast this morning. Just squeezed in a few minutes to make coffee." He pointed to the thermos on the passenger seat. His deeply creased face looked haggard, and his dull eyes were bloodshot and ringed with dark circles. He must have been plowing all night.

"I can't imagine how exhausted you are with storm after storm."

Oliver nodded after he set the container next to the thermos.

"I'd like more than a power nap. But I can't complain. All of this snow is good for business, you know?" He removed his denim baseball cap and ran his thick fingers through his gray hair. He'd been snowplowing for as long as Hope could remember and had seen countless nor'easters and blizzards.

"I get it." The endless hours of plowing were a bonus to Oliver's bottom line, while it was a loss to Hope's. But, what choice did she have? The snow needed to be cleared.

"I hope you enjoy the cookies." She stepped back from the beat-up old truck.

"When I'm done plowing, I'll shovel all the walkways. Thanks again for the cookies." Oliver slipped his cap back on and rolled up his window. He shifted into drive and got back to work.

"Good morning, Hope!"

She looked toward the end of her driveway where Gilbert Madison stood with his golden retriever. Gilbert dropped the hand he'd been waving to Buddy's head.

She pressed her lips together. She was torn between giving a pleasant wave and returning to the warmth of her home or walking to the road to be neighborly. Buddy tugged on his leash and whined, and Hope's heart melted. Going back into her cozy home would have to wait. She walked along the cleared section of the driveway toward her neighbor and his best friend.

"Isn't it ever too cold or snowy for you two?" Hope stroked Buddy's head. His brown eyes widened as he lapped up the attention.

"Nope." Gilbert's blue eyes gleamed. He was like the mail carrier, venturing out every morning like clockwork regardless of the weather. That morning he was dressed for the inclement weather in a heavy coat, earmuffs, and gloves. Buddy was also dressed appropriately for the bitter cold in a plaid coat that was coordinated with his beautiful golden hair with reddish highlights. Hope glanced at her dependable barn jacket and frowned. Its dull green color did nothing for her dark brown hair, which she'd gathered up in a messy ponytail. It was official; the dog was dressed better than her.

"I didn't think so." She pulled her hand away from

Buddy's head and shoved it into her jacket's pocket. "Are you going or coming back?"

"Coming back. We've done our three miles," Gilbert said proudly.

"Are you kidding me? Three miles in this weather?" Hope admired Gilbert's dedication to daily exercise, but it was barely ten degrees, with wind gusts making it feel like five below. A darn good reason to sit the morning walk out. Or, in her case, bake a batch of cookies and eat them for breakfast. On second thought, maybe doing some exercise wasn't a bad idea.

"We can rest when we're dead." Gilbert chuckled.

"You can rest now. It's not only too cold, but it can be dangerous walking with the icy patches and the town snowplows."

"No worries. I have a reflective patch on the back of my collar. And we walk slow."

Gilbert looked at his faithful companion and patted the dog on his side. "Though I think Mitzi agrees with you. She tried to get us to stay in this morning. She baked your French Toast Casserole. I told her she could warm it up when I got home." He winked.

Hope imagined the response from his wife of over forty years. Mitzi had a refined exterior but, on the inside, she was a spitfire. Yeah, maybe heading out for a long walk after the suggestion was a smart move for Gilbert.

"How's she doing? I haven't seen her in a few days."

The Madisons lived across the street and a few houses down from Hope. In the warm weather months, Mitzi spent her days outside tending to her gardens. From sunrise to sunset, she kept herself busy weeding, planting, and pruning. She had a large rhododendron plant she babied and rosebushes she nurtured. Hope wished she could give as much time and care to her own gardens as Mitzi gave to hers.

"She's taking Donna Wilcox's calligraphy class at the library. She's also planning the vegetable garden and trying to figure out how to expand the rose garden. Guess I'll have plenty to do in the spring."

"Sounds ambitious, like always." Hope's toes tingled. She needed to get going inside, otherwise frostbite was inevitable. She was certain of it. Apparently, her thick socks weren't thick enough for socializing in artic weather. She glanced at Buddy; he didn't look the least bit uncomfortable.

"I remind her she's retired now and doesn't have to work so much, but she doesn't want to hear any of it. You know how she feels about idle hands. Anyway, she's disappointed she didn't have enough free time to take your blogging class. I was thinking she could start a gardening blog."

"I'm bummed too about it." *And on the verge of losing feeling in my lower extremities.* "It would have been nice to have her in my class. Well, if she decides to pursue a garden blog, tell her to let me know." Hope attempted to turn toward her house, to make her getaway.

"Will do. You know, she mentioned last night she'd love to take a podcasting class. Do you have a podcast?"

"No. I don't." So much for her getaway. Now her interest was piqued. "Mitzi's into podcasts?"

"Oh, yeah. Especially true crime podcasts. She discovered a new one a few weeks ago. Let me see if I can remember its name. *Search . . .*"

"*Search for the Missing*?"

"Yeah, that's it. You listen to it too?"

"No. I just heard about it from Oliver."

"The host talks about cases of missing women. Mitzi is on the second season right now. She tells me it's called binge listening. What do I know?" He shrugged.

"I'll have to check it out." Though, over the past year, Hope had been involved in more than one true crime case in Jefferson. Hopefully, her unlucky streak was over, and the only connection she'd have going forward to any crime in town would be through her boyfriend, the chief of police.

"She can't get enough of it. I'd better get going and enjoy some of that French Toast Casserole. Have a good day, Hope." Gilbert tugged on Buddy's leash, and they walked away, crossing the road.

"You too," she called out before turning and hurrying back inside her house before she lost feeling in her whole body. She was interested in the podcast Gilbert mentioned despite having enough real crime to last her a lifetime, but she didn't have any spare time to search for it on her phone. She was dangerously close to running late for her meeting with Angela. And she hated being late. The podcast would have to wait.

At least for now.

Standing at the library's circulation desk, Hope snapped shut her trusty six-ring planner. There was no more satisfying sound than the closing of her beloved leather-bound book, knowing she was on top of all her to-dos. With her growing blog, increased freelance work, and home renovations, the planner was a lifesaver. Her latest and biggest actionable item on her list was the Blogging 101 class at the Jefferson Library.

During the meeting, Angela Green approved the curriculum and shared that she had to turn away people. She urged Hope to consider another session in the fall.

The excitement on Angela's face made it difficult for Hope to decline outright, so she said she'd think about teaching another class. While she would have loved to say yes, there were several projects coming up for her blog that were priorities.

"I hope I live up to all this buzz around the class." Hope slipped her planner into her tote bag and then pulled out her gloves.

"Don't be silly. You'll be great." Angela closed her leather portfolio and smiled. Her smile was reassuring to Hope, but she still had doubts.

"Those were one-hour presentations on specific topics. This is a full class on everything that goes into starting a blog."

So much had changed since she launched *Hope at Home*. Back then, when Hope published her first post, there wasn't the pressure of having everything perfect. She hadn't had a plan in place to build a following. Over the years, her favorite topic to teach was search engine optimization, SEO for short, because it was one of the most critical tools in her blogger toolbox. With over thirty million blogs on the web, the chances of a newbie getting noticed were low. She had to be careful how she shared that daunting statistic with her students. She didn't want to discourage them right out of the gate. She also wanted to make sure they were prepared for the work involved. Looking back, she was lucky, because she had the leisure of learning over time. New bloggers now didn't have that grace period.

Her belly quivered, and she tamped down her silly

nerves. She'd talked to a room of over a hundred bloggers, she'd given presentations to her publisher when she was a magazine editor, and she'd appeared on a national baking competition show. Surely she could handle a small class of wanna-be bloggers.

"I want to make sure everyone leaves with the ability to create their own blog."

"They will. You've laid out all the information in a clear, concise, logical manner. I'll have the Bishop room set up, along with the cables you'll need for your laptop."

"Good morning." Sally Merrifield approached the circulation desk with enthusiasm. She was bundled up in a dark-blue puffer coat and chunky white hat. The walk from her family's inn down the street left the tip of her turned-up nose and cheeks bright red.

"Is it still frigid out there?" Hope asked.

"It's not bad. Believe me, it's been colder." Sally removed her hat, revealing her cropped, salt-and-pepper hair, and shoved it into her plain black purse. She was from sturdy New Englander stock and boasted she'd never missed a day's work because of inclement weather and, now retired from her head librarian position, she wouldn't let a dip in the temperature keep her from her day of volunteering.

"How's the blogging class coming along?" Sally unzipped her coat, giving Hope a glimpse of the Fair Isle sweater she wore. It looked warm.

"We've just reviewed Hope's curriculum. It's fantastic." Angela stepped out from behind the circulation desk. She had on a tartan plaid blazer over a gray crew-neck sweater and dark trousers. The old library's heating and cooling system was fickle, so dressing in layers was a smart thing to do.

"I hope it doesn't end like the panel discussion last summer about blogging. Don't get me wrong, Hope, you were wonderful, and so were your blogger friends, but it ended like a circus. Norrie Jennings got the whole audience riled up about the murder, and then the news broke about an arrest. I knew I was right about it not being a good time for such an event." Sally shrugged out of her coat and draped it over her arm.

"I'm sure there won't be any problem with the class." Angela gave a firm nod.

"Guess we must wait and see. I better hang up my coat and get to work." Sally rapped her knuckles on the countertop and returned Angela's nod before stepping back. She turned and headed to the corridor that led to private offices and a break room for the library staff.

Hope watched Sally disappear before she glanced at Angela, who looked like she was suppressing a laugh. It was vital for her to maintain control as the head librarian, but Hope also knew Angela wanted to be respectful of Sally's long service to the library and the town.

"Oh, I almost forgot. I wanted to give you the list of students." Angela reached over the counter for her portfolio and removed a sheet of paper.

Hope scanned the list of students. Gail Graves. Laila Miller. They'd both gone to high school with Hope and her sister. Shirley Phelan. She was retired and volunteered at the senior center. The rest of the list contained familiar names and some not-so familiar. But there was one prominent name missing, and it surprised Hope.

"Elaine didn't sign up for the class?" Hope would have bet her brand-spanking-new, five-quart Le Creuset braiser the widow would have signed up for the class.

Last summer, Elaine had announced her intention to start a fashion blog because she needed a job, and since then, she'd barraged Hope with countless questions on the topic. However, she hadn't started the blog. Hope would be lying if she said she wasn't relieved by Elaine's procrastination.

Angela shook her head. "You don't know? She's in Bali. I heard she said she needed a break from all this snow." Angela's gaze drifted toward the front entrance of the library. Just outside were inches upon inches of snow being swirled up by gusty winds. "Her and me both."

"Tell me about it. Bali? I'm so jealous."

"The average temperature this time of year is eighty-one degrees."

"What a cruel fact to share." Hope laughed.

"Sorry. I can't help myself." Angela let out a delicate giggle as she returned to the other side of the circulation desk.

"Thanks for the student list." Hope folded the paper and placed it into her tote bag, then pulled on her gloves. "I need to get going. I promised Claire I'd stop by the shop before heading home."

Hope's sister, Claire Dixon, had opened Staged with Style in November, when she made an abrupt career change from real estate agent to home stager. Well, it seemed sudden to Hope. Unbeknownst to her, Claire had been toying with the idea for some time and even had a storage unit filled with home accessories she used to stage the homes she was selling. Everyone always complimented her excellent taste, so it made sense she was interested in pursuing staging full-time.

"How is the shop doing?"

"Business is a little slow. I'm sure once the weather gets nicer, it will pick up. Though she's been booked consistently for home staging. Maybe she can do a workshop."

Angela's eyes widened. "What a wonderful idea. Spring would be a perfect time. That's when most people get ready to put their homes on the market."

"I'll have her call you." Hope slung her tote over her shoulder and made her way to the lobby of the library and prepared herself for stepping outside. She found herself longing for warm spring days and short-sleeved shirts.

As Hope headed for the exit, she spotted Norrie Jennings approaching from the genealogy room. There was a short list of people Hope preferred not to run into at any time. Top on the list was her ex-husband, Tim Ward. Next was the overeager local reporter. She picked up her pace to make a quick getaway.

"Hope. Wait up."

Hope grimaced as she halted. *So close.* With no other choice, she turned to face the reporter. Barely out of her twenties, Norrie was fresh-faced, with a pixie cut and wide eyes. She looked more like a high school student than the ambitious journalist she was.

"Good morning, Norrie. I just finished up a meeting about a blogging class I'm teaching here."

"Interesting. Is it like a how-to class?" A hint of interest flashed in Norrie's amber eyes and disappeared as quickly. "Whatever it is, I'm sure Drew will be happy to cover it. I'm busy with another story." She leaned in. "I'm sure it will be another front-page byline for me."

Before Christmas, Norrie broke a story about an embezzlement scheme at the local branch of Emerson Bank. It not only got her several front-page articles in the *Gazette*, but they were also picked up by the wire service, garnering her national attention.

The only reason Hope knew all the details was because her best friend, Drew Adams, had drowned his sorrows over a plate of cookies—gingerbread and sugar. By the time he left her house, he was complaining he'd have to spend hours in the gym to work off all the calories he consumed during his pity party. He'd rebounded the next day and pitched an article on Donna and her calligraphy cottage industry. The article was a success. It was about a woman pursuing her passion later in life and it was about a Jefferson resident. After the article was published, Hope shared with her best friend that she believed it was one of his best works.

"Good luck with your new story." Hope turned toward the exit.

"It's not new. In fact, it's twenty years old. You were born and raised here, so you must know of the Joyce Markham cold case."

Even though she was inside the warm library, a chill wiggled through Hope at the memory. She spun back around to face Norrie.

"When I applied to the *Gazette*, I was concerned about writing for a small-town newspaper because, well, not much happens in small towns. I was wrong. The murders and scandals that have occurred here rival those in any big city. And who knew Jefferson had a twenty-year-old missing persons cold case?" Norrie's grin summed up how thrilled she was to use Joyce's unsolved disappearance as another career steppingstone.

Hope recalled the unusually warm Valentine's Day when word spread around dinnertime that Joyce was missing.

"It shocked us all. Her husband and daughters left home

in the morning, and when the girls returned home from school, the front door was open and Joyce was gone. Felice and Devon called their father, and when Joyce wasn't home by dinnertime, they called the police. Why are you interested in her case? As you said, it's been twenty years."

Norrie arched a brow. "You don't know?"

Chapter Two

Norrie had a smug look on her face, as if knowing something Hope didn't was some sort of lifetime achievement. The last thing Hope wanted to do was play twenty questions with the reporter.

"What are you talking about?" Hope asked.

"Joyce's daughter Devon has a podcast about unsolved cases of missing women. It's called *Search for the Missing*. The case she's doing now is her mother's," Norrie said.

Hope's mouth fell open. That was the podcast Oliver had been listening to and the one Gilbert mentioned. Why hadn't either one mentioned the host was Devon? Or that the case she was talking about was her mother's? They'd both lived through the months of searching for Joyce and all the false sightings of her, raising hopes only to be disappointed yet again.

"I had no idea."

"You should listen to it. Devon's quite a good storyteller. Captivating. Anyway, with Valentine's Day coming up marking the twentieth anniversary of Joyce's disappearance and now the podcast, I'm going to write a story. I'll look at the case with a fresh set of eyes. I want to get a telephone interview with Devon. I was thinking, you know her sister, Felice, right?"

Hope's surprise at finding out Devon had a podcast vanished while her guard, like a force field, shot up. Norrie was asking for a favor.

Her reluctance to answer must have been written all over her face because Norrie propped a hand on her hip, and she looked displeased.

"Come on, I helped you out last summer. Don't you remember, I gave you a lead when you were sticking your nose into that whole mess with Lionel?"

Hope recalled the unsolicited information Norrie provided under the guise of wanting to be helpful. Here was proof Norrie did nothing without some expectation of reciprocation.

"So, I owe you one?"

Norrie shrugged. "Well, if you want to put it that way." Her cell phone buzzed, and she lifted a finger to indicate she needed a moment. After pulling her phone out of her purse, she frowned as she read the text message. "I have to go. We'll pick this up later." She sprang forward, and in an instant, she was gone. Which was just the way Hope liked her.

Hope readjusted the straps of her tote bag on her shoulder. Helping Norrie was something she didn't want to do. Not only had she stepped over the line in some of her reporting regarding Hope, but she was also her best friend's archrival. Yes, that was what Drew had called her on more than one occasion. Childish? Perhaps. Accurate? Definitely.

She opened the heavy paneled door and stepped out of the stately, two-story brick building. The library was built in the early twentieth century after years of operating out of Frieda Bishop's small home on Main Street, just north of where the current police department was located. She lent books to friends and neighbors from her living room until Fred Merrifield and Louisa Dayton stepped in to help build a permanent library for their town.

The frigid air swooped down around her, making her coat feel like a thin sheet of cotton. The cold seeped inside her, sending bazillion chills up and down her body.

Bali sure sounded good, even if it meant spending time with Elaine. The social-climbing, career trophy wife who had perfected backhanded compliments, had on more than one occasion said Hope was her best friend. Another swoop of cold air whacked Hope, and she shivered. If Elaine honestly thought they were so close, why hadn't she taken her bestie to Bali with her?

Hope walked along the path from the library's entrance to the sidewalk, passing benches, where, in the warmer months, patrons lingered with their newest reads. Not paying attention, she slipped on a thin patch of ice, but was able to quickly regain her balance. Landing on her backside wasn't something she wanted to do right there on Main Street. To make sure she didn't have another slipup, she forced herself to stop daydreaming about Bali.

She fixed her gaze ahead. No looking up or sideways. Eyes on the sidewalk. As much as she'd like to focus on the picture-perfect scene ahead of her created by a lush blanket of snow, she couldn't. There was a landmine of ice patches just waiting for her to become distracted again. She continued along until a long-forgotten memory flashed in her head, bringing her to a stop.

She remembered what Main Street looked like the day after Joyce disappeared.

Thanks to a brief warm-up, the snow that had fallen days before had melted, leaving a slushy mess. Hope recalled navigating the puddles as she tagged along with her mother to run errands. Inside the General Store, the topic of conversation was Joyce. She recalled the prevailing theory was someone had abducted Joyce from her home. Beneath the armchair sleuthing there had been a ripple of fear. Everyone was asking whether some other wife and mother would be next?

A chirping drew Hope's attention upward, and she saw a cardinal fly to a nearby feeder. As much as she groaned about the weather, winter in the northwest hills of Connecticut was beautiful.

She pushed off, continuing her trek to Staged with Style, and her mind wandered back to Norrie's announcement that she'd be writing an article about Joyce. While she'd never been one not to want to see justice served, reopening the case seemed too cruel to Joyce's family. Whatever healing had been done was sure to be ripped apart. Then again, Devon was talking about her mother on her podcast. Maybe Norrie's coverage of the cold case wouldn't be a bad thing.

Hope tugged the blush-colored scarf around her neck tighter. Touching the soft cashmere brought a smile to her lips. It wasn't her first cashmere scarf, but it was the first Christmas gift she'd received from Ethan as his girlfriend.

She rolled her eyes. She was behaving like a lovesick teenage girl, getting all mushy about a gift. But after years of him being her steady rock, her anchor when her life turned upside down, they'd moved from the friend zone to romantically involved, and she couldn't have been happier. They were planning their first long-weekend getaway to celebrate Valentine's Day.

The short vacation had been in the works since Thanksgiving. They thought it would be easy and quickly learned how naive they'd been. Between his work schedule and juggling joint custody of his two daughters along with Hope's overbooked calendar, finding a stretch of free days was challenging. When they realized Valentine's Day was clear on both their schedules, they booked their room at a charming inn up in Vermont, and Hope made a promise to herself not to bring along her work camera. She'd also decided on a complete social media detox while away. No liking. No following. And absolutely no posting content.

She needed the time to recharge and relax.

She and Ethan both.

"Hope!"

She looked in the direction of her favorite coffee shop and saw her new assistant, Josie Beck, moving at a brisk pace toward her. Josie had two Coffee Clique to-go cups in her gloved hands.

Bless her.

Hope could use another cup of hot coffee. She continued forward, knowing she was risking a slip and fall because her eyes were fixated on the coffee cups.

"How did it go with Angela?" Josie's face was barely visible beneath a knit hat pulled down to her brows and a scarf covering her up to her chin. A transplant from

Florida, she wasn't used to New England winters. She handed a cup to Hope and then moved her scarf so she could take a sip from hers.

"Good. Class registration is full." She took a drink of the hazelnut coffee. Heaven. "You didn't have to do this, but I'm glad you did."

Josie beamed. Just two days on the job and Hope didn't know how she'd survived so long without an assistant.

"Everything is all set for the class?"

"Yes." Hope walked to the curb. "Were you able to set up the website I'll be using for the class?"

As a part of the curriculum, the students would create a website. Hope didn't want to demonstrate on her own, so she'd purchased a domain and website hosting for a site she'd use to teach with.

"All done." Josie walked alongside Hope. "When I get back home, I'll schedule the Facebook posts for the next two weeks. Then I'll pull together your newsletter and send it over for you to review."

"Good. Also, there's the Chicken Parmesan video that needs to be edited."

Josie did an air check with her forefinger. "Done first thing this morning."

"You're doing an amazing job. Where have you been all this time?"

"Working at a dead-end job at an insurance agency. Now working as a virtual assistant, I'm finding it is so much more rewarding."

"I wish I could give you more hours." Hope had more than enough work to delegate to Josie, who worked primarily from her apartment. What Hope didn't have was the budget to pay a full-time salary.

"I know. But in time you'll be able to. Besides, I have other clients, so I'm doing okay. Don't worry about me. I'd better get going. There's a bunch of work to do, and I'm freezing. I wish I had one of those automatic starters for my car." Josie waved and dashed back toward The Coffee Clique.

With both hands wrapped around the cup, Hope sipped her coffee while she waited for a break in the morning traffic. The hot beverage was just what she needed. In midsip, she saw a police cruiser pass by, and her heart did a little thump.

Ethan was at the wheel. He turned his head, and his gaze landed on her for a moment. He'd been away at a law enforcement conference and returned late last night. Exhausted from his flight from Colorado, he went straight to his house after landing at Bradley Airport. He texted her that he'd see her today. He smiled just before he returned his attention to the road.

He continued driving along until he flicked on his blinker and turned into the driveway of the police department. She dragged her gaze from his disappearing vehicle back to the task at hand—crossing the street. A break in traffic happened, and she hurried across the road, careful to avoid patches of icy snow. Back on the curb, she bustled to her sister's shop.

A self-moving cargo van was parked in front of Staged with Style. Making her way toward the entrance, Hope glanced upward at the rental apartment. She recalled her sister mentioning a new tenant would be moving in.

The charming, red-clapboard house was once home to Jefferson's first mayor and, in the middle of the last century, was converted into a retail space on the first floor.

The large front window showed a display of two toile-covered chairs and a small cherry occasional table topped with a crystal vase of fresh-cut flowers. She sighed. The furniture was lovely and far out of her price range these days. She consoled herself with the fact that it was also too formal for her farmhouse, which had a contemporary country vibe.

Hope entered the shop, and a warm blast of air greeted her, followed by a scowl on her sister's face. For a split-second, she considered backing out. Quickly. But the scowl and its cause would have to wait. She desperately wanted to let the warmth settle over her, and then she would find out what vexed her sister.

Claire stood beside the sales counter, its glass case sparkling with prisms of light caught from the morning sun shining in from the large window. Inside the case were small decorative items such as votive candles and a mother-of-pearl jewelry box Hope coveted.

"I don't have time for a coffee break." Claire dropped her hand from her hip and walked across the dark wood floor toward Hope. Dressed in a dove-gray sheath dress, she had a floral scarf perfectly knotted at the base of the ballerina neckline, and her shoulder-length blond hair was swept back into an elegant chignon. Hope doubted she'd ever look so pulled together if she owned a shop. Most days she barely got out of her yoga pants and hoodies. A casual dress code was a bonus of working from home.

"Good to hear, because Josie brought this for me." Hope sipped her coffee. She took her sister's snapping in stride. Claire was juggling a lot with her new venture, so Hope gave her a pass. This time. Okay, they were the closest of close sisters, so Claire had a lifelong pass as far as Hope was concerned. A shadow of disappointment crossed Claire's flawless face and her shoulders slumped, prompting Hope to hand over her cup. "Here. Finish it."

Claire smiled as she took the cup. She spun around and walked back to the counter with a little shimmy in her shoulders. After she took a drink, she set the cup on the counter.

"I needed this. You have no idea how lucky you are to have an assistant to get you coffee. I can't just dash out any time. . . ." She pressed her lips together, as if forcing herself to stop complaining. She lifted the cup and took another sip.

"Sure I do." Hope was certain Claire was on the verge of reminiscing about the days not too long ago when she worked at the real estate office and could run out any time for coffee without worrying who would stay behind for customers. Now, as a sole proprietor, she had to concern herself with those pesky little things.

"It's nice you've found someone who's working out," Claire said.

"You've had three employees since you opened. If you kept one of them, you could dash out when you needed a caffeine fix." Hope pulled off her gloves and dropped them into her tote bag. She then unzipped her coat and untied her cashmere scarf.

"Gloating does not become you."

"I'm not gloating, I'm simply stating a fact. You need help here."

Claire's head tilted and she gave a pointed stare. "As you are well aware, finding good employees is hard." She sighed. "Though I do need to find someone ASAP. I'm about to be up to my eyeballs in work. You won't believe the job I just landed!" Her manicured hands clasped together, and her scowl morphed into a full-on smile.

"What is it? Come on, spill it." Hope joined her sister at the counter. She slipped her tote bag off her shoulder and set it down. She was eager to hear all the details.

"The Landon House," Claire squealed. Hope couldn't remember the last time she saw her sister so excited.

The Landon House was a Cotswold Tudor Revival situated on twenty acres of prime horse property. The current owner was a recluse with eccentric tendencies. When Hope and Claire were little girls, everyone trick-or-treated at the house. Back then, Gloria Marshall's mother was alive and made sure the mood was festive and welcoming. Upon her mother's death, Gloria shut out the world and let go of all the traditions the Marshall family was known for.

Hope's eyes widened. "That old place is up for sale?"

"Can you believe it? Though according to Kent Wilder who has the listing, the house needs significant repairs. It's also dark and dated. This will be more than just a simple staging job. Gloria is very particular, and from what Kent told me, selling the house isn't her idea. She doesn't have the money to pay the taxes or maintain the property."

"Are you going to be able to handle the job along with running the shop?" Hope took a look around the shop, and her gaze landed back on her sister, whose brows furrowed, and the scowl returned.

Oh, boy.

"Of course I can handle it!" Claire squared her shoulders and marched over to the table where she had consultations with clients.

Stacked on the gleaming cherrywood were fabric swatch books. She grabbed the heftiest one and shoved it into the large canvas tote bag she took with her to job sites. She added two smaller swatch books and her portfolio.

"I know what I'm doing! I just need time to evaluate the space Kent wants staged and come up with a plan. Once I have the plan, everything will fall into place. You'll see."

Hope ignored her sister's outburst. She knew firsthand starting a new business was stressful. She imagined having your sibling question your decisions added to the stress of the situation. The last thing she wanted was to pile onto the pressure Claire must have been feeling, so she promised herself she wouldn't question her sister's ability to run her business anymore. It was time to move on to another topic.

"There's a moving van outside. Is it for the new tenant upstairs?" A safe topic, Hope thought.

Claire nodded, but didn't look at Hope.

Hope huffed. Her sister would not make it easy.

"Do you know who the new tenant is?" Hope asked, joining Claire at the table. With her sister still refusing to look at her, she peeked into the bag.

There were all sorts of things in the bag. Like Hope, Claire was always prepared. Tucked inside were two measuring tapes—you know, in case you need more than one—a leveler, because you have to make sure things are straight, and a camera. Claire photographed the rooms she was hired to stage. In the small back office, she had a bulletin board where she tacked up the photos so she could study them and make design decisions.

Claire turned her head toward Hope, her chin jutted

out. "No idea. I know it's a woman, and she's signed a short-term lease. My guess is she's moved for work or family and will look for something more permanent."

"Sounds like she might be interested in some of your merchandise." Hope pulled out a chair and sat.

Claire shrugged. "Maybe." She grabbed her canvas tote by the handles and carried it over to the counter. "What's on your agenda today? Are you all ready for teaching your first blogging class?"

Hope leaned into the chair. "I'm all prepared for the class. I have two recipes to make and photograph this afternoon. I also have to see what I need to take to Vermont. I have a few things for skiing, but I haven't looked at any of that stuff since I moved into the house. It's all still packed away."

"Don't forget, I have ski clothes—" The front door opened, letting in a blast of cold air as a woman entered.

The woman, dressed in a green parka with a black knit hat pulled over her chin-length, blond hair, looked vaguely familiar to Hope, though she couldn't place where she knew her from.

"I'm sorry to interrupt." The door shut behind the woman and she stepped farther into the shop. "I saw Hope coming in, and I wanted to . . . well . . . say hi. It's been ages." She stood there in awkward silence. "It's me. Devon."

Hope and Claire looked at each other, both clearly surprised by their visitor.

"Devon Markham?" Hope stood, still staring in disbelief at her long-lost friend. "It has been ages."

Devon nodded as she closed the small space between them and hugged Hope.

"It's really you." Hope couldn't believe her arms were wrapped around Devon after all these years. The last time they'd hugged was on high school graduation day, right before the newest graduating class went off to start their journey into the real world.

Devon had chosen a college in Oregon. Hope guessed she had wanted to put as much distance between herself and the bad memories of her hometown as possible. In Oregon, she'd be Devon Markham, a biology student. Not Devon Markham, daughter of a missing woman.

"It's so good to see both of you." Devon let go of Hope.

Now, looking closely at her, Hope realized Devon hadn't changed much. The same hair, the same freckled nose, and the same warm smile. Though she rarely flashed the smile after her mom vanished.

"Same here. I'm . . . we're surprised to see you. It's been too long." Claire gave Devon a quick hug.

"I agree." Devon waited a beat before continuing. "To tell you the truth, returning to Jefferson wasn't planned."

"Whatever has brought you back, I'm glad to see you after all these years." Claire gestured to the chair at the table, but Devon waved off the offer to sit.

"I can't stay. I have to finish settling in and return the van. Patrick just left. He helped me move in some of the stuff," Devon said.

"He and Felice must be happy to have you back in town." Hope returned to her seat. She wondered if it was the revisiting of the worst day in her life that had Devon returning to Jefferson. Talking about Joyce's disappearance on the podcast had to have stirred up difficult feelings. Had Devon decided to come back to find comfort from her sister?

Devon shrugged, and she pressed her lips together as if she was keeping herself from saying the first thing that came to mind.

"Like the two of you, they were surprised by my decision to come back after all these years. There's been a lot of hurt between us."

Hope nodded. She knew about the hurt. The most significant wound that divided the sisters was Devon's decision not to come back for Felice's wedding. Hope couldn't imagine not being there for Claire's wedding or vice versa, even though hers ended in a messy divorce.

"You're here now, and seeing that Patrick is helping you, it looks like you are all on the road to mending your relationships."

Devon shrugged again. "Felice has been pretty angry with me, but I'm hoping she'll find a way to forgive me. Patrick seems to be open to starting over. He's a good husband and a good brother-in-law. He offered to help with moving in, so I took him up on it." She looked around the shop. "I thought you were a real estate agent, Claire. Are you working here now?"

"It's my shop. I'm a home stager now." Claire rested her hands on the back of the empty chair. "Felice was in here last week and she didn't mention you coming back."

"She didn't know then. I only called her a couple of days ago. I don't know how long I'm going to stay. Thank goodness the apartment was available on a short-term lease option," Devon said.

"Does your podcast have anything to do with you coming back to Jefferson?" Hope asked.

Claire looked to Hope and then Devon. "What podcast?"

"A year ago, I started a podcast about unsolved cases of missing women. I've done three cases so far," Devon said.

"I've heard of true crime podcasts. But I've never listened to one. They sound fascinating." Claire grimaced. "I'm sorry, I didn't mean cases like your mother's are fascinating. It's not, it's horrible."

"I know what you meant. No worries." However, Devon's smile faded. "I figured it was time to cover the one unsolved case closest to me. My mom's."

"That's very brave of you." Claire's gaze drifted downward, and Hope knew her sister was kicking herself for the comment. She also knew her sister didn't mean to hurt Devon.

The awkwardness passed as quickly as it had descended upon them. Devon continued, not dwelling on a silly comment. She had bigger things to worry about. "There are all sorts of theories of what happened to my mother. I'm certain she didn't walk out on us. Someone took her. I intend to find out what happened to her twenty years ago."

"I don't think anyone believed she left on her own." Hope remembered her mother hadn't believed Joyce walked out on her family. But there were rumors she'd fled with a boyfriend or was forced into the witness protection program. Both those scenarios seemed unlikely, given Joyce had been a well-respected member of the community. Then again, Hope was only a teenager at the time and wasn't privy to information about Joyce's personal life.

"How do you plan on finding out the truth?" Claire asked. "It was so long ago."

Devon's baby-blue eyes hardened. "I'm going to turn this whole town upside down and shake as hard as I can until I find the person responsible for my mother's disappearance." A chirping noise came from her wrist, and she lifted her arm, pushing up the sleeve of her parka. She tapped her smartwatch. "I'd better get going or I'll be late returning the van. It's so good to see you both." She hurried out of the shop.

Claire followed, and when the door closed, she swung around to face her sister.

"Did you hear what she said? What she's planning on doing?"

"I did."

"Why didn't you tell me about her podcast? How do you know about it?"

"I only found out about it this morning. I ran into Norrie Jennings, who also knows about the podcast."

"Does she know Devon was planning on coming back to town?"

"I don't think so. Norrie said she's heard the podcast and wants to write a follow-up story about Joyce's case in time for the anniversary. She didn't mention anything about Devon being back in town."

Claire walked back to the counter and lifted the tote bag. "I'm not going to lie; I have a bad feeling about all this."

"Same here." Hope stood and moved to the window. She looked out to Main Street.

In the early morning light and the fresh coating of snow, the street looked charming. A quick glance and no one would ever suspect any evil acts occurring in the postcard-perfect New England town. Hope swallowed. She knew otherwise.

She'd been caught up in a few murder investigations over the past year, which meant she'd been face-to-face with evil. Her guess was Joyce also faced such, but unlike Hope, she never got the chance to tell the story.

"Wait until Maretta finds out Devon is back to reopen her mother's case. And of all things, with a podcast." Claire tsk-tsked. "Plus having Norrie write an article about it for the *Gazette*? Maretta is going to blow a gasket. You know how she feels about portraying Jefferson's image of the ideal destination for antiquing and leaf-peeping."

Hope winced. Her sister was right. The new mayor had been on the job since last summer and blamed Hope for the unfortunate murders that occurred recently in town. Why blame the murderer when you have a perfectly innocent food blogger to accuse?

Chapter Three

The timer dinged, signaling to Hope she was mere minutes away from enjoying one of her favorite meals, currently bubbling away in one of the double ovens.

When she renovated the kitchen, she and her contractor had gutted the entire space. She had compiled a lengthy wish list—or maybe it should have been called a dream list, because her budget wasn't large enough for everything she wanted. But the top on the list was the double-oven unit.

She hauled the heavy, nine-quart Le Creuset Dutch oven to the island. The aroma of the red wine, rosemary, and thyme mingled together with a thick slab of chuck roast had her mouth watering. Then she checked the timer for the upper oven, where a tray of carrots tossed with olive oil and coarse salt roasted. Once those finished, she'd garnish them with chopped parsley.

One-pot meals were easy and popular, but Hope didn't love the taste or texture of potatoes and vegetables cooked along with the pot roast. She preferred to serve the hearty slices of roast over a fluffy mound of mashed potatoes and a side of roasted carrots nestled on the plate. Hands down, that little change elevated the traditional pot roast.

Hope checked her watch as she finished setting the table. Her dinner guests would arrive shortly.

From an upper cabinet, she pulled out three mismatched plates—some of her favorite tag sale finds. She loved the treasure hunt of a good tag sale. Plus, there was no worry about breaking a dish and having to find a matching replacement. She also found props for her photography, DIY projects for her blog, and a few pieces to weave into her home. Like the plates.

She set the plates on the table, a not-so-vintage find at an estate sale right after her kitchen remodel was complete. While the table didn't have a provenance, it had charm and seating for six. Its lightly scuffed, warm wood tone effortlessly merged the kitchen and the family room together.

She retrieved three napkins from the hutch. The antique pumpkin pine floorboards creaked with her steps. She smiled. Others would have thought the sound annoying, but she found it to be endearing. Salvaged from a barn up in Vermont, she had them trucked to Connecticut and stored until the remodel of the opened space was complete.

The kitchen had been closed off from the family room when she purchased the house. The first order of business was to tear down the dividing wall between the rooms because she wanted a large, open living space. Now, she had a direct view to the fireplace that anchored the family room and to the wall of windows that looked out over her expansive backyard. For as far as the eye could see, the property was dotted with towering evergreens and oak trees coated with snow. In the early morning, she'd catch glimpses of the deer that settled down to sleep way back on the acreage. There was also a big, fat groundhog who ventured out, though she hadn't seen him lately.

The tapping of toenails approaching prompted Hope to look up from folding the napkins. Bigelow had appeared at the doorway of the family room. The medium-size dog paused for a moment before trotting over to her.

"What took you so long? You're starting to slack off." She laughed. Bigelow usually hung out with her as she prepared food, always hopeful he'd get a taste. Though today he seemed tired, and after she scrubbed the potatoes, he disappeared. She figured he went upstairs to her bedroom to nap on her bed. The aroma of the pot roast must have awakened him and his taste buds.

Bigelow yawned and then set forward in a trot and joined Hope at the island. He was a handsome combination of brown, white, and black. While her rescue dog had good looks and a kind heart, his manners needed work. At first, he wasn't a very good student, but in the past few months he'd greatly improved. Even so, Hope remained steadfast. He'd not get any food until after she and her guests finished their dinner. Then, and only then, she'd make him a bowl of shredded pot roast, carrots, and potatoes.

Rules were rules, after all.

"Drew and Jane are coming for dinner tonight. Are you going to be on your best behavior?"

Bigelow slanted his head and stared at her with his big eyes. He woofed.

"I'll take that as a yes." She gave him a pat on the head as she passed by on her way to check the carrots. She turned on the oven's interior light to look. So far, so good. Just a few more minutes.

Back at the island, she lifted the Dutch oven's lid and inhaled the aromatic fragrance the slow cooking of the roast produced. Every time she made the recipe, she was transported back to her childhood. The anticipation of having to wait hours for the roast to be fork tender never failed to build, no matter how many times her mom made the dish.

Bigelow woofed again.

"Be patient. You'll get some." Doubt flashed in his brown eyes, and he inched closer to Hope. "I promise." After setting down the lid, Hope used a tong and a spatula to maneuver the roast from the pot and set it onto a waiting platter. She covered it with a sheet of aluminum foil while she prepared the gravy.

After she gave the gravy a final whisk, there was a knock at the back door. She hurried through the mudroom and let her guests in.

Drew removed his coat and shook off the cold. He muttered something about freezing to death as he hung up his jacket and then reached for Jane's red wool coat after she slipped out of it.

He had swung by the Merrifield Inn to pick up Jane on his way to Hope's house. The seventysomething retired mystery author had given up her driver's license years ago, after she had an accident. Rattled by the experience, she chose to stop driving. Though the decision left her dependent upon others for transportation, mostly it was her sister-in-law, Sally, who chauffeured her around. Hope wasn't sure how'd she feel relying on friends and family for lifts to run errands or a night out for dinner. When the day came, she hoped she'd handle it as well as Jane seemed to be. Hope dashed back into the kitchen to check on the gravy.

"It smells heavenly in here." Jane followed Hope into the kitchen and stopped to greet Bigelow, who'd been waiting impatiently at the door. Jane's ivory sweater was a nice change from all the drabness of midwinter fashions. Hope glanced at her top. Dark gray. Could she get any duller? Jane cooed a few endearments to Bigelow, and he ate up the attention. Her white hair was cut short and wispy bangs grazed her brows. She had on her classic pearl earrings and her trademark pink lipstick.

"Pot roast? Good thing I went to the gym after work." Drew continued to the island and helped himself to the bottle of wine set out. A nice red to go along with their meal.

"You can't spend your life worrying about calories." Jane gave a final pat on Bigelow's head and then joined Drew. She slid one of the three glasses on the counter in front of him and waited. She wasn't driving, so she wasn't shy about enjoying wine. When Drew stopped pouring, she cleared her throat, prompting him to continue filling the glass.

Drew handed his travel companion the amply filled glass and slid Hope a can-you-believe-that? look. Hope gave a small shrug. She knew Jane enjoyed wine, especially red.

"I wish I didn't have to worry about calories." Drew sipped his wine. As the designated driver and conscientious about his caloric intake, Hope knew he would savor his drink. "I barely got into these jeans tonight." He glanced at the slim-fit, dark-washed jeans he wore with a navy crew-neck sweater.

"Dinner is almost ready." Hope rattled off the menu as she transferred the strained, thickened gravy into a glass gravy boat and set it on the table. Back at the roast, she began slicing. "Too bad Sally couldn't make it tonight."

"You know she won't miss a garden club meeting." Drew took his glass and the bottle of wine to the table. "Tonight they're making their plans for spring projects around town."

"It's her passion." Jane joined Drew at the table. She lived with her sister-in-law, and together they managed the town's only inn. It'd been passed down from generation to generation. These days, they had help for all the day-to-day tasks.

"Hope, we need to set up a time for me to interview you about the blogging class at the library. My editor assigned the story to me." Drew plucked a roll out of the bread basket before handing it to Jane.

Hope made a batch of garlic and herb dinner rolls a week earlier and froze them, so for dinner tonight she only needed to thaw and heat. Halfway through their baking, she brushed them with melted butter, so they'd get a nice, golden color.

She paused in slicing the meat, which was falling apart because it was so tender. Messy? Yes. But it was going to taste delicious. Drew didn't appear unhappy about being assigned to cover a run-of-the-mill, adult education class.

Though she was certain he'd prefer something juicier that could garner him a front-page byline.

"Anytime you want."

"Sally said she saw a moving truck out in front of Claire's shop earlier today." Jane buttered her roll. "It's nice to see the apartment has been rented. It's been empty for months." She took a bite of the roll, and her eyes fluttered.

Hope transferred the slices of the roast to a platter and then spooned the potatoes into a large bowl. The specks of red from the potato skins were a little pop of color. She carried the serving dishes to the table. With the bowl of carrots placed last, she pulled her cell phone out of her jeans' back pocket.

"This looks delish." Drew reached for the roast's serving fork.

"No!" Hope had her phone poised for a photo.

Visibly startled by Hope's directive, Drew almost dropped the fork. "What?"

"Can't you see she's trying to take a photograph?" Jane asked.

"Can't you see I'm trying to eat dinner?" Drew leaned back into his chair and pouted.

"Give me a minute. I need to take a photo before we eat." Hope angled the phone to get a shot of the entire table without the faces of her guests. When she posted "real-life" photographs of her meals, they garnered thousands of likes, so she shared more of those.

"Be sure to tag me." Jane reached for her wineglass.

Hope laughed and then promised she would. Much to her surprise, over Christmas, Jane joined the millions of users on Facebook. One of the employees at the inn, who handled the website and social media accounts, helped

Jane set up a profile, and now she was addicted to checking her news feed and being tagged by her friends. Most days being on social media felt like a chore for Hope, so it was nice to see someone enjoy it for a change.

"Can we eat now?" Drew still held on to the serving fork. When Hope nodded the okay, he placed three slices of roast on his plate and then two slices on Jane's before passing the platter in Hope's direction.

Seated, Hope spooned out a mound of potatoes and then added a few slices of the meat on top. She drizzled a little gravy and then broke off a piece of roast with a scoop of potato and chewed. It was better than she'd anticipated. The flavors of the potatoes mingled on her tongue. The spicy, pungent flavor of the garlic was mellowed by the silkiness of the cream cheese and the tang of the buttermilk, while the roast melted in her mouth and the gravy popped with the infusion of rosemary and thyme.

Bigelow came sniffing around the table and she quickly dispatched him to his bed in the corner of the family room. She'd never fed him at the table, but her niece and nephew had, so it made sense he'd try tonight. She craned her neck looking for Princess. Her fluffy white cat usually made an appearance when meat was involved. The little carnivore enjoyed a piece of beef or chicken but, like Bigelow, she'd seemed sleepy earlier. Hope guessed it was Princess's shredding of a roll of toilet paper that wore her out. Now Hope had to make sure the bathroom doors were closed when she left the house.

"You've outdone yourself, dear." Jane pierced a carrot. "The gravy is so smooth and flavorful. I hope this recipe is on the blog."

"It is. Getting back to the apartment over Claire's

shop." Hope gestured for Drew to pass the bread basket. She broke apart a roll and buttered it. "I'm sure you'll hear soon enough that Devon Markham moved into the apartment."

"No!" Drew leaned into his chair. The look of shock on his face mimicked the surprise in his voice. "She's back? Why? Did you talk to her?"

"I did. Briefly. She came into the shop while I was there." Hope popped a piece of roll into her mouth and chewed.

"I can't believe she's come back. I thought for sure when she left after graduation she'd never return. After what she and her family went through, who could blame her?" Jane asked.

"Me too. Back then, Devon seemed to take what happened and process it internally. She didn't talk about it with anyone. Unlike Felice. She told me she saw a therapist when her mother disappeared." Drew sopped up the gravy on his plate with half of his roll.

"We all handle tragedies differently." Hope topped off her wineglass. "But it seems now she's ready to talk about what happened to her mother."

"What do you mean, dear?" Jane tilted forward, and her eyes widened with interest.

Hope took a drink of her wine and then set down the glass. "She's started a podcast about unsolved cases of missing women. The current case she's covering is her mother's."

Drew's fork dropped onto his plate with a clank. "A true crime podcast? I love them. What's the name of it?" He pulled his phone out of his back pocket and then looked up expectantly at Hope.

"*Search for the Missing.* This morning, Gilbert told me

Mitzi listens to it. Oliver also listens to it. I guess it has a following." Hope reached for the carrots and scooped out a spoonful onto her plate.

Drew was busy tapping away on his phone. "Got it!" He tapped on the phone a few more times to finally bring up the podcast.

"We're going to listen to it now? I've never heard one before." Jane smiled.

"This is the latest one. Shush." Drew raised the volume on the phone.

Jane pursed her lips and gawked at Drew. Hope dipped her head to hide the smile that was curving her lips. *Drew just shushed Jane. Oh. My. Goodness.*

The dramatic music led into the introduction and Devon's somber voice followed.

> *"When I tell people I have a podcast they ask me why I started it. I tell them I started this podcast to help find answers to the sudden, unexpected disappearances of women like me . . . like you . . . like your mom . . . your sister . . . your wife . . . your friend. I started this podcast to work through the feelings that haunt me about my mother, Joyce Markham. Twenty years ago, she was a beautiful, smart, active mother of two girls and wife of a very successful man.*
>
> *"She'd entered her forties knowing it would only be a few years before her daughters would graduate high school and she'd have an empty nest. In preparation for this new phase of her life, she decided working as a secretary at a real estate agency wasn't enough. She wanted more. Who could blame her? She'd given so much to me and*

to my sister. Why shouldn't she have been able to follow her dreams? She wanted to be a real estate agent, so she started studying for the test. I remember her sitting at the kitchen table with a textbook. She was serious. She was going for it.

"I guess like any good student, she decided to push some boundaries. Do something a little daring. Something unexpected for a respectable wife and mother twenty years ago. My mom got a tattoo. That's right, my mom got a tat. It was a rose. A black rose."

Hope exchanged curious looks with Jane and Drew. They'd stopped eating.

"A black rose is mostly associated with death and mourning, but my mom told me they also have a more positive, inspiring meaning. Black roses can stand for the beginnings of new things and major changes. Little did my mother know, shortly after getting the tattoo she'd disappear."

Hope's jaw dropped open and a chill snaked down her spine. The feeling of foreboding she'd experienced earlier in Claire's shop returned and intensified.

"She had a black rose tattoo?" Drew paused the podcast.

Hope shrugged. "I never heard about it."

"It was probably a detail the police held back. You know, they always leave something out when they discuss a case with the public. Though I don't see what role it played in her disappearance." Jane forked a carrot and chewed. "I can understand the girl's need for answers.

Perhaps a fresh set of eyes on the case now will lead to the answers she desperately needs."

"This is great!"

"What are you talking about?" Hope stared at Drew, bewildered by his statement.

"Don't you see? I have a new story! The anniversary is coming up. Valentine's Day is right around the corner." Drew hastily wiped his mouth with his napkin. "I need to start right away."

"Drew . . . wait—"

"No time to wait, Hope." He sprang from his chair. "Do you mind giving Jane a ride home? I have to do research tonight so I can pitch this to my editor tomorrow."

Hope jumped up from her chair, jarring Bigelow from his bed, and he trotted to the table while she crossed the room to stop Drew from leaving.

"Wait. I need to tell you something."

"Later." He was already on the other side of the mudroom door. "Thanks!" he said before pulling the door closed.

"He's so excited when he gets a new story idea. I appreciate the ride home, dear," Jane said.

Hope spun around and her shoulders slumped. "No problem."

Jane set down her fork. "Oh, but there appears to be one. What's wrong, dear?" She gestured for Hope to come back to the table.

Hope lumbered back to her chair and sat. Bigelow made his way to her side and reared up, resting his front paws on her lap. He was trying to figure out what was wrong. She stroked him, hoping to reassure him there was nothing to worry about.

"Norrie told me this morning she was going to write a

story on Joyce's case. I was going to tell Drew after dinner. I had no idea he'd play the podcast and then rush out of here." She pointed to the mudroom door.

Jane's worried look diminished. "You need to call him later. You know how he gets."

"He'll be annoyed with me." Hope reached for her glass and gulped her wine.

She and Drew had been best friends forever. They'd shared secrets, commiserated over breakups, and gone antiquing together. Besties for life, they'd promised each other decades ago. The only other person she was closer to was her sister. And because she and Drew were so close, when they argued, it was ugly. Uglier than the Christmas sweater he made for her three holiday seasons ago when he was drunk. But it had taught them both a lesson: Don't ever operate a glue gun while under the influence. Because there really was such a thing as too many rhinestones. But she still had the sweater tucked away in a storage bin. She hadn't the heart to toss it out.

"Imagine what he'll be like if you don't tell him and he finds out for himself."

Hope sighed. "You're right. I have to tell him before he goes to work tomorrow. It won't be too bad. Right?"

Bigelow lowered his head to her lap and closed his eyes. Jane lifted her glass and took a long drink of her wine. There was no reassurance coming her way. It looked like she was on her own.

The next morning, Hope woke with a start. Her blogging class was happening. A mix of excitement, anxiety, and pride left her exhausted even after a good night's sleep. One minute, she was looking forward to sharing everything she knew with the students. A minute later, she was terrified she'd bore them with her lengthy explanations. How else could she explain long-tail keywords? And a minute after that, a swell of pride calmed her racing thoughts. She'd finally arrived at a place where people wanted to learn from her.

What she needed to do was to figure out a way to keep that last thought front and center for the rest of the day.

With Bigelow and Princess fed and her own breakfast dishes cleared and in the dishwasher, she gave clear instructions to her pets on her way out of the house.

The instructions were simple. They were to behave while she was gone. Bigelow, being the lovable pup he was, sat and listened intently, while Princess, being the diva she was, licked her paw and showed not one ounce of interest in anything Hope had to say. Typical.

She stepped outside with trepidation. Would it feel as cold as yesterday morning had?

With the door closed behind her, she walked along the shoveled path to the garage. No, it wasn't as cold as yesterday, but it was still plenty cold. If they got lucky, it would reach a high of twenty-five degrees. Woo-hoo! Time to strip off the long underwear.

A ruckus from the barn caught her attention. Hope didn't need to be inside there to know Helga, her four-pound Hamburg hen, was pitching a fit. The hen had a very distinctive sound, and she always seemed to be aggrieved by another chicken.

A rhythmic cackling announced that Beatrice was trying to oust an interloper from her nesting box. Hope grinned. Beatrice wouldn't quiet down until her space was cleared. The standoff could go on for the rest of the morning depending upon which bird was occupying the space.

The hens got along most of the time but, like sisters, they had different personalities, and they had disagreements from time to time. Helga was the top chick. She took her role seriously and would fiercely protect any other hen if she felt there was a threat. Poppy, a Rhode Island Red, was a gentler soul and preferred to hang out close to Hope's house, even letting herself inside occasionally.

The girls, as Hope called them, were a handful and a lot of work, just like the house and the blog. Over time, she realized she was taking on too much work for one person. After careful consideration, she'd hired Josie to help with the administrative work and Iva Johnson to help with the chickens, the new gardens, and work around the house.

Iva Johnson. Talk about a blast from her past.

They had gone to the same high school. That was all they'd had in common from those days. They'd traveled in very different social circles and had no shared interests. Throughout school, Hope was a perpetual volunteer. There wasn't a committee she hadn't wanted to organize. Iva, on the other hand, felt it was her duty to wreak havoc wherever she went. In that area, she excelled.

Looking back, Hope suspected Iva's unsettled home life had a big influence on how she behaved at school. Iva cut classes, smoked and drank, and barely got passing grades. She made it no secret she had cared little for Hope, the bookworm who loved to study for tests and bake cookies.

Now, they were working together. Never in a million years would Hope have believed such a thing would happen. But it did. Yes, pigs must have been flying somewhere.

Dropping out of high school thanks to an unplanned pregnancy, Iva had few job options, and when she lost her housekeeping job last summer, it hit her family hard. Hope needed help with the chickens and offered Iva a few hours a week. The work expanded to the gardens, which had been neglected by the last homeowner. During the early part of the fall, Iva worked on the long-dormant vegetable garden, preparing it for spring planting. With her help, Hope was optimistic she'd have a bountiful garden in the summer.

Things had certainly changed since high school. Seeing Devon the day before had stirred up memories about those four foundational years. The highs, the lows, the drama, the victories. Between her and her sister, she wondered how her mother survived those years. A small smile touched her lips. Soon, Claire would be the mom with high schoolers.

"Morning, Hope!" Iva waved from the barn door. She was dressed in her usual work outfit of a flannel-lined denim jacket and matching jeans. Her dark hair was covered by the jacket's hood, tied tightly under her chin to keep her neck warm.

"Good morning, Iva!" Hope waved back. She spotted several chickens inside the pen. She guessed they were deciding whether to free range today. After every snow-storm, Iva cleared a large section for the hens so they could move around.

Hope continued to the garage and pushed open the door. She aimed her key fob at her Explorer and unlocked the driver's side door as she hurried around the front of the vehicle. She wanted to sink into the heated seat and get a proper warm-up. Making her way around the car, she passed the floor-to-ceiling shelves erected along the back wall. Hope had turned lose her inner organizer when she designed the unit because she'd seen one too many garages become dumping grounds for all of life's must-haves, from fitness equipment to kitchen gadgets to outdated technology. She'd have no part of it in her garage.

Everything in its place, that was her motto.

"Hey, Hope, got a second?" Iva appeared at the door. Her face was barely visible beneath her hood and scarf. Her jacket was zipped up, and chunky socks peeked from the top of her well-worn work boots.

"Sure. What's up?"

"After I'm done in the barn, I'll get the first coat of paint done in the living room. You got the delivery of Shades of Greige, right?"

When the colder weather hit and Iva still needed a paycheck, Hope had asked if she'd be interested in painting. The downstairs powder room needed a fresh coat of paint, and Iva did a great job. Now she was tasked with painting the living room.

"I did." Hope set her purse onto the front passenger seat. She'd gone through countless shades of paint for the living room. She'd last settled on a crisp white, but it looked too stark against the medium shade of gray she'd painted the fireplace wall. Frye-Lily, a paint company she'd partnered with to write sponsored posts, sent her a can of Shades of Greige, and it was perfect. Finally! The soft tones of gray and beige blended together fit the image in her mind of how the finished room would look.

"Good. Hopefully, the animals will stay out of my way. The cat nearly knocked over the paint tray when I was working in the bathroom."

"A cat will be a cat." When Hope adopted Princess,

she'd expected a mild-mannered feline. After all, she'd lived with an elderly woman. How much trouble could she be? Apparently, appearances were deceiving, because Princess was a wild thing. She regularly tore through the house, knocking objects off surfaces on a whim and scratching furniture. Even with her challenging behavior, late at night she'd curl up with Hope on the sofa and purr as she slept. How could Hope not love the cat?

Iva sighed. "She should live out in the barn." Shaking her head, Iva turned and stomped outside.

Hope doubted her spoiled yet loving cat would allow someone to move her to the barn. An image of hissing, swiping with claws extended, and tiny sharp teeth flashed in her mind. She wanted no part of it. What she wanted a part of was surprising Ethan. A quick visit would help keep her mind from worrying about her class later that evening.

She slipped in behind the steering wheel and started the ignition. Her first stop was going to be The Coffee Clique.

Hope opened the door of The Coffee Clique and entered. A din of clipped conversations as the morning rush of caffeine-depleted people came and went greeted her. It took all of thirty seconds for her nose to wriggle at the sweet aroma of the coffee shop's most popular pastry, cinnamon buns. Her eyes zeroed in on the tray in the display case with precision. She had a flashback to the iconic scene in *Sex and the City*, when Carrie stared longingly into a store's window at a pair of fabulous shoes, and Carrie's words repeated in her head.

"Good morning, Hope!"

Those weren't the words Carrie had said. But they kept Hope from dashing to the display counter and pressing her face against the glass.

Hope's head turned toward the voice from the counter.

Laila Miller waved her over to the order station. From her cheerful voice and big smile, it was a good bet Laila had had her caffeine fix a couple of times over.

"Hi, Laila. Good to see you." Hope opened her purse and pulled out her wallet. "Two large. One hazelnut with milk and one regular black."

She glanced at the cinnamon buns again. The most perfect pastry. And her kryptonite. She chewed on her lower lip. One little cinnamon bun wouldn't hurt. No. She needed to be strong. She'd had a holiday season full of baking cookies and cakes, and now she was testing recipes for a new, digital cookbook of quick breads. She didn't need the extra calories the yummy pastry was packed with. She'd stay strong. No matter how much it hurt.

And it hurt a lot.

"You got it." Laila plucked two cups from the cup dispenser and filled them. Her moves were precise and efficient, a testament to her years of experience behind the counter. She'd pulled her shoulder-length, coppery-brown hair into a high ponytail, and her face was bare of makeup. Laila always had the natural, girl-next-door kind of beauty. She never had to work at it. "I'm looking forward to class tonight."

"Me too. I'm both thrilled and terrified. The class registration is full." Hope removed a debit card from her wallet.

"You have nothing to be terrified about. Me? I fluctuate between excited about starting a blog and dreading it.

I guess it's a normal feeling? But I've seen how success-ful some crafters are when they blog. There's this one knitter who has created an online knitting course, and she's making six figures a year!" Laila set the filled cups on the counter and placed lids on each. "Don't get me wrong; I enjoy working here, but I'd love to do some-thing that has more meaning to me. Like sharing the joy of a hobby I learned from my grandmother."

"The opportunities are endless, and you're such a tal-ented crocheter. It'll be a lot of hard work, but I think you can be very successful." Hope handed Laila her credit card and waited for her receipt.

"Gail was in here a few minutes ago for her latte. She told me Devon is back in town. And reminded me it's coming up to twenty years since Mrs. Markham disap-peared. I can't believe it's been so long." Laila handed Hope her card back, along with the receipt.

"News definitely travels fast, doesn't it?"

Laila nodded. "Who needs the *Gazette*? Gail wonders if Devon and her sister are planning a memorial of some sort for their mother. Wouldn't that be nice? For us all to be to-gether again and remember what a great lady Mrs. Markham was? Maybe Alec would come back for it." The hint of hopefulness in her voice reminded Hope of the wicked crush she'd had on Gail's brother in high school.

Hormones ran amuck back then, and it seemed Laila still carried a torch for Alec Graves.

The opening of the front door drew Laila's attention to the group of women entering the shop. "Have a good day. See you tonight."

Hope took her cue to leave. Outside, the temperature

seemed a little warmer and the wind from yesterday had diminished.

It wasn't too frigid to walk, so she decided to leave her Explorer parked at the curb and continued on foot to the police department. Back in New York City, she had walked everywhere regardless of the weather, and since returning to Jefferson, she'd found herself too comfortably settling into driving everywhere.

The sidewalk had been shoveled by the shop owners, leaving a clear path for her to stroll along. Signs of life started to show. Interior lights were on, "Open" signs were visible, and up ahead, Nathan was dusting the section of sidewalk outside his antique shop with granules she expected were some type of sand mixture.

As she passed by the florist, she paused to take in the lovely display of flowers for Valentine's Day. Next door, the clothing boutique had a love theme in their window, and The Bark Boutique, the place where Hope got her supplies for Bigelow and Princess, also had a love theme. The window display was filled with stuffed toys, heart-shaped beds, bowls, and the cutest sweaters. She wondered if they had Bigelow's size. She'd have to check later.

She followed the path leading to the main entrance of the police department and entered the reception area.

There was a small seating area to her right. Along the opposite wall was a brochure rack filled with information, from over-the-counter drug disposal to how to report scam telemarketers. She approached the partitioned-off dispatch center. Doug was on shift, operating the communication system, and was just finishing a call.

The small but efficient dispatch center opened to the back section of the main office, and she spied several empty desks and Ethan's office. The office door opened, and out walked a tall blonde wearing a black wrap dress that hugged her hourglass figure and showed off her long, tanned legs.

Hope's mouth fell open, and she inched closer to the glass partition.

What on earth was she doing there?

Chapter Four

Elaine Whitcomb was supposed to be in Bali. But there she was, standing in the doorway of Ethan's office, giggling, fussing with her bleached blond hair, and handing her coat to Ethan. Hope's mouth gaped open when he obligingly helped the young widow into the coat. She leaned closer to the partition when Elaine patted Ethan's hand after she'd slipped into her coat.

"He'll be right out." Doug glanced over his shoulder. "He's just wrapping something up."

"I can see that." Hope stepped back from the counter and moved closer to the door from which Ethan and Elaine would emerge in a few seconds. Any. Second. Now.

Ethan appeared first from the opened door, followed by Elaine, who was still giggling.

What on earth was so funny?

"Hey, Hope. This is a surprise." Ethan made sure the door was secure before leaning in for a quick kiss. She inhaled his clean and energizing, tangy scent. He had used the body wash and aftershave conditioner set she gave him for Christmas. The notes of citrus gave him a fresh-out-of-the-shower scent she adored. But because they were standing in the public reception area of the police department, she had to control her adoration.

"I'm sure it is." She slid a quick glance at Elaine. "I've brought coffee." She handed the black coffee to him.

"How thoughtful of you. Thank you, Hope." Elaine reached for the remaining cup in Hope's hand. "You're such a good friend. How did you know I was here?" She took a sip and then made a face. "Oh, honey, this is hazelnut, isn't it? You know it's not my favorite."

She handed back the cup.

"It's *my* favorite." Hope looked at the red lipstick mark on the cup. A perfectly good coffee, ruined. "Why are you here? I thought you were in Bali."

"I was. It's beautiful and warm. You should go there sometime. I can recommend the perfect hotel."

"Thanks for the suggestion." Hope doubted she'd ever be able to afford a trip to the tropical paradise, much less afford any hotel Elaine stayed in. The trophy wife, she'd gone from amateur status to pro by having four marriages under her Gucci belt, lived a lifestyle Hope couldn't fathom. Each of her husbands was a financial step up. Except for the last one. He'd left her finances a little murky. "What are you doing here?"

"My lawyer called and said there were matters I needed to take care of ASAP." Elaine shook her head and sighed, as if legal matters were a boring nuisance. After all, vacationing in the lap of luxury was so far more important than anything else.

"Sometimes you need to be present to deal with certain issues." Hope knew from experience. From her divorce to the sale of her condo to the purchase of her home, there were a lot of lawyer meetings. She was thankful that phase of her life was behind her, and now she only consulted with a lawyer about her business.

Elaine looked point-blank at Hope. "I reminded him that's why I have him on retainer. To take care of those matters. But I had to cut my vacation short and come back to the brutal cold."

"Elaine came in to register the new alarm system at her house." Ethan moved closer to Hope and sipped his coffee.

"All this paperwork. Who knew? I guess now being an independent woman, I have to learn all sorts of things." Elaine paused for a beat and then reached out her perfectly manicured hand and rested it on Ethan's arm. "Good thing I've found a great teacher." Her gaze flickered to Hope as she took back her hand. "He helped me fill out the form."

"I'm sure he did." *Found a great teacher*. Hope wanted to gag.

"You're lucky to have such a good man. Smart. Handsome. You'd better be careful, or some other lady might swoop in and snatch him up." She wagged a finger at Hope. "I'd better get going. I have a full-body massage in twenty minutes." She made a Vanna White move to emphasize the word "body." "Hope, we need to catch up. I'll call you."

"Great." Hope wasn't sorry to see Elaine leave. She couldn't believe the woman had the gall to be so overt about Ethan right in front of her. The giggling, the touching, the warning. She'd have to Google the price of a one-way ticket to Bali and buy one for Elaine.

"Toodles." Elaine waved her fingers and sashayed out of the building. Even beneath the coat, the swaying of her hips was noticeable.

Hope caught Ethan watching Elaine walk out the exit, and she whacked him in the stomach with the back of her hand.

"Ouch."

"You deserve it."

"You've just assaulted a police officer."

"If you keep looking at her that way, I'll really assault you."

A slow grin formed on his lips and he wrapped his free arm around her waist, drawing Hope closer to his solid chest. "How rough are we talking?"

She rolled her eyes and laughed. "I'm being serious. You know what she's like."

"Are you jealous?"

"No. Of course not. Now that she's single, she's on the prowl for a new husband."

"Don't worry. I know what kind of woman Elaine is. I also think she'll be looking for someone who earns substantially more than I do as Jefferson's police chief."

"But you're smart and handsome . . ." Hope tried to keep her voice light and playful, but she was anything but. Elaine had no boundaries when it came to flirting, and she didn't know her well enough to know how far Elaine would take the ordinarily innocent activity.

Ethan released Hope. "Thank you for the coffee. Sorry about yours."

Hope glanced at the cup. "How could she even think I

brought her a coffee? Like I knew she was here?" She stepped over to the trash can and dumped the cup. She'd pick up a new one on the way home. "How late did you work last night?"

"After midnight. Now I have a meeting with Maretta to update her on it, and see what funding we can get for them." Ethan had been away at a training workshop for the use of body cameras. And yesterday he'd spent all day catching up and preparing the proposal for those cameras.

Hope felt sorry for him. First Elaine and then Maretta Kingston. Not exactly the most pleasant way to start the day.

"Are they expensive?"

Ethan took a gulp of his coffee. "It's the data storage fees that are the financial concern."

"I never really thought about storing the video. I know what I pay to store my content in the cloud. Wow, it's going to cost a fortune, isn't it?"

Ethan nodded as he took another drink of his coffee. While he smelled all fresh and rejuvenated, his eyes told another story. Up close, they looked fatigued.

"It's not going to be an easy sell to Maretta or the Town Council."

"If anyone can convince them, it's you."

He broke out in laughter. "Thanks for your vote of confidence. Sorry, but I need to get back to my office to finish getting my notes together. How about dinner tonight?"

Hope frowned. "I have the blogging class. But there will be food to reheat, so if you want to stop by, you could also let Bigelow out."

"You had me at food to reheat. I'll stop over. Don't worry about Bigelow."

"Oh, you won't believe what happened yesterday. Devon Markham is back in town."

Ethan's head drew back in surprise. "I didn't think she'd ever come back. Didn't she miss her sister's wedding?"

"Good memory."

"I'm a cop. I remember everything. Sorry, but I gotta go." He kissed Hope on the forehead before returning to the office door. Doug buzzed him in.

Hope zipped her coat and then waved goodbye to the dispatcher as she left the police department. Her next stop was the library to check on the room where her class would be held. She followed the path back to Main Street. The sun was brighter, and it warmed her cheeks.

Her cell phone chimed, alerting her to an incoming text message. She reached into her purse, but of course the phone wasn't where it was supposed to be. Her fingers fumbled. Finally, she had to look down into the cavernous black hole, and because of that she didn't see the person approaching until it was too late.

"For goodness' sakes, you really should watch where you're walking!" Maretta Kingston glared at Hope from under her black fedora hat.

Hope sighed. Of all the people to run into. But on the bright side, she found her phone and pulled it out of her purse.

"I'm sorry. I should be paying more attention to where I'm walking." Hope's sympathy for Ethan skyrocketed. It seemed Maretta was in a particularly bad mood. "It's a beautiful day, isn't it? A little warmer than yesterday."

"Yes, yes, yes. Beautiful day indeed. I don't have time to chitchat. First, I had to deal with the broken furnace at the school this morning. It's working now, and school is opening in an hour. Now I have an appointment with Chief

Cahill, and I don't want to be late. I hope your visit here hasn't set him back either." She nodded in the direction of the police department's entrance.

So much for pleasant conversation.

Before Hope could respond, Maretta's body jerked, making Hope jump. She looked over Maretta's shoulder and saw three boys high-fiving each other.

"What on earth?" Maretta swung around to face the boys, and the back of her coat was covered with snow. "I see you, Billy Teager! Who are your hooligan friends?"

The boys responded with a chorus of hearty laughter and then took off running.

"This is outrageous!" Maretta turned back to Hope. She huffed. "I'll have to see what the chief will do about this blatant assault." She walked around Hope.

"Maretta, don't you think you're overreacting a bit?"

Maretta arched a thin eyebrow. She apparently went heavy with her tweezers. "You condone such behavior?"

"No, they shouldn't have thrown all those snowballs at you, but they're kids. I don't think the police need to be brought into this."

Maretta looked off in the distance for a moment and then met Hope's gaze. She nodded slowly, as if she were considering options. "Perhaps you're right."

Hope's eyes narrowed. What was Maretta saying? Was she agreeing with Hope? There was a first time for everything.

"This may not be a police matter. Rather, something I should take care of as mayor."

Oh, boy. Hope sensed Maretta wasn't agreeing with her. No, instead, Maretta's brain was churning with another thought. A part of Hope was curious to find out what Maretta was thinking while another part was scared.

"What are you talking about?"

"I'll introduce a ban on snowball throwing."

"No, no, Maretta, no. You can't do that."

"Watch me." Maretta's tone was severe, leaving Hope to believe she'd do what she said. Ban snowball throwing? A stupid idea on so many levels. Maretta turned and walked along the path to the building's entrance.

"She's out of her mind," Hope muttered as she swiveled around on the sidewalk. Billy Teager was an energetic kid with a mischievous streak, and he was also her nephew's friend. Thank goodness Logan hadn't been in the group of snowball throwers.

She was about to send Ethan a text warning him of Maretta's sour mood, but an SOS text from Claire stopped her.

Need help. Now!

What on earth was going on at the shop? She dropped her phone back into her purse. Her trip to the library would have to wait.

"Thank goodness you're here. I've been waiting." Claire, dressed in her coat, stepped out from behind the sales counter. At the table, she lifted the canvas tote bag filled with swatches and her supplies. "I'll be back as soon as I can."

Hope raised her palm to slow her sister down. "Wait. What's going on?"

"My walk-through at the Landon house got rescheduled to now." She raised her arm and pushed back her coat sleeve to look at her watch. "I'm barely going to make it on time. I have to go."

Hope joined her sister at the table. "If you're leaving, why did you ask me to come over?"

"Isn't it obvious?"

"You want me to watch the shop while you're out?"

"Thank you!" Claire hurried to the door.

"I'm not offering. I have work to do. I can't babysit your shop. Close for a few hours."

"And risk losing business or confuse my customers with erratic shop hours? I can't do that."

"Well, I can't stay."

"But you will, because you're my sister and you'd do anything for me. Besides, you can do all your work on your phone. Isn't that the beauty of being self-employed with an online business? You can work remotely anywhere, anytime. Thanks!" Claire didn't wait for Hope to respond. She hustled out of the shop and didn't look back.

How . . . ? What . . . ? Hope snapped out of her stupor and hurried to the door, but she was too late. Claire was long gone. She'd had her getaway all planned. Even parked her Mercedes in front of the shop.

Darn.

Hope counted to ten. And then added another ten.

"This is why I told her not to open a store. But did she listen? Nooo." Great. She was talking to herself.

She shrugged out of her jacket and draped it on the back of the chair along with her purse. She rested a hand on her hip and looked around the shop.

Her gaze landed on the tufted bench. Its pretty teal color would brighten any gray day. Too bad she didn't have a spot for it in her house. Her entry foyer had a coat closet, but not enough space for the bench. But she did have room for the hand-painted yellow, honeycomb-patterned vase.

Babysitting the store was going to be expensive on her

end. Before she reached for the vase, the door opened and Drew burst in.

"Why didn't you tell me?"

Shoot. She'd forgotten to call him first thing about Norrie's story on Joyce.

"Drew, I'm so sorry. I meant to call you this morning before you left for work, but I got busy. . . . I had an email from a PR firm I needed to reply to ASAP and then I totally forgot. I'm really sorry."

"What about last night? Why didn't you tell me then that Norrie was already working on the same story idea?"

"I tried, but you wouldn't listen, and then you left so quickly."

"So, it's my fault?"

"No, I didn't mean . . . no, it's not your fault." There was going to be no winning this argument. No matter what she said to defend herself, Drew would twist it around. He always did. There was only one way to try to keep the situation from escalating. "I like your hat." She prayed the compliment of his brown, faux shearling trapper hat would turn his mood around.

"Thank you. It was a Christmas gift from my sister." His rigid stance and clipped words told Hope his mood hadn't shifted one iota. He was still angry with her.

"She's always had good taste. Guess it runs in the family." Sure, Hope was laying it on thick, but she had no choice.

"Don't try to butter me up. Do you have any idea how embarrassing it was going into my editor's office to pitch a story he'd already heard? And from all people, Norrie?" Drew shoved his hands into his pants pockets and lowered his chin.

"I can't imagine it was a pleasant thing."

He shook his head. "No. She wasted no time in telling me about how she plans to write the story and how she's certain it'll get picked up on the wire service, thanks to the podcast." Drew trudged over to the table and dropped onto a chair.

Hope pulled out the other chair and sat, careful not to let her jacket or purse fall.

"She might be writing the story but remember, it's you who knows Devon. We all went to school together. We were friends."

Drew perked up. He made eye contact with her. And it wasn't the stink eye now. "You're right. I can use the connection to get Devon to talk to me."

Crisis averted.

Drew jumped to his feet. "She's living upstairs. I'll go see if she's home now. I can get the interview and write it up before Norrie realizes what happened. My editor won't care who got the story as long as he gets one for the front page."

Hope let out a whoosh of tension as her body relaxed. Drew had a new plan. More importantly, he wasn't upset with her any longer. She glanced upward and said a silent thank-you to whatever power helped her.

Outside the window, she saw someone approaching the door. It looked like it was time for her to play shopkeeper.

"Where's Claire?" Drew finally asked.

"You just now realized she's not here?"

He shrugged. "I was preoccupied by my career tanking."

The door opened, and Devon entered. Talk about perfect timing. Hope stood. "Good morning, Devon. What brings you by?"

"I'm looking for Claire." The door closed behind Devon as she stepped farther into the shop. She pulled a tissue from her jacket's pocket and wiped her nose. "I forgot how cold it gets here." She returned the crumpled tissue to her pocket.

"Claire's out at an appointment. Is there something I can help you with?" Hope asked.

"The light bulb in the hallway is out, and the landlord said Claire could contact the handyman if anything needed to be fixed."

"Hi, Devon. I don't know if you remember me. I'm Drew Adams." Drew extended his hand to Devon.

Leave it to Drew to jump into the middle of a conversation when there was a story at stake.

"I'm sure Devon remembers you," Hope said.

A flicker of recognition flashed in Devon's eyes. She reached out and pulled him in for a hug. "Of course I do. So glad to see you!"

Drew gave Hope a thumbs-up, and he smiled.

"How have you been? You were the editor of the high school newspaper. What are you doing now?" Devon let go of Drew and stepped back.

"I'm a reporter with the *Gazette*. And I'd love to interview you about your podcast and your investigation into your mom's disappearance."

"Another reporter has already contacted me. Norrie Jennings, I think her name is."

Drew's mood darkened again. Oh, boy.

"I haven't called her back. To be honest, I'm not sure how I feel about an interview. I'm not back here to promote my podcast. It's not a business, like Hope's blog. More like a passion project. Though it may be nice to talk about it and my mom." She was quiet for a moment, putting Hope's nerves on edge. She didn't want to live through the fallout if Devon turned down Drew's request. "Let's do the interview. I'll let the other reporter know I'm going with you, my old friend."

"Great!" Drew exchanged cell phone numbers with Devon.

"Hope, I was thinking we could have dinner if you're not busy tonight. Nothing fancy; I'm not a famous food blogger like you. I thought it would be nice to catch up."

"I'd love to, but I have my blogging class this evening at the library."

"How about after the class? Stop by for tea and dessert. I open a mean package of cookies." Devon chuckled. "Drew, please come too if you're free."

"Thanks, but I have a committee meeting to attend tonight, and I have to write up the article when I get back home. Can I get a rain check?"

"Definitely. So, Hope? Are we on for later tonight?" Devon asked.

"Yes. It sounds wonderful. See you later." Hope walked Devon to the door and closed it tightly to keep out the cold air. Drew came up behind her and wrapped his arms around her. "You got your exclusive interview with Devon."

Drew rested his head on her shoulder. "I did. Norrie will be reading my interview and weeping because I'll be back on the front page."

"Yes, you will." And Hope was out of the doghouse.

Chapter Five

Hope stood in front of her class of eager bloggers-to-be, all waiting to absorb the information she had to share, notebooks opened, tablets powered on. She welcomed them, gave them a brief overview of the course, and shared her journey from magazine editor to full-time blogger. Then it was time to get down to work.

She began with how to choose a topic to blog about. Some of the students had a broad idea, while others had niched down to a very specific subject matter such as crocheting or nature photography.

"We've covered choosing the topic for your blog. Now let's talk about choosing a domain name. The name of your website. I chose mine, *Hope at Home,* because I knew while the focus of my blog would be primarily food, I would include DIY projects, household tips, and other content regarding my home. I wanted a name that would be broad enough, yet still be easy to remember."

"How do we know the name we want for our blog is available?" Gail Graves sat in the front row and feverishly jotted down notes while Hope talked. She'd asked the most questions and impressed Hope that she was serious about blogging.

"Let's check one now." Hope had her AV set up, and at her laptop's keyboard, she navigated to the service she used to host her website. "You'll check here. Let's say you want to name your website *Hope at Home*." She typed the words. "The message the domain name has been taken comes up. You should have several options in mind."

Shirley Phelan's hand shot up. "What if the name I really want is taken? Can I buy it from the person who owns it?"

"You can. However, some domain names will be outrageously expensive. My advice is to have options and not have your heart set on any one name."

For the next sixty minutes, Hope covered choosing a blogging platform. There were two main ones, and she gave all the pros and cons. She then finished the class with a tutorial on how to select the company to host the blog.

The students had many questions, a reminder she needed to break down the information into even smaller chunks. She was, after all, talking to beginners.

When she wrapped up her presentation, she handed out a checklist that covered everything she'd talked about. Each student expressed their gratitude for the cheat sheet. She took a few minutes to review the homework assignment. There were a couple of groans, but they were in good fun, and it made her feel like a real teacher.

Hope gathered her notes as her students filed out of the

room. They all said good night to her when they passed by her table. She reminded them to do their assignment for the next class.

"Platform, hosting, framework. I think I have it all straight." Gail stopped at the table, holding her notebook against her chest. She was the same age as Hope but had a few more creases around her eyes, and her dull black hair had gray roots.

"I know it's confusing. The best way to think about it is that the framework is the construction of your blog; it's what everyone will see. The platform is like what building you live in. The hosting is the service you use to get your information out to the masses. Take it one step at a time and you'll be fine."

Hope slipped her computer into its protective case and then into her tote bag. All in all, it was a good class. Her nerves had settled once she began talking about how she started blogging and never returned.

"You make it sound so simple." Shirley Phelan arrived at Gail's side. In her midsixties, Shirley was retired, but had too much energy to sit around and do nothing. Her daughter, Amy, was a friend of Hope and complained her mother needed a hobby because she was spending too much time trying to fix Amy up. Hope felt Amy's pain. It wasn't her mom who was the self-appointed matchmaker in the Early family, it had been Claire.

"Once you get the hang of it, I promise it's simple." Hope zipped her tote closed after adding her notes inside. She reached for her coat.

Shirley nodded. "Too bad life can't be simple. I heard Devon is back in town."

There it was: the gossip train chugging full steam ahead. Hope wondered who'd tipped Shirley off.

"I wonder why Felice didn't tell me Devon was coming back." Gail looked put out. Since high school, she and Felice had been close. Practically inseparable back then. "It's all over town. She's renting the apartment above Claire's shop."

"I hope she's come back to make things right with her sister. What happened to their family is tragic, but they're still family," Shirley said.

"I don't think we're in a position to judge how any of them reacted to Joyce's disappearance." Hope shrugged into her coat and pulled out her gloves from the pockets.

"It would be nice if they repaired the rift between them." Gail started for the doorway. "I know Felice has missed her sister. I've heard something about a podcast Devon has."

"It's about unsolved cases of missing women. I listened to some of it last night." Hope reached the doorway with Shirley next to her.

"Oh, good Lord. Has she come back after all these years to dredge up the past?" Shirley halted. She looked worried. "Nothing good will come of it. Mark my words."

"If there's a chance she can find out what happened to her mother, you don't think that's good?" Hope asked.

Shirley shook her head. "I spent weeks, months wondering what on earth came of my friend. I cried so many nights because my thoughts always drifted to the worst-case scenario. But as the years passed, those dark thoughts faded. Now I remember her as the loving wife, mother, and friend she was. I don't want to go back to that dark time again." She lurched forward and hurried out of the room.

Hope and Gail exchanged a look. Hope couldn't remember the last time she'd seen Shirley so agitated.

"I feel sorry for her. She lost a friend." Gail's sympathetic voice matched the look on her face. "I couldn't imagine losing a close friend as she did."

"Neither can I. But I can't imagine living with not knowing what really happened. Come on, let's go." Hope flicked off the light switch as she and Gail passed over the threshold into the hall. The never knowing, the unanswered questions would haunt Hope if she were in Shirley's shoes. If Drew suddenly disappeared, she'd be scared for him and unrelenting in trying to find out what happened to him. So, why didn't Shirley want Devon to find answers to what had happened to Joyce?

Hope followed Gail out of the library's parking lot. Gail turned, heading toward her house, a quick drive from Main Street, while Hope drove to Staged with Style to have a cup of tea with Devon.

Hope parked her Explorer in a shared lot behind Claire's shop. She grabbed her purse and a container of Double Chocolate Oatmeal cookies. She felt her and Devon's long-overdue get-together was too special for store-bought cookies. With the container in hand, she pushed open the door and stepped out.

A border of plowed snow lined the lot, which had been empty except for what she assumed was Devon's compact car. She locked her car and then made her way around to the front of the shop.

The flight of stairs leading to Devon's apartment was lit by a bright bulb, proof that Claire had contacted the handyman. At the small landing, Hope knocked on the simple wooden door. Footsteps approached from the other side and, after a click of a lock, the door opened.

Devon's tangle of auburn hair fell below her shoulders, and her face was bare of makeup, allowing its natural brightness to shine. Long lashes framed her emerald-colored eyes, and she smiled.

"Come on in. It's a lot smaller than the place I had in Phoenix. But it's all I really need now."

Devon stepped aside to allow Hope to enter the apartment. In Claire's real estate lingo, she would have classified the space as cozy. Charming in a minimalist kind of way. The living area consisted of a combined seating and eating space, all in the confines of sad beige walls.

"It's cozy."

"Nice spin. The real estate agent who rented me the apartment said the same thing." Over ripped, baggy jeans, Devon wore an ivory fisherman sweater, and thick gray socks covered her feet. "What's in the container?"

"Double Chocolate Oatmeal. I baked them yesterday." Hope handed the container to Devon and returned her gaze to the rectangular, wooden table pressed against the wall. On top, a large bulletin board was propped up and covered with articles, photographs, and notes.

Devon moved to the table and swept a hand over it. "This is where I work, and this is all my research." On the dark surface were stacks of files, notepads, books, and copies of newspaper articles. Pens were strewn over the workspace, and a closed laptop computer was topped with a file folder. Set on a corner of the table were a microphone and recorder.

"You're quite thorough." Hope leaned forward for a closer look at what was tacked to the bulletin board. An article from a larger newspaper about Joyce's disappearance.

*"This case is the number one priority for
the Jefferson Police Department," Detective*

*Jim Voight said in a statement. "At this time,
we cannot comment on the progress of our investigation."*

Hope didn't recognize the article. What she recalled
clearly about the incident was the anxiety her mother and
her friends had felt, and the days Devon and Felice hadn't
come to school. It had seemed like forever, but they'd
returned one week after their mother's disappearance.
While Hope was happy to see her friends in school again,
she didn't understand how they could be at school not
knowing what happened to their mom. Hope's mother
had explained that the Markham family needed to get
back to their routines, their schedules.

They needed some type of normalcy.

*"Searchers are looking for any sign of Joyce Markham in
the wooded area near the Markham home,"* another article
said.

Hope couldn't fathom how Devon had found any normalcy after people searched the woods for her mother.

"When I select a case to discuss on my podcast, I need
to know it inside out."

"It must be more difficult when it's your mother."

"I thought I knew everything about it because I lived
it. Turns out, I pushed the memories away for so long,
I've become fuzzy on some of the details. I needed to go
through the articles and other documents. Just like I did
for the other missing persons cases I've covered."

"I can't imagine it's easy." Hope skimmed the board
again. Was it healthy for Devon to be staring at all those
articles and photographs every day?

"No, it's not easy."

"This photo." Hope pointed. "It's the kitchen from your house on Greenhill Street. Why is it on the board?"

Devon stepped closer to the table. "Something seemed off about the kitchen when I got home from school. I still can't pinpoint it." She walked to the sofa and set the container of cookies on the coffee table. There were two mugs of tea already set out. "There's no doubt in my mind. My mother was abducted and murdered."

Devon's bluntness caught Hope off guard. Then again, Devon had been living with the event for twenty years.

"The police never found a suspect or a motive." Hope draped her jacket and purse on an armchair before joining Devon on the sofa. "Nor did anyone come up with a reason why your mother would simply run off."

"Exactly! I remember one afternoon the detective who handled the case came to our house. My dad told Felice and me to go upstairs. Felice, always the Goody Two-shoes, went to her room. I, however, stayed downstairs and eavesdropped." Devon handed Hope a mug. "The detective wasn't hopeful my mom would come back home. He told my dad he had no leads, no suspects, no reason why someone would want to hurt my mother. He wished he could do more."

Hope wasn't sure she heard the last part of what Devon said correctly. "Wished he could do more? It sounds like he was giving up on your mother's case."

"I thought the same thing. Eventually, the searches stopped, and my mom's disappearance moved from the front page to the inside of the newspapers. Then the reporting stopped altogether. Except around Valentine's Day. It always reminded me of those articles you see online about actors . . . where are they now." Devon inhaled a deep breath, her green eyes watering. "Instead, the headline was something along the line of 'still missing, a local woman's disappearance remains unsolved.'" Tears streamed down Devon's oval-shaped face.

Hope leaned forward and patted Devon on the knee. "Are you sure you want to do this?"

Devon's head bobbed up and down as she wiped away the tears. "I don't have a choice. I need to know the truth. I quit my job to do this."

"You did?"

"Yes. I needed to devote as much time as possible to the podcast. I worked as a staff writer for an equestrian magazine, and now I freelance for them. It gives me flexibility and helps pay the bills. Felice thinks I'm crazy."

Hope lifted her hand and leaned back. "She's your sister. She's worried about you." Just like Claire was when Hope decided to pursue *Hope at Home* as a full-time career. From where Claire sat, blogging was an uncertain way to make a living, while working as a magazine editor offered a regular salary and benefits.

"I'm a big girl. I can take care of myself. It's not only my career decisions. She doesn't understand why I'm back here now, reopening Mom's case. What I can't wrap my head around is her reluctance to want to find out the truth."

"Sometimes the truth is painful."

"Not knowing is always painful. I can't let the fact that I may find something I don't want to know stop me. It's a risk I'm willing to take." Devon dipped her head, shielding her face. Her hands, resting on her lap, were shaking.

Hope's insides twisted. A part of her wanted to pull her old friend into a protective hug, while the other part wanted to know what Devon was keeping from her.

"What's wrong? What is it?" Hope asked.

"I think I know the reason Felice doesn't want me stirring up the past." Devon lifted her head and, with her hands, wiped her face dry. "I think she's trying to protect our father. I've come across information he'd been having an affair at the time of my mother's disappearance."

Hope took a drink of her tea. She needed a moment to process what she'd just heard. From what she'd seen on the news, it always seemed the husband was the responsible party when a wife disappeared. Had Joyce been another statistic?

"Are you certain?"

Devon's brows furrowed, causing a deep crease between them. "I wouldn't have said it if I weren't." She stood and went for a tissue. After blowing her nose and discarding the tissue, she returned to Hope. "There's also something my mom said a few times about Oliver Marchant."

"Oliver? What about him?"

"He mowed our lawn back then, and Mom said he creeped her out. But she never elaborated on what it was he did."

"Did she ever tell your father?"

"I think so, because I remember hearing him tell Mom Oliver was affordable and he wouldn't pay more to have the lawn cut." Devon shrugged. "I asked her once, and she said it wasn't important."

"Did you tell the police after your mom disappeared?"

"Sure. I don't know what they did with the information." Devon shifted on the cushion. "Hope, I need your help. I've kept up on what's been going on in town, and I follow you on your blog. I know about your knack for solving murders."

Hope's took another drink. She shared none of her

sleuthing adventures on her blog or any of her social media platforms. Rather, they'd been written about in newspapers and on celebrity news websites. Her former producer of *The Sweet Taste of Success*, Corey Lucas, believed any publicity was good publicity. However, her current agent didn't share the same philosophy. Laurel would have preferred Hope spend less time chasing down killers and more time developing recipes.

"I don't have a knack. Looking back at those few incidents, I think my curiosity led to the killer making a mistake. If they knew how little information I knew at the time, they certainly wouldn't have wasted any energy on me."

"You're selling yourself short. Your curiosity is an asset, and you have an ability most people don't. Like the detective who I believe botched my mother's case. I need your help, Hope. Think about it. Please say you'll think about it."

"Yes, I will. Though I can't promise anything else." Hope glanced at her watch. She hadn't realized how late it was and how uncomfortable she was feeling. "I should get going." She stood and grabbed her jacket and purse.

"Of course." Devon stood and walked Hope to the door. "Thanks for stopping by and for the cookies."

"I'll call you." Hope stepped out into the hall, but she wasn't ready to leave yet. She had one more thing to say. "Whatever happens, let's not wait so long to see each other."

Devon smiled and it broke out into a laugh. "I promise. Be safe getting home." She closed the door, and Hope shrugged into her coat before she descended the narrow flight of stairs.

She reached the vestibule and opened the door. Usually, the stillness of this part of the northwest hills was comforting, but tonight the darkness over Jefferson was eerily quiet.

She followed the cleared footpath back to her vehicle.

Looking for any sign of Joyce Markham in the wooded area.

Her imagination was taking over. Visions of volunteers combing the woods for Joyce's body, dead or alive, played like a movie reel.

Was it possible Joyce had been alive but died from exposure out in the woods? Or was she murdered and her body dumped there? Or Joyce was abducted and taken out of state. Maybe she was living under an assumed name. Perhaps she went into the witness protection program.

A shrill interrupted the darkened silence. Hope's hand clutched her chest until she realized it was her phone. The ringtone belonged to Corey. She wasn't sure what his title was these days, but she knew what he was hired to do. His job was to connect Hope and the other bloggers in the agency with brands.

She fumbled for her phone. Her purse had an interior pocket that was the perfect size for her phone, but did she keep it there? *No.* Her fingers finally grasped the phone, and she tapped it on.

"Good evening, Corey. What's up?" She'd learned a long time ago small talk was wasted on the hyper New Yorker.

"Just calling with an update." His nasal voice seemed far away. "Yeah . . . yeah . . . extra soy sauce . . . Sorry, I'm picking up dinner on my way home. Tomorrow I'm having lunch with the people from Mama Mia Pasta. It's looking good. Also, Frye-Lily is partnering with Allied

Home Centers for an autumn campaign, and they'd like to bring you in. You'll do a few DIY projects for your blog and their website."

Hope unlocked her Explorer. Whatever Corey's title was, he was doing a great job at raising her profile among companies.

"I'd love to continue working with Frye-Lily."

She balanced the DIY projects on her blog by adding recipes to the post. When she wrote about painting the entry of her house, she also shared a recipe for one-bowl brownies. Because after a long day of home reno, you needed a treat.

"Awesome! It's a great way to get in front of Allied Home. They like working with bloggers."

Hope squeezed her eyes shut as she smiled. Landing a sponsorship with Allied Home would be huge! She opened her eyes and forced herself to remain calm. One step at a time.

"Call me after you meet with Mama Mia. And keep me updated on Frye-Lily." She tossed her purse onto the passenger seat and climbed into the SUV.

There was silence on the other end.

"Corey?" Then the sounds of Midtown traffic, horns, sirens, loud voices, reminded Hope of her years living in the city. She glanced around the empty lot. New York was still alive and vibrant, while Jefferson, like her, was getting ready to tuck in for the night.

"Sorry . . . lost you there for a moment. I'll call you when I have news."

Before Hope could say good night, the line went silent. Again. Corey had disconnected the call without so much as a goodbye. Nothing new there.

Hope dropped the phone into the console and then started the vehicle. Warm air streamed from the vents, and she eased back into the heated seat.

While her body warmed up, she thought about Devon's request. In high school, they studied and did their math homework at Hope's house. They'd breeze through their assignments so they could spend the rest of the time doing other things. Fun things. Hope smiled. She could still see them in her bedroom. Thin as a rail, Devon had her waist-length hair pulled back into a ponytail, and she snapped bubblegum while they decided which songs to add to their mixtape. Hope cringed. What could she say? They were teenagers, and that's what they did back then. Now, her classmate was all grown up and wanted her help to track down a potential killer.

During the blogging class two days before, Hope did her best to present all the positives of writing a blog. Her reasoning was simple. Publishing a blog for the long haul was hard and rife with setbacks, obstacles, and a boatload of competition, and she wanted to make sure her students saw the good things and remembered them. Otherwise, when faced with an unpleasant task, they could easily give up.

One of the most tedious yet essential tasks she did regularly was edit her cooking videos. The process from start to finish to upload took hours, and she was now able and willing to hand off the task to her assistant.

Seated at the kitchen table, Hope had her laptop open and her phone next to it. She was on speaker with Josie.

"Great job editing the *How to Bake Even Cake Layers* video." Hope closed out of one tab and opened a new one. She wanted to check her views for yesterday's recipe post.

"Really? I'm so glad you loved it." Josie's enthusiasm came across loud and clear. She had a little experience with editing, and she welcomed the challenge of building a new skill. The how-to cake video was short, less than two minutes, and the perfect one for Josie to edit solo, like the Chicken Parmesan video. In no time, she'd be tackling Hope's more in-depth videos.

"I watched it while having coffee earlier. It's perfect."

"I'm excited to do more."

"Well, you saw the schedule. We have a lot more videos to produce." Hope leaned forward and tapped her keyboard. Her calendar for the month came up, and there were five video shoots scheduled by the end of February.

Bigelow barked, announcing his arrival in the kitchen. Coming up behind him was Princess. She paused for a nanosecond before continuing to the table, where she jumped up onto a chair. Hope eyed her, wondering if the cat would leap up to the table. Hope didn't have many rules in her house, but one nonnegotiable rule was that Princess wasn't allowed on tables and countertops. From the glint in the cat's eyes, it looked like she was thinking about breaking that rule.

"Before I let you go, have you seen my charm bracelet?" Hope looked around the kitchen. She remembered wearing the sterling-silver bracelet three days ago, when she was filming her Beef Bourguignon recipe. She'd removed the bracelet when she realized how much noise the charms made when she moved her arm. Now she couldn't find it.

"You had it on when you made the Beef Bourguignon. You took it off and set it on the counter by the sink."

"It's not there now. I thought maybe you moved it

someplace safer. It's been crazy the past few days; I probably moved it. Guess it'll show up." The mudroom door opened, and Hope glanced over her shoulder. "Claire's here. I have to go."

"Okay. I'll schedule the cake video to make sure all the social media links are done for it too. Remember, you have to give me the list of the older posts you want me to work on so the links can be updated. I hope you find your bracelet."

"Me too. I'll keep looking. It has to be here somewhere." Hope ended the call and swiped off her phone.

"What can't you find?" Claire dropped her purse on the counter and unzipped her puffer coat. She walked to the coffee maker and poured a cup. At the refrigerator, she pulled out a carton of milk and added a drop to her coffee. Bigelow trotted over to her and sat by her side, his head tilted up. "Good morning. What do you want?"

"Maybe a pat on the head?" Hope suggested.

"Needy much?" Claire patted the dog on his head, and his tail wagged excitedly. "Oh, he likes this." She continued to pet him.

"Look at the two of you, getting along." It was about time. From the first day Hope brought Bigelow home, he and Claire had had a rocky relationship. He liked to jump on humans, while Claire preferred not to be jumped on. Their goals definitely conflicted with each other.

"He might be growing on me," Claire said reluctantly.

"Of course he is." Hope stood to refill her coffee cup and reached for the milk. After adding more than a drop—unlike her sister, she didn't like her coffee dark—she returned the carton to the refrigerator. She closed the stainless-steel door. "What brings you by so early?"

"I never got the chance to properly thank you for staying at the shop while I went over to the Landon House. I appreciate your help."

When Claire had returned, there were three customers browsing, and Hope was ringing up a sale for a fourth. Hope had been in a hurry to leave because she had to get ready for her blogging class, and since then, they hadn't had the chance to catch up.

"Thank you. Just make sure it's not a regular habit." Hope took her cup back to the table, and Bigelow followed. He lay down beside her feet.

"You didn't answer my question. What can't you find?" Claire asked as she approached the table. She noticed Princess, who'd curled up on the chair rather than leap up onto the table. "It's like they own the place." Claire pulled out another chair and sat.

"They live here." Hope didn't want to answer the question about what she was looking for because she didn't want a lecture. But it seemed Claire wouldn't let go of the topic. "My charm bracelet. It's missing." Claire went to say something, but Hope cut her off. "Don't say it."

Claire looked offended. "Say what? Say Iva has always been a thief? Say you should have never hired her?"

"Exactly."

"I'd be gloating if I said those things. I was simply going to ask if you'd let Iva into the house recently."

"You know I have. She's been painting inside."

Claire lifted the cup to her lips and took a drink. She didn't say a word, though the look in her eyes didn't leave Hope any doubt of what her sister was thinking. Someone had accused Iva of stealing from the homeowners she'd cleaned for. One of those homeowners was Claire. Though there wasn't any proof Iva had stolen.

Hope wanted to change the subject. Fast. She had the perfect topic.

"You texted me your thanks last night. What's the real reason you're here?"

Claire set her cup on the table. "You know how much I dislike gossip."

"Since when?"

"Not funny." She traced the rim of her cup with her index finger. "Anyway, last night when I was closing the shop, Devon was outside. She was on her phone, and she got pretty loud. Devon said she had no intention of leaving Jefferson until she finds the person responsible for her mother's disappearance."

Hope took a long drink of her coffee. Devon had said those same words to Hope. She wondered who Devon had been talking to on the phone. Possibly, Felice. A disagreement with a sibling could cause raised voices. Lord knows, Hope and Claire had had their share of arguments over the years.

"She could have been talking to her sister. I don't think Felice wanted Devon to come back and stir up the past." Hope didn't want to share everything Devon had said, and she certainly didn't want to tell Claire about Devon's request for her help. Hope still hadn't decided yet.

Claire shrugged. "Could be. I'm worried about her. I have a feeling she'll be hurt no matter what the outcome is."

"If it was us and Mom disappeared, wouldn't we both risk being hurt to find out the truth?"

"I don't like thinking . . . yes, I see your point. We would risk anything. You were close to Devon back in school; can you talk to her? Make sure she's okay?"

"I will." Hope had to give Devon an answer anyway. "Let me finish some work, and then I'll call her."

Claire looked relieved. "Thanks. I should get going. I have to open the shop. Call me after you talk to her." She stood and grabbed her purse on the way out of the kitchen.

Hope heard the back door close, and so did Bigelow. He stood up and stretched. Then he looked at Hope with those big, loving eyes. She knew what he wanted. He wanted to go for another walk.

"We already took our morning stroll." She'd learned early on not to say the word "walk" unless she wanted to go on one. While his manners had been so-so, his understanding of certain words was excellent. "You're supposed to be napping now."

His gaze intensified.

"How about I give you a cookie, and then you go take your nap?"

His ears perked up. "Cookie." See, another word he understood.

She went to the container on the counter where she kept the peanut butter cookies, aka bribes, she baked for him. He trotted over and sat.

"Good boy! Here you go. Enjoy." She handed him the bone-shaped cookies, and he trotted to his bed in the corner of the family room, crunched it, and ate every single crumb.

Meanwhile, she grabbed a filled, reusable bottle of water from the refrigerator before returning to the table. Princess was still curled up and snoring. Lucky cat.

Back in her seat, Hope checked the weather forecast for the hundredth time. The likelihood of snow in Connecticut on her and Ethan's weekend getaway had increased to forty percent. Snow was guaranteed up in Vermont, but it was the local weather that concerned her. If a snowstorm hit, Ethan would feel obligated to stay in town. While she admired his dedication and his commitment to the citizens of Jefferson, she also wanted a break and some alone time with him.

She closed the browser so she could get back to work and reached for her water. She transitioned from coffee to water early in the morning. As much as she loved coffee, she didn't want to overcaffeinate. She set her fingers on the keyboard, and her gaze landed on her bare wrist again. Was Claire right about what happened to the piece of jewelry?

Maybe it was a coincidence the bracelet had disappeared at the same time she'd had Iva inside the house working.

Her stomach flip-flopped. Would Iva really steal from her? There was only one way to find out. She had to speak to Iva about the incident in the most diplomatic way possible so as not to come off accusing the woman of stealing.

She leaned back and crossed her arms over her chest. Was there a way to tactfully ask someone if they stole your jewelry? She uncrossed her arms and reached for the keyboard. Time to do an internet search.

Scrolling down a list of search results for how to talk to an employee about theft, Hope stopped when her phone blared "Girls Just Want To Have Fun," her sister's ringtone. She reached for the phone and accepted the call.

"I'm sorry, I haven't called Devon yet." Hope minimized the computer screen, and up popped her screensaver, a photo of her and Ethan. She smiled. They'd snapped the photo during a hike. He was tall with broad shoulders, dark hair, and a strong jaw. She was a few inches shorter, with shoulder-length dark brown hair and a lighter complexion. In her humble opinion, they made a cute couple. Her smile broadened.

"Forget about calling her. I think something is wrong. I'm at her apartment door now, and it's open, and I looked inside. It looks like someone has searched the place. I don't think she's home."

"What? Why are you up there?"

"I wanted to check on her. Hope, I think something may have happened to her."

"Don't go in! Go back to the shop, and I'll be right over." Hope shot up from the chair, startling Bigelow with her quick movement. She mumbled a reassurance to him that everything was fine, but his eyes were filled with concern as he raised to all fours and rushed toward her. Maybe having a dog with her wasn't a bad idea. She tapped her leg for him to follow.

In the mudroom, she slipped on his coat and then harnessed him. With Bigelow all set to go outside, she shrugged into her coat. She slipped the phone into her purse and took out her key fob. They stepped outside, and she pulled the door shut behind them. Together, they raced to the garage. Bigelow seemed to think they were going on an adventure. But the pit growing in her stomach told Hope otherwise.

Chapter Six

Hope and Bigelow arrived at Staged with Style in record time. She usually didn't speed, but under the circumstances, she made an exception. Even though Claire wasn't
in any danger, Hope's protective instinct had kicked into
high gear. Devon's angry phone call last night, her apartment door left open, and the place appearing to have been
searched. It was all unsettling, and Hope didn't want Claire
there by herself.

"Why did you bring him?" Claire pulled the shop's
door closed behind her. She'd been peering out the shop's
window when Hope arrived.

"Protection." Hope patted Bigelow's back. He was
small but mighty. Not too long ago, he'd leaped into action when Hope's life was at risk, and she was grateful he

was there at the time. He may not have been large or mus-
cled, but he wouldn't let anyone hurt her.

She stepped toward the door that opened to the vestibule,
and the three of them ascended the staircase. Bigelow's toenails tapped on the creaky old wooden steps, and when he
reached the landing, he lifted his nose and sniffed.

"What's he doing?" Claire asked.

"Smelling."

"Like for a dead body?"

Hope shrugged. "Canines have a more acute sense of
smell than we do. So who knows what he's smelling now?"

"God, I hope Devon wasn't murdered here. Do you
have any idea how hard it is to rent or sell a property where
there's been a murder?"

Hope looked over her shoulder. "Actually, I do. Remember that house I was almost killed in? It's still on the
market. And I'd think we should be more concerned
about Devon than the rental future of this property."

"You're right. Sorry."

"Did you hear anything this morning?"

"No. Since she moved in, I've heard her moving
around sometimes, but nothing today."

The apartment door was ajar, and there was no sound
coming from inside the tiny apartment. Hope stretched
out her hand and pushed the door open wider. She immediately pulled her hand back. Fingerprints. While she hoped
this was all a big misunderstanding, that Devon was safe
somewhere, running an errand, she could be stepping into
a crime scene.

A messy crime scene.

If someone hadn't searched the apartment, Devon must
have been in a frenzy looking for something. Hope could

identify with that. She'd spent last night turning her own house upside down looking for her missing charm bracelet. Anything to avoid having to ask Iva about it.

Sofa cushions and pillows were tossed on the wood floor, the area rug was scrunched up, and the dining chairs were strewn across the small eating area. Even the kitchen cabinets were open, and canned items were on the floor. The other evening, everything had been tidy and orderly. Even the piles of research on the table had had some order to them, though Hope would have preferred neatly arranged filed folders hung in a desktop file container. Now there was nothing to organize. All the research was gone. The bulletin board was empty.

"Devon! Are you home? It's Hope and Claire!"

Bigelow barked. Hope guessed he didn't want to be left out.

"No answer, just like before. I have a terrible feeling about this." Claire had followed her to the table. "Isn't this breaking and entering?"

"No. It's just entering. Don't touch anything." It was a reminder for herself. Touching the door was a rookie mistake. Hope should have known better. She headed to the bedroom with Bigelow. The bed was made, but Devon wasn't in there. She returned to the living area.

"What was this for?" Claire was looking at the bulletin board, which now lay flat on the table. The pushpins that held the newspaper articles and photographs were scattered over the board and table. It looked like somebody had ripped those documents away in a hurry.

"Devon's research. Newspaper articles, photos, police interviews. Devon is thorough."

Claire fingered the heart charm on her necklace. "I don't remember the newspaper articles. What I remember is the six o'clock news and a photo of Joyce up on the screen." She swallowed. "It terrified me. I thought Mom would disappear next."

Hope wrapped her arm around her sister's shoulder and gave a reassuring squeeze. "Me too." They stood silent for a moment until Hope let go of Claire. "We have to figure out what's going on here."

Claire nodded. "If Devon is right about someone abducting her mother and that person is still here in Jefferson, I think he or she wouldn't want her to be revisiting the past."

"You're right. You know, the more I've thought about it the past few days, the more I agree with Devon. I don't think Joyce walked out on her family."

"But if I remember correctly, there wasn't any sign of a struggle or a crime at the Markham house. Unlike here." Claire looked around the apartment.

"It could have been someone Joyce knew and wasn't afraid of. Maybe that person lured her out of the house under false pretenses."

"Doesn't sound like she had anything more concrete than the police had."

"I know. I think that's why Devon asked for my help."

Claire gave Hope their mother's look. The one when the two girls knew they'd been caught by their mom, who was waiting for an explanation before sentencing them to an unbearable punishment. Hope hated that look.

"Help with what, Hope? Finding the person who probably kidnapped and murdered Devon's mother? And now she's . . . we don't know where she is, but someone ransacked her apartment. Tell me you aren't considering it."

Hope lowered her gaze, and that's when she saw Drew's business card peeking out from beneath the bulletin board. She pulled out her phone from her purse and called him. He picked up on the third ring.

"Hey, have you talked to Devon recently?" Hope asked.

"Yesterday. We started her interview. I've been trying to schedule the rest of it, but she hasn't returned my call."

"After you met with her yesterday, do you know where she went?"

"She mentioned her next stop was to talk to the detective who worked Joyce's case. He's retired and living in Milford now. What's going on?"

"Not sure. Thanks." Hope ended the call. She looked at Claire. "We need to call Ethan. First, let's get out of here." The apartment was giving her the willies. She shepherded her sister and Bigelow out to the hall and down the stairs.

The good news was Ethan answered her call. The bad news was, he was on his way into another meeting with the mayor and the town's attorney. The really bad news was, he sent Detective Sam Reid to check out Devon's apartment.

Detective Reid wasn't fond of Hope's amateur sleuthing adventures. He'd made it abundantly clear she had no business poking her nose into police matters. He also never let the fact that she had a personal relationship with Ethan stop him from threatening to arrest her for interfering with a police investigation. Several times in fact. And now here he was.

Why couldn't Ethan have sent a patrol officer?

"I can see why you're concerned." Detective Reid stepped out of the apartment into the hallway where Hope, Claire, and Bigelow waited. He pulled the door closed. "Mrs. Dixon, did you hear anything this morning from up here?"

"No. Nothing. It looks like someone searched the apartment. Do you think it's connected to her mother's disappearance?" Claire asked.

"I'm unable to speculate at this time. For all we know, Ms. Markham could have left early this morning before you opened the shop, and she didn't securely close the door." Reid towered over Hope and Claire. His thin frame, courtesy of marathon running, was covered in a black trench coat. The unbuttoned coat revealed a dark gray turtleneck over black trousers and gave a glimpse of his badge attached to his belt.

"What about the mess inside?" Hope stood beside her sister, and Bigelow was seated, pressed against her leg. He'd positioned himself between her and the detective. Few things ignited the dog's ire, but Reid was one of them.

Reid shrugged. "A simple explanation could be that she's messy."

"That's not messy!" Hope pointed to the apartment door. "I was in there two nights ago, and other than paperwork cluttering the table, there wasn't any mess. No, Devon didn't do that. What about all her missing research?"

"She could have taken it with her. Why were you here the other night?" Reid pulled out a small black notepad from his coat's interior pocket, along with a pen. He flipped the notepad open to a blank sheet of paper.

"To catch up. Devon asked me to come over after my blogging class at the library." Hope watched the detective jot down what she'd said.

"I heard about the class." Reid looked up from his notepad.

"It was the first class, and I think it went well. There

were a lot of questions, and I think the students were confused when I talked about platforms hosting—"

"I don't think he's interested in your class," Claire
said.

"Right. Sorry. Back to Devon."

"Thank you, Miss Early." A rare smiled appeared on
his lips. His sharp facial features usually didn't reveal what
he was thinking. So, seeing something like a smile was
indeed surprising.

"Devon wanted to catch up." And to ask her to help
with her investigation. But she decided not to share that
part until her sister poked her in the side with her elbow.
"Ouch." She glared at Claire.

"Tell him or I will."

"Tell me what?" Reid asked.

Hope gave her sister a I-will-not-forget-this look.
"Devon asked for my help with her investigation of her
mother's case."

"She did, did she?" Reid smirked. "And what was
your answer, Ms. Early?"

"I didn't give her an answer."

"Why not? It should have been a big, fat no," Claire
said.

"I know what you think." Hope turned her attention
back to the detective.

"Do you? What am I thinking now?" Claire's tone was
aggravated.

Reid cleared his throat, interrupting the squabble.

"Sorry." Hope glared one more time at Claire. "I called
Drew, and he said he met with Devon yesterday. He's
writing a story about her podcast. After their meeting, she
told him she would talk to the detective who handled her
mother's case. He's retired now."

"Sounds like you're investigating," Reid observed.

"Exactly!" Claire threw her arms up in the air.

"All I did was call Drew. Look, we should be concerned about Devon right now," Hope said. "Last night, Claire overheard Devon talking on the phone."

"She sounded upset. I heard her say she wasn't leaving Jefferson until she found out what happened to her mother," Claire said.

Reid jotted down more notes. His dark eyebrows drew together, and he closed his notepad. "Given the situation, I will file a missing persons report because it appears someone has searched the apartment."

"A report?" Claire propped her hand on her hip. "Can't you do more?"

"In all honesty, filing the report at this stage is all we can do until we're certain whether Ms. Markham is missing or not. I'll contact her sister to see if she knows where Ms. Markham could be." Reid took a step forward, and Bigelow stood up on all fours.

Hope patted her dog on the head as the detective passed by and walked down the stairs.

"What good is a report going to do?" Claire turned and tramped down the staircase. Her steps were heavy with frustration, and Hope sighed. She didn't like the outcome either. She'd hoped for more, but Devon was an adult who could be anywhere doing anything and not in any danger.

Perhaps they were overreacting. Then again, did Devon, her family, and the police think they were overreacting when Joyce was first discovered to be missing? Did they all think she was an adult who could be anywhere doing anything and not in any danger?

Hope led Bigelow down the stairs. It wasn't unreasonable to think Devon went out first thing in the morning as Reid had suggested. In fact, most likely that was what happened and Devon would return home at some point. If that were the case, why did the hairs on the back of Hope's neck prick up?

The warmth of the inn's lobby prompted Hope to unzip her jacket. She found Jane busy at the reception desk, a fixture in the inn since the once private house was turned into a charming bed-and-breakfast. The couple Jane was speaking to was asking about skiing in the area. Jane handed them two brochures and then explained the differences between the two ski destinations. The couple smiled and thanked Jane for her advice and, on their way out of the inn, patted Bigelow on the head.

"I'm sorry to interrupt." Hope guided Bigelow to the reception desk.

Jane waved away the silly notion. "No worries at all, dear. I was just about to take a break. And it's wonderful to see the little guy." She whisked Hope and Bigelow into the back parlor.

The room was a private space where Jane and Sally retreated from their guests.

Jane's husband, Sally's older brother, had died a decade ago, leaving her alone in their big house. Sally had been living in her house north of Main Street but spent most of her time at the inn. One day, they came up with the idea of moving in together at the inn. It made sense. Both of them were already spending a lot of time there, and they'd save money by not maintaining separate homes.

Jane set Hope on the deep-cushioned sofa before shuffling out of the room to prepare a pot of tea. The hot beverage was Jane's cure-all for everything from physical ailments to broken hearts. Hope preferred coffee. But she wasn't about to argue with Jane. She'd have a nice cup of steaming-hot black tea, hopefully English breakfast tea, with a little milk and maybe one of Jane's muffins.

Bigelow lay down beside the sofa and rested his head on his front legs. He looked like he'd made himself quite comfortable on the area rug. In subtle tones of green, brown, beige, and cream, the intricate pattern grounded the dark furnishings.

While she waited for Jane to come back, Hope eased back and relaxed into the jewel-toned sofa. A bookcase lined the wall opposite the fireplace. Sally and Jane crammed the shelves with books, many first editions, and Jane's novels were also displayed.

Over the firebox, where a crackling fire burned, was a carved mantel covered with knickknacks passed down from generation to generation in the Merrifield family. They weren't the only family with deep roots in the town. Devon's family was also deeply rooted in Jefferson. The Markham family tree didn't go back to the eighteenth century, but it went far enough to have made Greg Markham a prominent member of the town and Joyce one of the busiest volunteers during her marriage.

Jane returned, expertly balancing the tray of tea. "Here we go. A fresh pot of chamomile tea."

Hope did her best not to wrinkle her nose at the choice of beverage.

"This will do you a world of good." Jane set the tray on the oval-shaped coffee table. She glanced up at Hope and smiled. She wore her signature lipstick. Hope would never have the guts to wear such a bold pink color; matte nudes were her preference. "I also have a little something for Bigelow. We don't want him to feel left out."

Hope scanned the tray. There was one dog biscuit, but no muffins. However, there was lemon cake. Okay, she could endure the chamomile tea if it came with cake. Her mood brightened.

"Here you go." Jane handed Bigelow the treat, and he chomped hard, breaking it in half. "Now, tell me, what's going on? You have a worried look on your face."

Jane knew Hope all too well. When Hope was a teenager, she'd been a member of the mystery book club Jane organized at the library. So, it wasn't a surprise she could read Hope so easily. After Hope left Devon's apartment, she walked in the direction of the inn. Where she needed to be was home and back at work, but what she wanted was a little comfort and reassurance.

"Claire called me a little while ago. Something is wrong with Devon."

"This sounds serious. Good thing you came over. I sliced you a piece of lemon pound cake. My niece, Elnora, lives in California and sends me a big box of lemons every year from her trees. I squeeze the juice and freeze it so I can bake and cook with it later." Jane handed Hope a cup and saucer. "Drink up, dear."

Hope took the cup and saucer. She wasn't sure about Jane's claims about the tea, but she was dying to dive into the slice of lemon cake on the tray.

She sipped the tea and then told Jane what had happened at the apartment. From Devon's call, to finding the apartment a mess this morning, to Detective Reid filing a missing person report.

"My mind keeps bouncing back and forth between

Devon being perfectly fine and busy chasing down leads, to her spending the day at the mall, to her being left for dead in the woods. See, I'm all over the place. So far, she hasn't replied to any of our voice mails."

"This is some predicament. It's understandable for our minds to instantly jump to the worst-case scenario, given the circumstances around Devon's return to Jefferson." Jane sipped her tea and then leaned into the upholstered chair. Her winter white sweater dress looked comfy and warm, as did her suede loafers.

"I wish we knew exactly what her plans were for today. Drew told me she planned on visiting the detective who was assigned to her mother's case." Hope eyed the cake. Would it be rude to help herself?

"There was one case Barbara Neal became entangled in where a classmate didn't want any help. She insisted she could handle the situation all on her own."

Sipping her tea, Hope looked over the rim of the cup. She knew what was coming next. Jane was about to draw another comparison between her fictional sleuth and Hope. She had a habit of doing that. But as long as Jane understood Hope wasn't her imaginary creation, she guessed all was good.

"Barbara didn't know what to do. She wanted to help her friend, yet she wanted to respect her friend's wishes."

Hope set her tea on the tray. "Devon wanted my help."

Jane nodded. "You're thinking if you agreed to help her, she wouldn't be missing now."

"What did Barbara do?" Hope couldn't believe she was asking the question.

"She helped, of course."

Of course Barbara did, otherwise the book would have been very short.

Jane reached forward, set her cup on the tray, and then handed Hope a plate with a slice of cake and a fork. She then took her own plate.

Hope broke off a piece and chewed. The texture was moist and light, and the burst of brightness from the lemons elevated her mood. She ate another piece and allowed her body and mind to relax. There was no reason at this point to suspect foul play. Devon was just out for the day and not checking her voice mails.

The door opened, and Bigelow lifted his head. Sally entered carrying a basket filled with cleaning supplies. The inn had a staff, but Sally liked to take care of the parlor herself. She said it kept her busy, especially in the winter months, when her gardening was limited to the houseplants.

Her face was weathered, and her body was toned from a lifetime of gardening. Though her hands were showing signs of arthritis, and every so often Hope saw a flicker of irritation in Sally's eyes from the joint pain. She wasn't a woman who liked to slow down. So any physical limitation was a source of contention for her.

"Good to see you, Hope." Sally topped a pair of jeans and sneakers with a yellow sweater. She set her basket on top of a cabinet and pulled out her dusting cloth. She reached down and gave Bigelow a pat on the head. "Hello, little fellow. What brings you two out for a visit?"

Jane answered for Hope, leaving her to finish her cake. Sally listened as she wiped the lamp on the end table.

"Sounds like both of your imaginations are off and running. Devon probably forgot to charge her phone."

"I want to believe she's okay, but you didn't see the apartment. It really looked like someone searched it," Hope said.

Jane's brow arched. Intrigue was written all over her face. "What's missing?"

"All the research I saw the other night." Hope finished the last piece of her cake. Now she was sad. Sad and worried.

"I've been listening to Devon's podcast. I've gotten to the episode where Devon revealed she believed her father was having an affair at the time of Joyce's disappearance," Jane said.

"She told me she didn't know who the woman might have been. Was there any gossip of an affair back then?" Hope looked to both women. For as long as she could remember, the Merrifield women had had their pulse on everything that happened in Jefferson.

Both women shook their heads.

"Never heard a peep about it." Sally put down her dusting cloth and walked to the sofa and sat. "Joyce always seemed happy when she came into the library. She'd stay and chat for a bit."

"Chat about what?" Hope asked.

"The usual stuff. Weather, her girls, and school. She usually stopped by on her way to work at Alfred's agency."

"Joyce worked for him?" Hope had forgotten which real estate agency Joyce worked for. *Oh, boy.* Not only would Maretta be up in arms about a podcast showcasing a twenty-year-old unsolved disappearance in town, but now her husband's company would be connected.

"She'd worked there only a few months before she disappeared." Jane's blue eyes glimmered. "Do you think someone at Alfred's company had something to do with Joyce's disappearance?"

Hope knew that glimmer she was seeing all too well. It meant Jane's mind was concocting a theory.

"A jilted lover perhaps? A scorned admirer who was rejected by Joyce? Or maybe it was work-related. Real estate is a cutthroat business, as we all know." Jane took a triumphant bite of her cake.

Hope figured Jane's reference was related to the murder of a real estate agent last year. She'd been a newcomer to town and an agent with a reputation of being a shark when it came to deals.

"Joyce was a secretary. I'm not sure she would have gotten involved in any of the transactions." Hope wondered if Devon had reached out to Alfred Kingston yet. If she had, what had she learned about her mother's employment record?

"I'd better get back to my cleaning." Sally patted Hope's knee and then stood. She walked to her basket and pulled out a spray bottle and spritzed the mirror over the console.

Hope glanced at her watch. It was getting late, and she had work to do.

"Thank you for the tea, Jane." Hope reached for Bigelow's leash and stood.

"Any time, dear. Be sure to let me know when you hear anything about Devon. I'm very concerned."

"She'll be fine. Like always, you two always jump to the wildest theories." Sally stretched to wipe the mirror from top to bottom.

"We've had good reason in the past, haven't we, Hope?" Jane stood and walked to the door. "In fact, because of our so-called overactive imaginations, murderers have been brought to justice."

"I think Maretta would disagree. She'd probably say it's your busybody tendencies that were involved." Sally chuckled.

"Don't pay her any mind. We're not busybodies. We're concerned citizens." Jane opened the door.

"I'll call you when I hear something." Hope and Bigelow exited the parlor and made their way through the lobby to the front door. As they left the inn, they passed another young couple on their way inside. Seeing them reminded Hope she had to decide what to pack for her weekend getaway with Ethan. A buzzing from her phone alerted her to an incoming text; it was from Josie. A gentle reminder she had class tonight. Hope picked up their pace to get home. She was so far behind.

Chapter Seven

Hope spent the rest of the day on pins and needles, waiting to hear something, anything, about Devon. Because there were no incoming calls about her friend, she made some of her own.

Her first call was to Detective Reid. Nothing new there. The next call was to Devon's sister. Felice sounded upset and worried. She hadn't heard from her sister since move-in day. After Hope hung up, she had one more question added to her long list: if Felice hadn't spoken to her sister in two days, who had Devon been arguing with on the phone last night? Hope's final call before she dashed out to the library was to Claire to check if Devon had returned home. She hadn't.

Hope arrived at the library fifteen minutes before class was supposed to start. She used the time to set up and mentally prepare. All thoughts of Devon needed to be put on the back burner. At least until after class.

Her students arrived and took their seats.

She did a quick head count. They all came back.

Plus one.

What on earth was *she* doing there?

Elaine strutted to the front of the class in her knee-high boots. How she had navigated the slick patches of ice in those four-inch heels baffled Hope. Didn't the woman own any sensible winter shoes? Hope glanced at her sturdy black ankle boots designed for real life, not runways.

"What are you doing here?" Hope asked, dragging her gaze upward.

Elaine unbuttoned her faux fur jacket and revealed her form-fitting red sweater. The woman had curves, and she knew how to use them to her full advantage. Hence, her four husbands.

"I figured because I had to cut my vacation short, I might as well learn about blogging." She scanned the two tables where the other students had settled. "Where should I sit?"

"Registration is full," Hope said.

Elaine blinked, giving Hope full view of her expertly applied eye makeup. From the skilled application of winged eyeliner, to the depths of a smoky eye, to lush false lashes, Hope couldn't fathom the time spent. She barely had time to apply one coat of mascara.

"No worries. I worked it out with Angela. I'm auditing the class."

"Auditing? This isn't a college course."

"Of course not, silly. Ooh, there's a seat." Elaine sashayed away to a seat next to Phillip Rafferty, who looked pleased to have her next to him. But his look quickly changed when she gave him a cold glare that had back-off written all over it.

Elaine took off her jacket and draped it over the back of her chair. Next, she pulled out a notebook from her designer bag.

"Don't you like to start class on time?" Elaine tapped her blinged-out watch.

Hope heaved a heavy sigh. It would be a long class.

"The assignments you all turned in were great." Hope moved back to her laptop. Before the class, each student had emailed their completed assignment for her to review. She wasn't grading; there were no passes or fails. Though she did provide feedback to them.

She forced herself to stop staring at the newest edition to the class and dwelling on how long class would be. When her gaze moved from Elaine, she saw Laila beaming. Her assignment had been the most thorough. It was clear that Laila wanted more out of life than whipping up cappuccinos every morning for tired customers. Hope continued scanning the class. Gail's chapped lips curved up into a satisfied smile. Her assignment was light on detail, but Hope could see her student had a clear vision of her blog. Two seats over was Shirley. She didn't look pleased. Hope was puzzled because Shirley had turned in a solid assignment.

Hope absorbed the excitement that bounced off her students. As any long-time blogger would tell you, it was easy to get caught up in all the minutiae and lose sight of what first attracted them to blogging. Seeing the activity through the eyes of newbies was invigorating. Their enthusiasm was refreshing.

"Tonight we'll cover how to design your blog. For

this, we'll be working on the back end. I expect this will be our most intense class. But trust me when I say it's important for you to understand how it works behind the scenes."

Elaine raised her hand. "Do you think I could get a private lesson to cover what I've missed so far?"

Hope cleared her throat. "We can work something out. Now, back to what I was saying about designing your blog." She wasn't a website designer, but she believed for any blogger to be successful, she should be able to do simple tasks on her blog without having to pay a designer.

She tapped a key on her laptop's keyboard and an image of the website's dashboard came up on the screen, and as she expected, confused looks appeared on everyone's face.

"This is the dashboard. It's not as scary as it looks." She scanned the class. Her words had fallen on deaf ears from the collective puzzled looks on their faces. She was losing them.

Quick, say something. Now.

"This is where you will spend most of your time as a blogger. Remember what I told you about blogging not being glamorous? Well, here's why." She gave a little laugh, and the class joined in. Feeling more relaxed, she continued with the lesson.

By the end of the class, there were a lot of glazed eyeballs, but to their credit, each student was still enthusiastic and eager to work on the new assignment—ten ideas and outline the first two posts.

All in all, the session could have turned out worse. At least no one was racing to the door.

She was thankful they kept her mind off Devon. She did a quick check of her phone. Still no update. Not even from Ethan.

He'd been in and out of meetings all day. Then he had a retirement dinner to attend for the police chief in the next town over.

"Well, that was a lot of information to take in." Shirley stopped at Hope's table.

Hope looked up from her phone and then set it down.

"I promise, it's not too bad once you start using your website. Do you have a minute?" Hope had been churning over Devon's theory that her father had been unfaithful to her mother at the time of the disappearance. Maybe Shirley could shed some light on it.

"I suppose so. What's up?" Shirley set her purse on the table.

"You were friends with Joyce. Did she ever confide in you that she suspected her husband was having an affair?" Hope asked in a low voice as the last of the students left the room.

"Why are you asking?" Shirley's thin lips clamped down and her gaze narrowed, signaling to Hope their conversation would not be pleasant.

It wouldn't be the first unpleasant conversation she'd had. There was the divorce conversation with her ex-husband, the time she had to explain to Detective Reid why she trespassed onto a crime scene, and the chats she had with killers when she got into their crosshairs. So, Shirley's warning look didn't have the impact she'd expected it would have on Hope.

"Devon said she believes her father was having an affair."

"I can't believe she'd say such a thing! Outrageous! I'm surprised you'd be repeating such nonsense." When the look didn't work on Hope, Shirley raised her voice, prompting the last of the students walking out the door to look over their shoulders.

Hope gestured to them that everything was okay and then turned back to Shirley. "Devon doesn't believe it's nonsense. If she did, I doubt she'd say it publicly."

"I've said it before and I'll say it again, it does no one any good to dig up the past. My goodness, Greg's not here to defend himself. Talk about unfair."

"Don't you think what happened to Joyce was unfair?" Hope countered.

"You have a reputation of stirring up hornets' nests, and I strongly suggest you stay out of the Markhams' business." Shirley yanked up her purse and stormed out, passing by Gail, who was reentering the room.

Gail gave Hope a curious look and then pointed to her seat. "I forgot my notebook."

"She's right about you having a thing for stirring up hornets' nests." Elaine approached the table. "Like you did when my sweet Lionel was murdered. But I know you can't help yourself." She tilted her head sideways and smiled. Though the smile didn't feel sincere to Hope.

"Is Shirley okay?" Gail, with her notebook in hand, joined Hope and Elaine.

"I'm not sure." Hope grabbed her coat. What she was sure about was that Shirley wasn't behaving like her usually perky self. She always had a sunny disposition, like her daughter, Amy. It didn't take an experienced detective like Sam Reid to realize there was something about Joyce's disappearance that Shirley didn't want to discuss.

"I don't think I've ever seen her storm out of anywhere." Gail shoved her notebook into her tote bag.

"Hope can have that effect on people. Though she means well," Elaine said.

Hope bristled at being spoken about as if she wasn't even there. "We should get going." Her tone was sharp and her patience short.

"Are you feeling a little tired? Ethan says you're working so much. You know, I have a concealer that will work wonders for your under eyes." Elaine dug into her purse and pulled out a small tube. "Try this. It's a life-saver. Especially these days. There's so much to do, settling into my new house."

"New house?" Gail asked.

"I found a rental I love. It has an option to buy. So I'm giving it a test drive, so to speak." Elaine looked at Hope. "Ethan was so kind as to help me with my alarm system."

"I'm sure helping you fill out the paperwork to register the system wasn't too much for him to do." Hope eyed the concealer. Did she really have dark circles under her eyes?

"Oh, he did way more than that." Elaine gave a breathy laugh as she handed the tube of concealer to Hope. "He helped me with the system. I got all flustered with how to use it. He showed me how to do it just right. The man is a wonderful teacher. Toodles!" She waved as she sashayed out of the room. That was how Elaine went through life—sashaying and batting her false lashes.

"She's a piece of work," Gail observed.

She most certainly is.

When had Ethan gone to Elaine's house? Why hadn't he told Hope? It wasn't like house calls to set up alarms were a part of his job description. She tamped down her irritation with both Ethan and Elaine.

"Anyway, it was a great class. I'm looking forward to brainstorming post ideas," Gail said before she walked out of the room.

Hope shrugged into her coat after she gathered all her papers into her tote along with her laptop. With all her belongings plus the tube of concealer, she walked to the doorway. Before she left the room, she looked back at where Shirley sat during class.

A niggling feeling reinforced her suspicion that Shirley was hiding something.

The next morning, Hope's alarm went off, but all she wanted to do was pull the covers over her head. She reasoned she didn't have the oomph she needed to get up and head out for her run. Then a little voice in the far recesses of her mind reminded her of all the indulgences she enjoyed over the holiday season. While the holidays were long over, the aftereffects still lingered on her hips. Plus, a ramped-up schedule of recipe-testing had also tilted the scale in the direction she didn't like.

Adjusting her reflective headband over her ears, she prepared herself for a long, grueling run thanks to a lack of sleep and it being freakin' cold outside. After she tied her sneakers, she patted Bigelow on the head. He'd stayed curled up on her bed, sleeping. He never seemed to have restless nights.

Passing through the downstairs to the mudroom, she found Princess curled up on a chair in the family room. It was hard to imagine her as the wild child she was a few months ago. She looked so peaceful and angelic. They grew up so fast.

Hope packed her waist belt with her bare necessities and pulled open the back door and was greeted by a slap of cold air. Walking to the road, she turned on her playlist, then picked up her pace.

She'd thought her morning run would snap her out of her sleep-deprived fog. It had. During the three-mile run, she was anything but sleepy thanks to the frigid February air. The best part about running in the winter months was, her speed increased because she was freezing her glutes off. But an hour later, seated across from Jane in The Coffee Clique, her eyelids were heavy, and her yawns were increasing.

Hope tried to fight it, but she was powerless against it. She covered her mouth with her hand as she yawned again.

"Didn't sleep well, dear?" Jane asked before she broke off a piece of her glazed apple walnut muffin. She'd called Hope midway through her run and suggested they meet at the coffee shop.

The idea had perked Hope up. A hazelnut coffee would be the perfect reward for finishing her workout. Without hesitation, Hope said she'd be there. With a prize at the end of her run, she had dug deep into her reserves to power through and arrived at The Coffee Clique right after Jane had.

Hope suppressed another yawn as she nodded. Too bad The Coffee Clique didn't have a megasize coffee cup. The large she ordered just wasn't doing it for her. She needed another one. Or two.

"I kept tossing and turning all night." Between worrying about Devon, being annoyed by Elaine barging into her class, Ethan's secret visit to the widow's house, and dreading having to talk to Iva about the missing bracelet, Hope's mind had raced a mile a minute once she'd lain her head down on the pillow.

Her bed was normally her sanctuary. While she saved money where she could in her house remodel, she splurged on her bedding. She indulged in cloud-soft pillows and luxurious linens, including a down comforter that had an eye-popping price tag. She spent long hours every day on her feet, either recipe testing or working on some DIY project around the old farmhouse, and when it came time to sleep, she wanted to be cocooned in comfort.

Too bad her sleep cycle didn't get the memo that she was supposed to be relaxing and dreaming about kittens overnight, not fretting about everything that happened the day before.

"Still no word about Devon?" Jane wiped her mouth with a napkin and then set it down on the table. She wore a lavender-colored scarf tied around her neck and a matching hat. Her red wool jacket was draped over the back of her chair.

"No. Ethan texted me after he got back from the retirement party. There wasn't any news." Hope chugged her coffee. When she received the text, she was tempted to ask about Elaine's alarm system, but she resisted. The conversation should happen face-to-face. She kept her thoughts from spiraling out of control because she knew the kind of man he was. They'd known each other since high school. Ethan was a straight-up guy who didn't cheat on his significant other or his taxes. But she'd been married to a man who did, and the experience had left her wary.

"It feels like her mother all over again. One day she's there and the next she's not."

Those haunting words had Hope's thoughts shift from Ethan back to Devon. She knew her relationship with him was solid. Nothing to worry about. But Devon? There was a lot to worry about there.

"I'm glad you called because I wanted to ask about Shirley. You've known her for a long time, haven't you?"

"I have. Though we aren't close friends. Amy was in one of my reading groups at the library. Shirley would stop and chat when she picked Amy up." Jane sipped her tea. Yes, she was more refined than Hope was.

"Why are you asking?" Jane asked.

"Last night she got all weird when I asked her about Devon's claim that her dad was having an affair. She made it clear no one, not even Devon, should dig up the past." Hope went back to drinking her coffee like a normal person. Setting down the cup, she caught a glimpse of the pastries.

"Well, I doubt Shirley would have been eager to talk about something so private even if Devon was shouting it all over the internet with her podcast." Jane's blue eyes, generally filled with curiosity and warmth, turned serious and changed the whole demeanor of her rounded face. "It's not in Shirley's nature to discuss such matters."

"I understand, but you'd think if she and Joyce were such good friends, she'd want to find out what happened. Wouldn't you?"

"Wouldn't you what?" Drew approached the table holding a tall coffee cup and a plated bagel smeared with cream cheese. His messenger bag was slung crossbody over his navy jacket. He set his breakfast on the table and removed his bag, then sat.

"We're talking about Shirley's lack of interest in finding out what happened to Joyce." Jane finished the last piece of her muffin.

"How could she not be interested? Weren't they like best friends back in the day?" Drew bit into half of his bagel with a vengeance. Hope guessed he'd hit the gym already and worked up an appetite.

"Believe me when I tell you, she was adamant last

night that what happened in the past should stay in the past." Hope lifted her cup and leaned back. "If it were me and one of you disappeared, I'd want to know what happened."

"Thank you, dear. I appreciate knowing you'd move heaven and earth to solve my disappearance." Jane finished her tea.

"Yeah, right back at you, Hope. On a different matter, have you heard Elaine's back in town?" Drew asked between bites.

Hope nodded. "I saw her the other day at the police department and last night at the library. She's auditing my class."

Drew gave her a confused look. "Really, for an adult education class? Does she even know what the word means?"

Jane laughed. "Don't be too harsh on her. She lost her husband a few months ago, and her life was turned upside down."

"It feels like wherever she goes, things get turned upside down. She wants me to give her a private lesson so she can catch up with the other students." Hope took a breath. She didn't want to talk about Elaine anymore. Except with Ethan. Definitely with Ethan.

"Moving on. Have you heard about Maretta's bright idea?" Drew asked with a touch of sarcasm after he took a drink of his coffee.

Hope and Jane glanced at each other and then shook their heads in unison. Jane's wispy bangs fluttered.

"In her infinite wisdom, she's decided to move forward with her proposal to ban snowball throwing. And the police paid Billy Murphy's parents a visit."

"Absurd. Children love snowball fights," Jane said.

"I can't believe the police spoke to his parents. He and

his friends weren't being malicious. I was there." They didn't need a visit from the police, just a reminder not to throw snowballs at people who weren't playing along. Hope pulled her phone out of her jacket pocket and checked her messages. None from Ethan or Claire or Reid. And where the heck was Devon?

"Can she really ban throwing snowballs?" Jane asked.

"She has to go through the Town Council. They'll do just about anything not to have to deal with her. I have a feeling her mayoral term is going to feel like forever for all of us." Drew took another bite of his bagel.

"My thought exactly on election day." Hope drained the last of her coffee and seriously considered a refill. She had a feeling she'd be testing how much caffeine she could ingest before becoming too jittery.

"The one good thing about Maretta being the mayor is that the Town Council meetings are now a lot more interesting. The last one had—" Drew was cut off by the chime of his cell phone. He retrieved it from his messenger bag and read the screen. "Oh. My. Gosh."

"What? What is it?" Hope leaned forward.

"They found Devon's car in a ditch off Hargate Hill Road." Drew didn't look up; he kept reading.

"Who says?" Jane asked.

Drew finally looked up. "My source."

"Who's your source?" Hope asked.

Drew returned his phone to his bag. "Does it matter? The police are on scene. I gotta go." He stood, slung his bag across his body, and gathered up what was left of his breakfast.

"I'm going with you. I'll call you later, Jane." Hope rose to her feet, grabbed her coffee cup, and ditched it in the trash can as she followed Drew to the exit.

"You understand I'll be gathering info, so you'll be on your own while we're at the scene." Drew held the door open for Hope.

"Got it."

They walked to Drew's sports car. It wasn't the most practical vehicle for winter months in Connecticut, but it sure was sleek, and the way it drove made her swoon. And that's why she drove an SUV.

"Did your source say anything about Devon?" Hope snapped the seat belt buckle into place.

Drew glanced at his side mirror and then pulled his car out of the parking space and headed north on Main Street. "No."

"Where on Hargate Hill did they find the car?"

"Past Swamp Hollow."

Hope winced. She knew the spot well. It was an isolated stretch of road with a sharp curve. Beautiful in three seasons of the year and treacherous in the winter.

Several turns and ten minutes later, they were on Hargate Hill Road. She glanced at Drew. He'd drawn silent. She sensed he was keeping something from her. Something his source had shared with him, but he didn't want to share with her.

The stillness of the cold air blanketed the hilly landscape as the morning sun struggled to break through the thick patch of clouds above, ice glazed over the jagged edges of the rocky wall they drove by, and snow weighed down the limbs of the bare trees. They were getting closer to Swamp Hollow Road when the tires of Drew's car did a little hula dance. Instinctively, Hope's hands reached out for the dashboard and pressed hard as she looked to Drew.

"Just a little slip. Nothing to worry about." He pulled the steering wheel back and regained control. "Up ahead."

Hope nodded. The crime scene was coming into view. Among the various rescue vehicles was Hank Padgett's tow truck.

"Hank's your source, isn't he?"

"Maybe." Drew parked his car on a small patch of packed-down snow. The spot also made sure his vehicle wouldn't be in the way. "I can leave the car running so you'll stay warm." His finger hovered over the Start button.

"You really think I'm going to stay in here?" She opened the door and stepped out. The frigid air gave her pause to reconsider Drew's offer.

"You're not dressed for the elements or terrain in your running shoes. Be careful! We don't need another rescue!" Drew closed the door and walked toward the scene. His stride was fast and confident. He was in his glory. Being first on the scene, getting an exclusive, doing what he loved. She'd asked him countless times why he chose to stay at the *Gazette* when he had the talent and skill for a larger publication. He always said the same thing: he loved Jefferson and didn't want to live anywhere else.

The one big downside to living and reporting in a small town was, eventually the big news of the day would be about a friend, neighbor, or relative.

Like today.

Devon was the story.

A man's voice shouting instructions distracted Hope from thinking about the possibility that Devon was in the car when it went off the road and didn't survive the accident.

She couldn't think like that. At least not yet.

She came around to the front of Drew's car and shoved her hands into her jacket pockets. A pit of coldness settled in her stomach. It wasn't the kind of coldness that could be warmed up, like adding another layer to her jacket. No, the coldness inside her just sat there, expanding with every minute that passed, and it hurt.

The strobe lights on the rescue vehicles lit up the gray morning, and the constant sounds of radios squawking with what sounded like garbled conversations disturbed the usual quietness of the wooded area.

"Come on! Keep moving!" A uniformed police officer, bundled up in layers and a thick hat, directed traffic on the now one-lane road. The cars passing by moved at a slow speed so the drivers could get a glimpse of what was happening. Human nature at its finest.

Amid the controlled chaos of the scene, Hope spotted Drew walking back toward her, and Ethan was beside him.

Ethan's jaw was set and his shoulders were squared. He was in full cop mode. If Hope didn't know better, she would have been nervous.

"What are you doing here?" he asked.

Ouch. He was channeling Detective Reid.

She tried not to take his abruptness or tone personally. He was the police chief and on the scene of an accident. He didn't have time for chitchat. Not even a simple hello to his girlfriend.

"I was with Drew when he got the tip someone found Devon's car." She raised to her tippy toes to see over Ethan's shoulders. He was blocking her view of the scene.

"Why did you bring her?" Ethan asked Drew.

"Do you really think I could have stopped her?" He gave Hope a double take and shrugged as he mouthed, *Sorry.* He looked back at Ethan. "Who found the car?"

He had his cell phone out and tapped on the recording app.

"Jimmy Lightfoot. He was out walking his dog when the dog broke free from the leash and wandered into that area." Ethan turned and pointed up ahead, where there was a break in the fencing. "He spotted the car when he was getting his dog out of there and called us."

"Is he still here?" Drew did a full 360 turn, scanning the scene.

"He's finishing up his statement." Ethan turned his attention to Hope. "I wish you hadn't come with Drew." His stern look softened, as did his tone.

"I won't get in the way." Hope folded her arms over her chest. Drew was right; she wasn't dressed for the weather, at least not for standing in place.

"I didn't think you would." Ethan looked back to where the first responders were working. Several had huddled at the break in the fence where it looked like the car hit before plummeting down the hillside. He looked back at Hope and held her gaze for a solemn moment before he cast his eyes downward.

Hope gasped. "Devon's in the car, isn't she?"

He closed the small gap between them and touched her arm. "I'm sorry, but I can't confirm the identity of the victim at this time. Not until the next of kin has been notified."

Hope's hand covered her mouth. Devon was dead. She was certain of it.

"They're bringing up the body now. Are you going to be okay?"

Hope stared at him for what seemed like a lifetime. Everything went still around her. Around them. And silent. She wanted to cry, to scream, to wake up from this nightmare. But she couldn't. It wasn't a dream, it was real. Devon was dead. She fought back the tears. She couldn't cry. Not then. Ethan and Drew had work to do. They didn't have time to console her. She wanted them to do their jobs and not worry about her.

She dipped her head to compose herself and then looked back up. "I'll be fine. Don't worry about me. Go back to your officers."

"Wait, before you do. Can you tell me if the victim's death was a result of the accident?" Drew asked.

"At this time, I can't comment. There will be an autopsy to determine the cause of death," Ethan said. "Also, under no circumstances are you to reveal the victim's identity."

"Of course not. No way I want to be responsible for a family member learning about a loved one's death via my article. Can you tell me if there was any sign there was foul play involved?" Drew asked.

"Again, I can't comment at this time. We'll do a full investigation and then release our findings," Ethan said.

"Chief!" an officer from the section of the broken fence called out.

Ethan raised his hand to acknowledge he heard. He took a step closer to Hope. "I have to go. There's nothing out here for you to do or see. Go back in the car. You're shivering. I'll call you later." He squeezed her arm before turning away and walking toward his officer.

Hope opened her mouth to protest but didn't say a word. How could she argue with him? He was right. Maybe it would have been better if she'd stayed at the coffee shop with Jane.

"I'll be a few more minutes." Drew followed Ethan and then changed course. Hope saw that he'd spotted Jimmy

Lightfoot on the other side of the road. He wasted no time in getting his exclusive interview. She scanned the scene, and everything seemed to go into slow motion, and the shouts from the first responders seemed to fade as the body bag came into view.

Hope's stomach somersaulted, and her hand flew up to cover her mouth to stifle her cry.

What happened on Hargate Hill? How long had Devon been in that ditch? Was she alive when her car careened through the fencing? The questions repeated until they became a never-ending loop in her head.

She looked away, refusing to look back at the disturbing scene. She leaned against the driver's side of the car. The body was out of view. A few minutes later, Drew joined her, and nudged her with his shoulder.

"You okay?" he asked, concern filled his voice. "It's okay if you're not. She was a friend."

"We were. Though we hadn't seen each other since high school. Maybe 'friend' isn't the right word." Hope looked at Drew. They'd gone through life's ups and downs, like her divorce and very public loss on *The Sweet Taste of Success*, and her first-ever recipe video going viral. They *were* friends. Best friends for life.

"Maybe not. Still, you and Devon were friends in high school. You had a connection with her. I can't imagine being here is easy for you."

"What about you? You were friends with her too, back then."

Drew wrapped his arm around Hope's shoulders and pulled her close to him. "I'm here doing my job. I'm a professional. I have to be emotionally detached."

"I see. So, what does your emotionally detached, professional brain tell you about all this?"

"That's easy. I suspect this wasn't a simple accident."

"Exactly what I'm thinking. I mean, it's too much of a coincidence Devon shows up here to find out what happened to her mother and then disappears the day she's supposed to talk to the retired detective and then she's found dead in a car accident."

"I don't believe in coincidences."

"Neither do I." Hope pulled away from Drew and the car. She walked to the hood. "I think someone staged this to look like an accident." She looked over her shoulder. "I think someone murdered Devon."

Drew opened his mouth to say something and then clamped it shut, his lips thinning into a grim line. Hope followed his gaze. Approaching from the other direction was Norrie Jennings.

"Oh. No. She's not going to steal my story." Drew's voice went up a notch, and he stood up straight.

"I thought you were in a professional, emotionally detached mode?"

"Not when it comes to her." He lunged forward, but Hope grabbed his arm. He glowered at her.

"Drew, you have your quotes and your photographs. You need to get back to the office and write up your article before she writes hers. Come on, let's get out of here."

Drew was standing firm.

Hope tugged his arm. Still no movement on his part. She pulled, harder, and it yielded to him caving and walking back to the driver's side.

Behind the wheel, he navigated his car through a four-point U-turn and then drove back to town. Hope welcomed the heated seats and nestled her head in the soft, leather headrest. By the time she'd get dropped off at her house, she expected to be thawed out.

"We need to find out if Devon made it to Milford to speak with the retired detective. Can you check?" The warmth from the seat spread throughout Hope's body, chasing away the cold that clung to her.

"I can. I'd love to get my hands on her research notes. I wonder if she had copies or saved them to the cloud? Maybe Felice knows?"

"Felice! She'll be devastated when she finds out what happened." Hope's heart broke, thinking about the news Felice would soon be receiving. "Who's going to tell her?"

"Ethan was heading over to Felice's house with another officer."

Knowing Ethan would be the one delivering the devastating news gave Hope some comfort. He'd be gentle, compassionate, and would stay if Felice needed him to.

She swiveled her head and looked at Drew.

"She asked me to help her. Maybe if I had said yes right away . . ." Her throat choked with emotion.

"Hey, don't do that to yourself. You're not in any way responsible for what happened. Who knows, if you had said yes, we could be pulling your body out of a ditch." Hope knew his words were supposed to be supportive, but they painted a gruesome picture instead. He must have caught her grimace. "Sorry, I didn't mean to get all dark on you. But you know what I mean."

"I do." Hope shifted her gaze back to the road ahead. "I can't shake the feeling I let her down."

"Oh, boy. You're not thinking of doing what I think you're thinking of doing, are you?"

Hope huffed. "I can't just sit around doing nothing. Devon was murdered."

"We don't know for certain." He flicked on his turn

signal. "Look at me being the sensible one. Not leaping before the facts are in."

"Yeah, didn't think it was possible," Hope quipped.

"Hey! I have feelings, you know."

She stretched out her hand and rubbed Drew's arm. "I do know. So, are you going to help me?"

Drew eased his car to a full stop at an intersection and waited for the pickup truck coming from the other direction to drive through before pressing on the accelerator.

"Like you even have to ask. Let's find out what happened to Devon and her mother."

Chapter Eight

"You're doing great, Hope." Josie gave a thumbs-up from her spot beside the tripod. A camera and external microphone were attached to the tripod placed in front of the island.

Hope checked her watch one more time. It was almost time to go. But first things first.

Even though it was a Sunday, one more segment of the Broccoli-Spinach Soup recipe needed to be filmed. Being self-employed meant Hope worked long hours and on weekends. But she hadn't expected her assistant to work.

Josie had arrived an hour ago and gotten right to work. Luckily, her schedule was flexible, and she had no plans for the day.

"You nailed the intro. Ready for the outro?" Josie looked at her boss expectantly.

As soon as the outro was filmed, the recap of the recipe video, Hope would be off to visit Felice and pay her condolences. She hated those visits and felt she'd made too many of them, in her estimation. So she tried to celebrate the person's life instead of dwelling on the death, and it helped ease the grief and heartache. But not by much. While filming the soup recipe, all the things she'd liked about Devon in high school ran through her mind. She wanted to cling to those memories and not the fresh one of the accident scene the day before.

Hope cleared her throat, relaxed her shoulders, and looked at the camera. "I'm ready."

A moment ago, she'd wanted to cry, but looking to the camera gave her a jolt of fortification she desperately needed. Beyond the camera lens were her faithful followers, who read her blog every day and watched her new videos when she uploaded them. The last thing she wanted to do was to let them down.

With that kick in the pants, the smile she'd been struggling for eased onto her lips and the words came to her.

"All right, my friends, there you have my Broccoli-Spinach Soup. It's perfect for a cold, wintry day. The recipe is easy, and you'll find a link for it on my blog. Also, don't forget to share a photo with me on social media when you make the soup. Be sure to tag *Hope at Home*. I love to see your success in the kitchen."

Hope held her smile for another beat, and then Josie clicked off the camera and microphone. "Great job, boss. I'll edit the video and schedule it to go live when the post goes up." She stepped away from the camera and walked to the table, where her laptop was open.

"You'll also create the pin image?" *Hope at Home* had

a presence on all social media platforms, and juggling all those outlets was another reason she'd hired Josie.

"Of course." Seated, Josie looked over the top of her computer. "Are you sure you're okay? Do you want me to drive you over there?"

Hope ladled the soup into large containers. She planned to take the soup, along with a loaf of her sourdough bread to Felice's house. She'd already prepared a salad, and it was in the refrigerator to go along with the soup.

"Thanks for the offer, but I'm doing okay. A lot better than Felice, I'm guessing. It's not going to be easy. From what Devon told me, her sister wasn't thrilled with the reason she returned home. And now this." Hope wiped the containers with a paper towel.

"I don't understand. If it were me, I'd want to know what happened to my mother. But I guess families are complicated." Josie returned her attention to the keyboard and typed. "Did you find your charm bracelet?"

Hope groaned. With everything that had happened, she'd forgotten about her bracelet. And about the talk she had to have with Iva.

"I take it you haven't," Josie said with a sympathetic smile.

Hope put the two containers into the refrigerator, then dashed upstairs to change into more appropriate clothes for a condolence call. Maybe later she could think about how to approach the delicate subject with Iva. Or she could conduct one more, in-depth search for the bracelet. But in light of Devon's death, it seemed like such a minor loss. Yes, she could delay that uncomfortable talk for a little longer.

* * *

Hope grabbed the basket's handle and removed it from the Explorer's cargo space. She stepped back as the cargo door closed and looked upward. Big puffs of gray hung overhead, making for another glum day. She walked around her vehicle, and when she reached the brick path to the front door of Felice's house, she stopped.

A sadness reverberated off the Victorian home. From its drawn curtains to its quietude, it was as if the house was prepared for somber visits.

Before Hope pressed the doorbell, the door swung open and Felice pulled her into an embrace.

"I'm so glad you're here." Felice's voice was thick with emotion.

"I'm very sorry for your loss." Tears pricked Hope's eyes and she squeezed them shut. She wouldn't cry again.

"I can't believe this has happened. I don't understand it." Felice let go and gestured for Hope to enter the house. She closed the door. She was well under forty, so Felice's long, silver hair was a product of visits to the hair salon. She'd joined the granny-gray hair trend, and with her mid-toned complexion and dark eyes, the hair color worked for her. "You brought food? How thoughtful of you."

Hope lifted the basket. "I did. Soup with sourdough bread and salad."

Felice covered her heart with her hand. "I don't know how I'd be getting through this without my family and friends." She reached for the basket. "Let me put this in the kitchen. I'll be right back. Go on in the living room." She walked past Hope and disappeared down the hall.

Hope entered the spacious room with an arched ceiling and a working fireplace. The warmth from the fire felt good, and its crackling sound was comforting. She shrugged out of her coat and set it, along with her purse, on the sofa.

She crossed the polished wood floor to the fireplace and held out her hands to warm up.

"I thought you might like a cup of coffee." Felice entered the room carrying two mugs and handed one to Hope. She then took her mug to the sofa and sat. She tucked her bare feet under her legs and sipped her coffee.

"How are you doing?" Hope joined Felice. Seated, she took a drink of coffee.

"I think I'm still numb. Ethan told me about the accident and finding Devon's body, but I don't think it's sunk in yet."

"You're not alone here, are you?"

Felice shook her head. "No, Patrick's here. He's in the kitchen, making calls."

Hope had only met Felice's husband a few times over the years. He seemed nice. After college, he'd moved to the area to teach music at a private school in Litchfield.

Felice took a drink before setting the mug on the coffee table. "Devon told me she talked to you. I'm sure she told you I was against her reopening our mother's case."

"She did. If you don't mind me asking, why were you against it?"

Felice's lips quivered. "I didn't want to relive the pain all over again. The day I came home from school, I expected Mom to have been back from work. She wasn't." Her voice trembled and her gaze flickered away for a moment. "Dad called the office and found out she hadn't shown up for work. Realizing something bad went down was the most painful thing I'd ever experienced."

"Reliving it through the podcast and having the media attention on it would open wounds you'd already started to heal," Hope said.

"Exactly. Now it sounds selfish, doesn't it?"

Hope reached for a coaster on the coffee table and set down her mug. She scooted closer to Felice and took hold of her hands. "No. Not at all. You needed to protect yourself. Devon was your sister. She understood."

"I'm not sure she did. I want to try to make things right." Felice squeezed Hope's hands.

"What do you mean?"

"I want to continue with what Devon was doing. I want to find out what happened to our mother. There's a part of me that believes Devon's accident wasn't an accident."

Hope was speechless. Felice was also suspicious of the circumstances around Devon's death.

"Patrick thinks it's the shock of the news. But I think if the detective who handled my mother's case all those years ago had done a better job, we'd know whether my mother walked out of our lives or she was abducted and murdered."

"I hate to play devil's advocate." Hope surprised herself. Just yesterday she was all-in to investigate what happened to Joyce and Devon. Now, she was about to try to talk Felice out of doing the same thing. "The roads are slick and snowy, especially the section of Hargate Hill where the accident happened. Devon wasn't used to driving in those types of conditions any longer."

It'd taken Hope a whole season to get back into the skill of winter driving, even though she'd come back to the northwestern Connecticut town regularly for visits. Even with the all-wheel vehicle she owned, there was a learning curve to driving in her section of the state. Devon had been driving a rental car. Who knew how reliable it was?

"Patrick said the same thing last night. It's a valid point. As is the fact that Devon was digging into a missing persons case. My hunch is the person responsible for my mother's vanishing is still here in Jefferson and wants the past to stay right where it is."

"Patrick is a smart man."

Hope and Felice's gazes shifted to the direction of Shirley's voice. She stood in the doorway with her hands clasped and a stern look on her face. She advanced into the room and gave Hope a curt nod in passing. Her destination was to Felice's side.

"I didn't hear you come in." Felice's voice was shaky.

"I made a lasagna. I thought it would be easier to go to the kitchen door. Patrick let me in. He'd just gotten off the phone with your aunt. She's on her way down from Vermont. Would you like some more coffee?" Before Felice could answer, Shirley swiped up the mug.

"You don't have to wait on me," Felice said.

"It's no bother. I'm here to help you. At least until your aunt arrives. Patrick said she'll be here by this evening," Shirley said.

"Many people care about you. We're going to help you get through this." Hope patted Felice's knee before she drew back her hands to her lap.

"Those who truly care want to keep you from any more pain that the past presents." Shirley shot Hope a take-that look.

"I've been kidding myself all these years. The not knowing is what's painful. The difference between Devon and me was that she did something about her pain. And I think it got her killed."

Shirley gasped. "You can't believe she was killed because of what happened to your mother? From what I heard, it sounds like it was a tragic accident."

"The police haven't completed their investigation," Hope said.

Shirley gave Hope a quick, sharp glance. What was going on with Shirley? Hope's curiosity grew. She had to find out, but it wasn't the time or place to pry.

"When they do, I'm confident it'll be ruled an accident. Felice, I strongly urge you to be careful and not make any rash decisions or spout unfounded accusations. Let the police do their job." Shirley's face softened. "I'll get you more coffee," she said before turning and walking out of the room.

Hope glanced at her mug. Shirley hadn't offered her a refill. She took that as a cue to leave.

"I should be going." Hope stood.

"I appreciate your visit and the food. Patrick loves when I make one of your recipes from the blog." Felice stood and hugged Hope.

Amid the sadness and grief, a zing of happiness shot through Hope. She loved feeding people. It was impossible to feed everyone, so sharing her recipes on her blog was the next best thing.

"Take care and call me if you need anything. I mean *anything*."

"I will," Felice whispered.

Hope showed herself to the front door, buttoning her coat quickly to ward off the cold air. However, the chill outside was no match for the icy reception she'd gotten from Shirley. Her thoughts drifted to the coming days. She'd been looking forward to her weekend getaway with Ethan. Now, she would be attending Devon's funeral. It was a reminder how life could turn on a dime.

She started to walk past a hybrid car parked in the driveway when the driver's door flew open, revealing Norrie.

"Do you know everyone in town?" A dark hat was pulled down over her hair and a coordinating scarf was tied around her neck.

"When you're born and raised in a small town, you pretty much do."

"Huh. I'm still getting used to the small-town thing. Being from Chicago, I didn't know everyone. I barely knew my neighbors."

Hope wanted to ask how the *Gazette*, as small as a small-town newspaper could get, was able to lure a skilled reporter like Norrie, but she resisted. She didn't want to know that much about Drew's archrival.

"Would you like to share a quote about Devon for our readers? Perhaps a memory?" Norrie unzipped her cross-body bag.

"Thank you for the offer. But not at this time." Hope walked past Norrie toward her car. She was being rude, and it went against everything her mother taught her. Neither she nor Claire was raised to be bad-mannered. Elizabeth Early had instilled in her daughters to be kind, polite, and extend grace whenever possible. But Norrie never made extending grace possible in her book.

Sorry, Mom.

Hope slipped in behind the steering wheel of her car and started the engine. She gave the car a moment to warm up. She watched Norrie approach the house as hot air blasted through the vent. She didn't know how Norrie or Drew did their jobs. Knocking on the door of a grieving family looking to get a quote. When the door opened, Hope shifted her car into gear and drove out of the driveway.

* * *

Hope sipped her coffee and pushed her cart along the produce section of Donegal's Supermarket. The grocery store had a café, which was her first stop when she entered. The mundane chore of grocery shopping soothed Hope. The typically mindless task of walking up and down the aisles was anything but boring. She always discovered a new product, and her mind would run wild with possibilities for new recipes.

Why on earth would anyone order their groceries online? A supermarket run was as cathartic as baking for her.

Donegal's was her favorite place to shop for produce because they had the best quality. And it was only ten minutes from Felice's house. So a quick dash inside to pick up a few things wouldn't put her too far behind schedule.

She browsed the produce area for mushrooms to go with the steak she planned on making for family dinner. There were the all-purpose button mushrooms. They had a less intense flavor than the others. For her steak dinner, Hope wanted a little extra pop of flavor. She loved portobello mushrooms, but they were better for grilling or stuffing, sometimes both. Her eyes lit up when she saw the shiitake mushrooms. They'd be perfect. They had a light, woodsy flavor and aroma. She added them to her cart, along with the fresh basil, rosemary, and oregano she'd use for the compound butter. For most of the day, she hadn't had an appetite, but thinking about the sizzling steak covered with the mushrooms and drenched with melted herb butter had her tummy grumbling.

A sale sign for onions caught her eye. A big pot of French onion soup sounded delicious. Well, at that moment everything seemed delicious. She added several onions to her cart and moved on along to the tomatoes, where she found Jane squeezing a Big Beef tomato.

"Looks like we both needed to do a little shopping." Jane's cheeks were flushed from the cold, and her wispy bangs peeked out beneath her black hat.

"I thought I'd stop in because I was close by. I was at Felice's." Hope continued down the aisle and reached for a bag of the Yukon Gold potatoes she'd mash and serve with the steak. The little, yellow-fleshed potatoes were fluffy and slightly buttery in flavor, making them the perfect potato to mash.

"Poor thing. First her mother and now her sister." Jane set the tomato along with two others in her cart and joined Hope, then reached for a bag of russet potatoes. Hope intercepted and placed the heavy bag into Jane's cart. "Thank you, dear. How is Felice doing?"

"Not good. She told me she feels numb." Hope returned to her cart and walked along with Jane as they perused the produce. "She also said she regrets opposing Devon's decision to reopen their mother's case. She's changed her mind. She wants answers. Felice believes her sister's death wasn't an accident."

"It would be far too coincidental if it were an accident. I believe Devon had been in contact with the person responsible for her mother's disappearance before her own death."

Now, if that wasn't enough to send all sorts of chills and willies through her body, Hope didn't know what was.

She sipped her coffee as she tried to picture whether there had been a planner among Devon's research material. Who had Devon spoken to before the car accident? The police would have her cell phone and access to her records. If there were a planner, it was probably stolen, along with everything else.

Jane continued to the apples. "I've done some thinking about all those years ago. Joyce was close to Shirley and Donna Wilcox. I recall Donna was adamant that Joyce would never have left willingly."

"My mom said the same thing."

"Donna wasn't shy about casting blame on Greg Markham, I think because one of Donna's uncles killed his wife. She may have been projecting." Jane inspected an apple. "Or she may have been right."

"I really don't remember Greg well."

"He was always working. Most of the functions Joyce attended, she was alone because he was traveling. This morning, after church service, Donna mentioned she wants to do something in memory of Devon. She's thinking about a scholarship fund to help students interested in journalism or writing."

"Sounds like something Donna would do."

"Perhaps you should visit her. You're superb with fund-raising, and I'm sure she'd like to reminisce about Devon as a child and also about Joyce."

"You're not very subtle."

Jane laughed. "I wasn't trying to be. I'd better get a move on. Sally will be here in a few minutes to pick me up." She patted Hope on the arm and headed toward the checkout.

Hope lingered in the produce section a little while longer and debated over whether to buy apples for a dessert. She could whip up a pie. She liked that idea. A rustic apple pie would be an excellent way to finish the day. With a scoop of vanilla bean ice cream. Her tummy rumbled again. Pie it was.

With her groceries paid for, Hope was back at her Explorer. She set the last grocery bag along with the two others already placed inside her cargo space. The canvas market totes were designed with her blog's logo. She gave them away to promote the website. Giveaways were always happening, whether on social media or her newsletter or on the blog itself, and the totes were the most popular. Probably because everyone needed bags for their weekly shopping.

"Good afternoon, Hope."

Hope looked over her shoulder and saw Maretta standing there with a shopping cart. Her gray coat was buttoned all the way up to its mandarin collar, and a plain black hat covered her drab brown hair. Just a few months ago, her hair had seemed to be a shinier shade of brunette. Now it appeared to have reverted to its lackluster old self.

"Hi, Maretta. How's it going?" Instantly, Hope realized the question was a mistake. She stepped back and closed the cargo door.

"How's it going?" Maretta repeated.

Hope was right. If only she could take the question back. Heck, if she could do that, she'd rewind enough so she could be inside her Explorer and backing out of the parking space before Maretta came out of the store.

"Since you ask, I'll tell you."

Lucky Hope.

"Chief Cahill notified me of a fatal car accident, and no doubt we'll have press about it. Now, it seems we're going to get hammered by another snowstorm. You have no idea how difficult it is governing a town. All the decisions I need to make daily, and making sure my subordinates follow through on what they're supposed to be doing."

Leave it to Maretta to turn a tragedy and weather event to be all about her.

Hope had no intention of giving Maretta what she wanted. She refused to feed her ever-inflating ego.

"I saw Felice a little while ago. She's devastated about her sister." Hope rested her gloved hands on the cart's handlebar.

"The Markham family seems to have more than its share of sadness. Though I suspect now all the hoopla about Joyce's disappearance will finally go away. The last thing Jefferson needs is for the past to be dragged back out. It's not good for our image."

Hope blinked. Had she heard correctly?

"Don't look at me like that. My job is to look out for Jefferson. Tourism is vital to our town."

"Devon was trying to find out what happened to her mother, which should trump how Jefferson looks to the rest of the world."

Maretta's eyes narrowed. "Oh, please don't tell me you're sticking your nose into that old case? What we need to focus on is spring tourism. It's right around the corner. If there has to be a podcast about Jefferson, it should be about our wonderful shops. Who wants to vacation in a town where women vanish?"

"You'd rather have them stay in a town where justice isn't served?"

"Must you be so dramatic? I'm warning you, Hope. Leave this alone. Joyce was a flirt. She went looking for trouble, and my guess is, she found it and then ran off so she wouldn't have to face her family and friends."

"What? What kind of trouble?"

"There's only so much innocent flirting a woman can do before she finds herself in a compromising position.

Mark my words, she took off because she was ashamed of herself." Maretta pushed her cart and continued down the row of parked vehicles.

Stunned by the comment, it took Hope a moment before she could make a move to go after Maretta. She wanted to know more about Joyce's flirting. But thanks to Maretta's sensible snow boots, she was already at her sedan. Maybe it was for the best. What she'd hear would probably just be gossip. Twenty-year-old gossip.

She navigated her cart to the corral as Maretta backed her vehicle out of the parking space. She couldn't dismiss everything Maretta said as gossip. And she couldn't help but wonder how Joyce had gotten herself into a compromising position. While Maretta made everything about herself, she sure seemed to take Joyce's behavior personally, even after all these years. Could the missing woman have flirted with Maretta's husband, Alfred? Or more?

Chapter Nine

Getting Bigelow's harness on was no easy feat for Hope. Her energetic pup was doing his happy dance because he was going out for a walk.

"Come on, sweetie, stay still." She almost had the leash attached, but whatever Bigelow heard her say had him licking her face, which made her giggle, thus making the whole process longer. But she didn't care; the laugh was very much welcome. She returned the kiss on his forehead and, steadying him for that second, she managed to get on his harness. Phew!

She'd returned home thirty minutes earlier, put away her groceries, and then got the French onion soup started—peeling and slicing onions and then sautéing them in her multicooker.

Once they were a deep golden color, she added the rest

of the ingredients and switched to the slow cooker setting. Hope loved when her appliances were versatile and efficient.

By the time she finished, the clouds had parted, allowing the sun to peek out and making for a more delightful afternoon. It wasn't much, but it was something, and Hope was grateful for the small ray of sunshine. And for the chance to get Bigelow out for another walk. He had a lot of energy. Walks were a good way for him to expend as much of it as possible.

She zipped up her jacket, and Bigelow stood by the door, looking up at the knob with anticipation. Hope opened the door, and Bigelow hurried out, pulling on the leash. He knew better and she gave a tug, signaling to him to slow down. His head dropped a little, and so did his speed.

On the patio, they found Poppy perched on a patio chair. Hope had put away all the outdoor furniture except for this one chair because the Rhode Island Red hen liked to sit there to be close to the house.

"Hello, Poppy." Hope walked to the bird with Bigelow by her side. He always behaved well around the chickens. She had expected him to chase them, but he never did. Rather, he slid into the role of protector. Having a dog around the chickens helped keep predators away.

Poppy tilted her head and looked at Hope with her beady little eyes. The bird's rust-colored feathers and curious personality endeared her to Hope. However, her inquisitiveness had her entering the house on more than one occasion. Bigelow hadn't minded, but Princess wasn't pleased by the interloper. Hope was amazed by how daring the hen was, walking in like she owned the place.

"Don't stay out too long. It's cold." Hope gave a stroke to the bird's back and Poppy replied with a "buh-rup" vocalization as she stretched out her wings and settled back down.

Hope and Bigelow set off on their walk. She'd dressed him in a plaid wool coat. He wasn't thrilled the first time she'd put the coat on him, but he got over it. Now he tolerated the coat, and she appreciated it.

She'd changed into her running clothes, though she wasn't going to run. She wanted to be comfy, and the layers also kept her warm. Her gloved hand kept a tight hold on the leash, and she led Bigelow out onto the road.

The wind had picked up again. The bare tree branches swayed side to side. The spot of sun she saw before heading out was still up there, but it wasn't doing much to warm the day. Bigelow didn't seem to mind one bit. He was in his glory. His ears flapped as his body moved swiftly along the road. His head was high, and Hope could swear he was smiling. So what if she was a little cold? He was having fun.

The little guy didn't have a care in the world. Well, except maybe for Princess. Hope had caught her taking a swipe with claws extended at Bigelow's nose the other night. It seemed they were still working out their boundaries.

Which reminded Hope that she had something to work out with Iva.

She groaned. If it weren't for Bigelow, Hope would have stopped in her tracks. The weight of having to talk to Iva about her missing charm bracelet came crashing down on her shoulders, making each step forward feel more like slogging through quicksand than walking along the snowy road.

She realized she'd been using the blogging class and

what was going on with Devon to avoid sitting down with Iva and having an honest conversation. During her time as a magazine editor, she'd mentored editorial assistants, helped them find their voices so as not to be overlooked for assignments and promotions. Speaking to Iva about the missing bracelet should have been easy for her to do. Sure, she expected it would be awkward, but she'd had the unpleasant task of firing employees before. And she wasn't even going to fire Iva. Well, if Iva stole the bracelet, she'd have to be fired. If she didn't, then Iva would think Hope didn't trust her. And it would wreck the friendly relationship they were developing after all this time. And Iva wouldn't like her.

There it was.

The one thing Hope wished she could change about herself: her need to be liked. She was sure it was the reason she'd learned to cook at a young age. You made people food, and they loved you.

Claire, on the other hand, hadn't cared if people liked her. She had no interest in feeding people. She had no deep-seated need to see their faces light up when they were presented the most perfect cookie. Nope. Not her.

Bigelow jerked on the leash and yowled. It was a unique sound, between a bark and a howl, and it had a lyrical ring to it. Albeit, a very loud lyrical ring. Hope happily pushed aside her thoughts about talking to Iva and about her own flaws to see what was causing her pup's excitement.

She should have known. Gilbert was approaching with Buddy tugging on a leash, his tail wagging.

"Good afternoon, Hope." Gilbert reached out to Bigelow, but he was too busy greeting Buddy to pay the older man any attention. "Brisk day for a walk."

"It certainly is." A chill wiggled through Hope. It was time to head inside and give the soup a taste test.

"I heard about Devon. It's such a shame. I remember her as a little girl." He stared down at Buddy and stroked the dog's head. He lifted his gaze back up to Hope. "She and her sister would come to the house every year selling cookies. Mitzi always chastised me for ordering too many boxes of Thin Mints." Gilbert chuckled.

"I saw Felice this morning. The whole situation breaks my heart."

Gilbert nodded in agreement. "I worked with Greg for years before he moved on to a new company. You know, he was a born salesman. He had the gift of gab, but he also had what my mother called a restless soul."

Hope's interest was piqued. She hadn't known Gilbert and Greg worked together.

"How so?"

Buddy sat while his owner pushed back his wool cap and then shoved his hands into his coat pockets. Hope sensed it would be a long story. Gilbert could chat for hours on end.

"He never seemed to fit into the family-man role. He'd prefer to travel than attend his kids' sports games or go cut down a Christmas tree with his family. He loved traveling so much, he turned down a promotion that came with regular hours and no travel. That's when he left for the other company."

It sounded like Greg had a bit of wanderlust. Hope couldn't help but wonder if he had wanted his freedom so much that he killed his wife and disposed of her body, never to be found.

"Everything okay, Hope? You have a funny look on your face."

"Yeah, everything is fine. I remembered I needed to add something to my to-do list," she lied. She couldn't very well tell him what she was really thinking about.

Gilbert chuckled again. "You never slow down, do you? Well, I'd better give Buddy his walk." He looked down at Bigelow, who looked expectantly up at him. "Why don't I take Bigelow with us?"

"Thanks, but we're just coming back."

Bigelow looked up at Hope. Calling her out on what she deemed a decent walk. Up and down their street? Sure, it wasn't their longest walk ever, but it was all she had time for.

"He looks like he's up for a little more, aren't you, boy?" Gilbert's question had Bigelow's head tilting and his eyes widening. He was practically nodding.

"I'm sure he'd love to go, but I'm heading out." Hope had it all planned. The soup would continue to cook in the slow cooker, giving her time to visit Donna before supper. See, that was why she loved multifunctional appliances.

"No problem. I'll keep Bigelow with us until you get back. Come over when you get home." Gilbert reached out and took Bigelow's leash.

"Thanks." Hope gave Bigelow a kiss on the head and hurried back to her house.

Inside, she checked the soup. She spooned out some broth and a sliver of onion and gave it a taste. It needed a little more pepper. She added a pinch of black pepper before she returned the lid to the pot. Up next was the crust for her rustic apple pie.

She gathered a stainless-steel bowl, the dry ingredients, and measuring spoons. She'd been making the same pie crust recipe since she was a little girl, so she had it memorized.

Within minutes, she had the dough formed into a flattened disc and wrapped in plastic wrap to set in the refrigerator.

She did a quick cleanup before calling Donna, who was pleased to hear from Hope and even more pleased by the offer of homemade broccoli and spinach soup. They agreed on a time, and Hope went upstairs to change clothes. She opted for a pair of jeans and a cozy sweater. It took a few minutes to pack up the soup and a loaf of sourdough bread and then she was off to drive across town. Hopefully, Donna would be able to shed some light on why she believed Greg was responsible for his wife's disappearance.

Twenty minutes later, Donna Wilcox swept Hope into her downsized home. It was a far cry from the massive, two-story Colonial she once lived in with her family. Her shoulder-length gray hair was gathered in a ponytail, and she wore a pair of lounge pants and a coordinating top. Donna looked like she was enjoying a relaxing afternoon.

"I'm glad you thought of me. Now I don't have to worry about what to make for dinner. Come on, let's go into the kitchen."

"I always end up with so much food after recipe testing and cooking for videos." Hope followed Donna into the cheerful kitchen.

Decorated with splashes of yellow and warm reds, the room had a French country flair to it. Especially the two white counter-height stools at the peninsula. Their turned legs and weathered finish were a nice touch to the elegant yet comfortable room.

Hope set the basket on the peninsula and then removed her jacket. She set it along with her purse on a stool.

"Would you like coffee? I also have flavored waters."

"Water, please." Hope took the soup container and the loaf of bread out of the basket. Every time she carried the basket with food in it, she felt like Little Red Riding Hood minus the wolf. "I love your kitchen."

"Thank you." Donna set the glass of water in front of Hope. Pushed aside on the countertop were the newspaper's crossword puzzle, a pen, and a pair of reading glasses.

"You do the crossword puzzle in pen? Impressive." And so neat. Even in those small boxes, Donna's handwriting was immaculate.

Donna shrugged. "Don't be too impressed. I have my phone beside me when I do the puzzle. Google is a wonderful thing."

Hope sipped her water. She wasn't sure how she felt about robust search engines. It would have been nice if they forgot about her ill-fated attempt to win *The Sweet Taste of Success*, her messy divorce, and her recent encounters with a few murderers. Then again, those same search engines helped her build her business.

"This soup looks so vibrant and healthy." Donna took the container to the refrigerator. "Having extra food must be a yummy perk for you."

"It is. And I love sharing it all."

"I'm happy to receive anytime you want to share." Donna rested her hands on the edge of the peninsula's countertop. In her midsixties, she had the expected signs of aging around her full face: deep creases across her forehead and a web of tiny lines around her alert eyes. But what she had that wasn't typical was a boundless amount of energy. She had an enormous amount of oomph that propelled her into a fulfilling second act as a patient advocate and an entrepreneur.

She'd turned her hobby of calligraphy into a small business and expanded to teaching others how to do it. Between juggling her job and side hustle, Donna was a member of Jefferson's Planning and Zoning Committee. She was an inspiration to Hope that it was never too late to start over again.

"I ran into Jane earlier. She mentioned your plan to start a scholarship fund in Devon's name."

Donna swallowed her drink of water. "The response has been overwhelmingly positive, so I think it will happen. I've spoken to Felice about it, and she's given her blessing. The high school is also on board with awarding the scholarship for writing." She'd definitely been busy. Big or small, there wasn't a fund-raiser she couldn't make successful. "It seems like yesterday when I got the call about Joyce being gone. You never think it will happen to someone you know."

"Who called to tell you about Joyce?"

"Shirley. I was back here in Jefferson, visiting my mother-in-law. In fact, Joyce and I were supposed to meet for brunch at the diner that morning."

"What happened?"

"I got there first, like usual, and waited. She didn't show up and I was a little irritated. My visit here was only for a few days and I really wanted to see her. Finally, I left and drove past her house, but I didn't see her car parked in the driveway. I figured either she forgot, or she had to run a last-minute errand for one of the girls. Then, the next morning, I got the call from Shirley. As soon as I hung up with her, I called your mother. Back then, we didn't have cell phones, and there were no texting groups. Oh, gosh, how I hate getting caught up in those."

Hope nodded in agreement. There was nothing worse than getting trapped into a conversation you cared nothing about. She'd yet to find a way to exit gracefully without offending someone. It was like a modern-day hostage situation.

"Devon told me she'd found evidence her father was having an affair at the time Joyce vanished," Hope said.

Donna pushed aside her glass and leaned forward, resting her forearms on the countertop.

"I'm not surprised one bit. After I moved, Joyce and I kept in contact. We talked at least once a week. Joyce wasn't happy, so I doubt Greg was."

"Unhappy in their marriage?"

"I can't speak to Greg's feelings because I didn't know him well. Though if the wife's not happy, how can the husband be? Anyway, Joyce wanted more out of life. I know it was only twenty years ago, but things were different for women like Joyce."

"How so?"

"She was in her forties, married, with teenagers and no real career experience. She worked as a secretary, and most people would have thought it was enough. Joyce hadn't thought so. She wanted to be a real estate agent, the person closing the deal and cashing the commission check."

"Sounds like she was ambitious."

Donna straightened and lifted her water glass. "Today she'd have more options. Look at you. You started a blog, and you're earning a living from it. We couldn't imagine such a thing back then. Today, women have so many options. We don't have to settle."

"Do you think Joyce was so unhappy she left on her own?"

"No. She wouldn't have done such a thing. Joyce was looking forward to going back to school for a real estate license. She'd talked to Alfred about changing jobs at the agency. Plus, she had her daughters." Donna gave a deep, weighted sigh.

"What is it?"

"I wasn't sure if becoming an agent would have made Joyce happy. I think there was such a profound emptiness in her that a new job and money couldn't fix it. Maybe that's why she flirted so much." Donna straightened up and topped off her glass with more water.

"Flirted?" Hope recalled Maretta saying the same thing and suggested Joyce had gotten into a compromising position. So maybe it wasn't just Maretta's imagination or idle gossip, as Hope had thought.

"Oh, yes. Joyce was a big-time flirt. My guess is the attention she got from flirting made her feel better; well, at least momentarily. Like a self-esteem boost."

This was all news for Hope. She hadn't heard about Joyce's flirtatious nature before that day. If her mother knew, she'd kept it to herself.

"I don't believe the girls were aware of their mom's flirting. She saved it for grown-up parties. Let me tell you, Greg didn't like it. One time he dragged Joyce out of the room, and we could hear his raised voice. They returned to the party, but the incident was a downer."

"She was looking to make him jealous?"

Donna shrugged. "I knew Joyce very well. She never cheated on him. Never."

"Devon mentioned her mom got a black rose tattoo.

Do you know why she did it? Did she ever say anything about it?"

"All I know is, it was on a whim. She didn't plan on getting one. It was so unlike her. But, hey, guys get close to their midlife, they do crazy things—buy useless sports cars, marry younger women. Women can have those impulses too. I guess getting a tattoo isn't the worst thing she could have done."

Hope glanced at the wall clock. If she wanted to bake the apple pie to have for dessert tonight, she needed to get home.

"I should get going. Let me know what you need for the scholarship."

"I can always count on you. Thanks again for the food."

Hope put on her jacket before grabbing her purse and basket. She followed Donna to the front door and said goodbye. The day was growing darker and colder. Inside her Explorer, she blasted the heat and then backed out of the driveway.

On the drive home, Hope couldn't help but wonder how, with all the research Devon had done, she didn't know about her mother's flirtatious side. It had been evident to other people. Maybe people wanted to spare Devon's feelings and withheld that from her. Or maybe Devon had known but chosen not to say anything about it to Hope.

Yet she had no problem in telling the whole podcasting world her father had cheated on Joyce.

Had Devon idealized her mother too much? Too much so it left her vulnerable and unprepared to recognize a threat when it was presented to her? Like the person responsible for her death. The more Hope was learning, the more convinced she was that Devon's death wasn't the result of an accident.

Hope drummed her fingers on the steering wheel, waiting for the red light to change. While she sat tight, her eyes narrowed on the street sign up ahead. Forest Trail.

Oliver Marchant's street.

The light changed and she drove through the intersection. Careful not to accelerate too fast on the slippery road.

She was approaching the turn for Oliver's street. Her checkbook was in her purse, and it would only take a few minutes to swing by to pay him for his recent plowing services.

Even though there was no one behind her, she flicked on the blinker and made the right turn. She traveled along the road past charming Cape Cods all nestled in for the winter surrounded by thick blankets of snow. Up ahead, there was the turnoff for Oliver's driveway, and she eased her vehicle over the unpaved strip of earth toward his house.

A bump jostled her, and she tightened her already death grip on the steering wheel.

The one-story home set on a stone foundation came into view. And it wasn't the prettiest view. The house's cedar shakes were in disrepair, discolored and damaged. They looked like they'd seen one too many winters. Taking care of his house hadn't seemed to be a priority for Oliver.

The plow truck wasn't in sight. She guessed it must have been parked in the garage, which was in the same condition as the house.

She wondered if Joyce had felt uneasy around Oliver

because she flirted and he misinterpreted the signals, leading to a "compromising position," as Maretta put it.

Hope exited her vehicle with her purse and walked to the oversize deck attached to the front of the house. It was an unusual spot for the poorly built structure, but she figured he didn't have much of a backyard on the sloping property.

She climbed the two rickety steps and carefully treaded across to the front door. A solid slab of wood, function clearly winning out over decoration, wasn't exactly welcoming. Neither was the mat. Maybe Oliver thought the "Come Back with a Warrant" welcome mat was a cute decoration.

Ignoring the so-called greeting, she knocked on the door and waited. When there was no response, she shuffled over to the window and peered in, cupping her hands around her face.

With no drapes or blinds impeding her view, what she could see inside was a typical bachelor pad. A big screen television and a leather sectional with cup holders in the arms dominated the room. Smack in the middle was a square coffee table covered with sports magazines.

A tap on her shoulder sent her jumping. She spun around, expecting to see that Oliver had snuck up on her.

"Drew!" Her hand rested over her thumping heart. "You scared the daylights out of me. What are you doing here?"

"Why are you skulking around?" He stepped back and grinned.

"I'm not skulking. I came here to pay Oliver for his services. Now it's your turn. Why are you here?"

"I'm here to interview him. You haven't heard? He was out plowing and found a stray dog with a litter of puppies. He rescued them and took them to the shelter. Human-interest story. It'll sell a bunch of newspapers."

"Aww, that's sweet." Her racing heart calmed down and began to melt at the thought of a bunch of rescued puppies. Then another thought shoved the first one away. Would a man who rescued a mama dog and her pups have anything to do with a woman's disappearance? "So, where's Oliver?"

Drew shrugged. "Not sure. Guess he's running late."

"Where's your car?" Hers was the only one parked on the gravel pad.

"Back by his other garage. He said to meet him there; it's where he parks his plow truck. I don't know how much longer I can wait. It's freakin' cold." As if right on cue, fluffy snowflakes started to fall. "And now it's snowing."

"That I did hear. And it's supposed to turn to sleet and ice." Hope shoved her hands into her jacket pockets.

"You still haven't told me the real reason you're here, and don't say it's only to pay your bill. Spill, sistah."

"Fine. I wanted to talk to him about Joyce's disappearance." Hope looked over Drew's shoulder to make sure they were alone. "Devon said her mom felt uncomfortable around Oliver and I'm hearing now that she flirted a lot. Maybe he got the wrong message from her."

"You think he made a pass, she rejected it, and he killed her?"

Hope shrugged. "It's possible. It happens all the time. Well, not the killing part. But misunderstandings do happen." She also knew her theory was complete conjecture and would never hold up in court. Heck, forget about court. It wouldn't hold up with Ethan or Reid. Neither one would act on her theory.

That was why she needed something more concrete.

"He does live in the perfect location to dump a body. His acreage goes way back behind his second garage."

She tilted her head and stared at the one-bay garage. "Why does he need two?"

"He stores his work vehicles in the back one."

"Then it means he has nonwork vehicles. I've never seen him in anything but the pickup truck he plows with. Have you?"

Drew's gaze shifted to the small garage. "No."

"Then what is he keeping in there?" She pointed to the building, just feet away from them.

Drew angled himself so he had a full view of the structure. "Maybe a twenty-year-old corpse?"

His question sent a shudder down Hope's spine. Was it possible Joyce's remains had been hidden away all those years inside a garage not too far from her home?

"Looks like there's only one way to find out." Hope pushed off, crossing the deck without any concern for her safety. If a board broke, then so be it. She was too eager to see what was inside the garage. She hurried down the deck steps and kept the same speed to reach the double-door entry of the garage.

"Are we going to break in?" Drew came up beside Hope and gestured to the padlock on the doors.

"I don't think so." Not deterred, Hope stepped to her right and looked down at the side of the building. Determined to get a look inside, she plodded through knee-high snow to reach the window. The coldness of the snow seeped through her jeans, but she didn't let it stop her.

On her tippy toes, she tried to get a look inside. Years' worth of dirt and grime obstructed her view into the building.

"What do you see?"

"Not much. How hard is it to clean a window?"

She was able to see a shelving unit filled with paint cans, rollers, and other DIY supplies. A workbench stretched the length of the back of the garage and was covered with hand tools and discarded rags. In the center of the space was a collection of snow blowers, all different sizes, but what drew Hope's curiosity was a drop cloth draped over something long.

"Let me look." Drew nudged her out of the way so he could peer in the window. "A workshop. No wonder it's locked."

"Do you see the drop cloth? What's it covering?"

"Dunno." Drew pressed his nose against the glass. "You think it's a skeleton?"

"I wonder how tall Joyce was."

"What's going on here?"

Hope jumped, again, at an unexpected voice. She turned and found Oliver standing at the front corner of the garage with a pile of firewood in his arms. Despite being in his late sixties, he was still strong enough to carry all that wood. Twenty years ago, he easily could have been strong enough to dispose of a body.

Drew stepped back from the window. "Oh, hi, Oliver. We were looking for you."

"You thought I locked myself in there?" Oliver asked.

Busted.

Drew laughed. It was a nervous laugh Hope had heard before. They were caught snooping. But Hope was curious to hear Drew's answer.

"No, no . . . you know, if now isn't a good time, we can reschedule." Not much of an explanation. Drew trudged toward Oliver and then dusted the snow off his legs.

"Nah, it's good. Might as well do it now, before the

next round of snow and sleet hit. I just needed some more wood for the stove. Looks like I lost track of time. Now what about you, Hope? What brings you by?"

Drew cocked his head sideways. He was waiting for her answer. And she knew he was thinking the same thing she was just a moment ago. He was curious to hear her explanation.

"I was on my way home when I realized I was passing by your house, so I figured I might as well drop off your check. It'll save me a stamp." She slogged through the snow to reach both men. And then she whipped out her checkbook and pen. She saw Oliver smile, so it looked like he believed her story.

"They keep raising the prices on those things. Remember when they were under thirty cents?" He walked to the deck and set down the firewood.

"I certainly do. What was the price twenty years ago?" Hope followed Oliver with Drew beside her.

Yeah, real smooth, Hope.

Drew shot her a questioning look and she waved it away.

She didn't dwell on her not-too-subtle reference to the time period when Joyce disappeared. She wrote the payment and signed her name.

"Twenty years ago? Who remembers?" Oliver pulled off his work gloves and accepted the check.

"So many things happened twenty years ago. Y2K. Julia Roberts won Best Actress," Drew said.

"Who? Oh, right, the actress. Thanks, Hope. But you didn't have to drop it off. I trust you. You've always paid on time."

Drew's cell phone rang and he excused himself to answer the call.

"I guess it's a benefit of living in a small town and having been in business for as long as you have."

"It has been a long time. Not always easy, but I've made a living. This place isn't much." He was at his house. "But it's all mine."

"You've earned it. You've worked hard. I remember when you mowed the grass for my parents. You never missed a week. Guess it's why people always refer you to their friends. Say, didn't you also mow the Markhams' grass back then?"

Oliver folded the check and slipped it into the pocket of his flannel-lined plaid shirt. "Yeah, yeah, I did. Thanks again for stopping by. I appreciate it."

"Maybe that's how my parents ended up hiring you. My mom was friends with Joyce. She probably referred you to my mom."

Oliver's face clouded and he grew quiet.

"Mom always relied on word-of-mouth referrals."

"I didn't work for the Markhams for very long. Barely knew them."

"No? How come?" Hope fidgeted with the straps of her purse.

"Hard to remember so far back. Thanks again for the check. You drive safe going home." Oliver turned and climbed the steps up to the deck and picked up his fire-wood. "Tell Drew we'll have to reschedule the inter-view." He walked to his front door.

Hope turned and headed to her vehicle. Oliver had had a quick change of mood once she mentioned the Markhams. As she climbed into the driver's seat, she noticed Oliver giving her a final look over his shoulder before he entered the house. Her breath caught. Was the stare supposed to be a warning?

A tapping on the passenger window forced her to shake off Oliver's eerie gaze. She turned on the ignition so she could lower the window for Drew.

"What happened?" he asked.

"He got weird when I started talking about Joyce. He also said to reschedule the interview. Sorry."

Drew sighed. "Me too. Do you really think he's involved with Joyce's and Devon's deaths?"

"I honestly don't know." When she looked back at the house, Oliver was nowhere in sight. "I'd better get going. Do you want to come for dinner tonight? Claire and the kids are coming. Ethan's bringing the girls too."

"Sounds like fun. See you later." If Drew was upset about losing the interview, he didn't show it. Hope suspected he was as curious as she was about the garage and what the drop cloth covered.

Ethan's ringtone interrupted them. "I'd better take this," she said.

Drew gave a nod and then pulled back from the vehicle. He walked away in the direction of the second garage. She grabbed her purse from the passenger seat and fumbled inside for her phone.

She lifted the phone to her ear, all the while keeping her gaze on Oliver's house.

"Are we still on for dinner?" Ethan asked. In the background, she heard his daughters squabbling over something she couldn't make out.

"I'm heading home now."

"Oh? Where are you?"

Hope cringed. *Shoot!* She didn't want to lie to him, but she didn't want to tell him what she was up to either. At least not yet.

"I stopped by Oliver's to pay him. Claire said she's

coming for dinner with the kids." She hoped he wouldn't fixate on her sudden need to pay for plowing in person.

"Good. The girls enjoy spending time with Hannah . . ." Becca's wailing drowned out the rest of what Ethan was saying. "Molly, give Izzy back to Becca."

Izzy was Becca's favorite doll in the whole wide world, and they were never separated. Except when her older sister snatched the doll.

"Not until she says sorry!" Molly demanded.

"I gotta go. See you in a few, babe." The line went silent.

Hope set the phone in the console and drove to the end of the driveway. She stopped and looked in both directions for oncoming traffic. Before she pulled out onto the road, she glanced over her shoulder. Oliver's property was secluded, a perfect place to bury a secret.

Chapter Ten

Hope made it back home in time to bake the rustic apple pie. Though peeling and slicing the apples didn't go as quickly as she would have liked. Her mind kept drifting back to her conversations with Donna and Oliver, forcing her to stop and wipe her hands clean so she could jot notes in her composition notebook.

When she was a member of the library's mystery book club, she had used a notebook to jot down observations, clues, and notes about the story. She'd been determined to uncover the killer's identity before anyone else in the book club. Apparently, old habits die hard.

And they also slowed down her pie-making process.

Despite the distractions, she was able to get the pie into the oven just as Claire and Logan arrived. Her sister brought her usual dinner contribution—a salad. Not that she was a bad cook; she just preferred not to. And she was more than happy to give her sister props for being the best cook in the family.

Logan raced in looking for Bigelow and begging his mom for a dog while Princess made herself scarce.

By the time the table was set, Drew had arrived, followed by Ethan with his daughters. The girls were giving each other the silent treatment. Claire nudged Hope as the girls moped. It was like gazing through a looking glass at their childhood. How many times had they quibbled themselves into silence?

"Hope, can Izzy eat with us?" Becca looked up while holding her doll tightly to her chest. She had her father's dark eyes and her mother's loose curls.

"I'd love for Izzy to join us for dinner." Hope reached out and tousled Becca's light brown locks.

Becca beamed. "Thanks!" She swung around and ran to the table, ignoring Ethan's reminder only a few moments before not to run through the house.

"Daddy said not to run," Molly said with her hands on her hips and a pointed stare at her little sister. Molly's hair was darker and straight. She favored Ethan more than Heather in appearance and temperament. Molly was a by-the-books six-year-old.

"You going to tattle?" Becca climbed onto the chair and placed Izzy on her lap.

"Remind you of anyone?" Claire grabbed the salad, which Hope had dressed with a simple raspberry vinaigrette.

"Oh, yeah." Hope laughed. Even with the bickering, she loved when the girls visited. They livened up the house in a way she could never have imagined. It was like when Bigelow came to live with her. She hadn't realized how much her home needed a dog. Now she realized how much her heart needed the girls.

"Molly doesn't have to tattle because I saw you run after I told you not to." Ethan approached the table from the family room.

"Sorry, Daddy." Becca gave her father a sad face, and Hope was sure it melted his heart. How could it not? Hers had melted, and she wasn't the one doing the scolding.

"I'm about to pull the soups out of the oven. Everyone to the table." On her way to the double ovens, Hope grabbed her oven mitts, while Logan and Drew hustled to the table from the family room.

"I miss having Hannah here." Hope pulled out the first tray of the French onion soup ramekins, perfectly broiled on top. She set the tray on a cooling rack.

"I know. She wanted to hang out with Becca and Molly. But her friend is having a rough time. Her parents announced they were divorcing, and Hannah said they had a huge fight in front of Anneliese. She'll be here next time."

Claire placed the serving platters next to the cooling rack while Hope transferred the bright red pots of bubbling hot soup and they carried the platters to the table.

"Here we go." Hope set down her platter and served Becca and Molly. "Let them cool. They're very hot." She then set a ramekin on Ethan's place mat.

"Thank you." Ethan picked up his spoon and poked the edges of the melted cheese, allowing the thick, hearty soup to rise to the surface.

"This looks so delish." Drew rubbed his hands together as Claire set a ramekin in front of him. She placed her soup and Logan's down next.

"I'll take the platter." Hope reached for the creamy white oval dish from Claire and stacked it on top of her platter. She returned both to the island and hurried back to her seat. She'd been thinking about the soup since she picked up the onions at Donegal's.

Ethan set down his spoon to help Becca with her soup. Her eyes nearly popped out of their sockets as she watched a long string of cheese pull away from the bowl. Hope had cut the amount of cheese in half for the girls' servings so it would be easier for them to eat.

"Have you had French onion soup before?" Ethan asked Molly, who was busy slurping a spoonful of broth.

Molly shook her head. "Never in my life. Why is it French?"

The adults at the table chuckled.

"Well, going back to the eighteenth century—" Hope began until she noticed the blank stare from Molly. "It's a recipe from France."

"Oh. That's the place with the trifle tower." Molly dipped her spoon into the soup and sucked up a sliver of onion and then smiled.

"It's called the Eiffel Tower." After his gentle correction, Ethan scooped up a serving of soup.

Hope's heart swelled. The girls liked the soup, and they were all gathered around the table, eating together as a family. Bigelow's head lifted, and he sniffed the air, but he remained on his bed in the family room. Hope guessed he was biding his time until she served the steaks. Princess was still nowhere in sight. The girls had searched the downstairs looking for her when they arrived but had no luck in finding the cat. Princess probably had found refuge upstairs in a bedroom.

"My friend, Billy, got grounded for a week." Logan looked up from his soup bowl. "A whole freakin' week."

"Watch your language," Claire warned.

"Sorry. But it makes me angry," Logan said. "He got into trouble for throwing a snowball."

"He and his friends threw several snowballs at Maretta's back." Ethan's tone left no doubt he considered what the boys did a serious infraction.

"Did the police have to go to his house?" Logan asked. "It's not like they hurt her."

"You have to realize, Maretta wasn't taking part in a snowball fight." Claire wiped her mouth with a napkin before she reached for her water glass.

"She's a mean old lady." Logan's brows drew together, and he scowled.

"Be nice," Claire said.

Logan shrugged. "Sorry. But she can be mean."

No one at the table disputed his statement. Maretta had always been difficult, and more so now that she was mayor. Hope suspected she realized how out of depth she was in the position. She'd made an impulsive decision to run for office last year. Hope knew all about hasty decisions. Like Maretta, she hardly ever made them. She relied on long-term planning and pros and cons lists. Until she made the unexpected decision to appear on *The Sweet Taste of Success* and quit her magazine editor's job. In a way, she empathized with Maretta. Appearing on the show with twelve other contestants who seemed far more skilled at baking than her, Hope had to sink or swim, and Maretta seemed to be doing the same.

Maybe someone needed to toss her a life jacket.

Logan set down his spoon with a clang. "You all heard she wants to make it illegal to throw snowballs. That's crazy talk."

"It seems over the top even for Maretta." Drew had been quiet so far because he was enjoying his soup. Claire shot him a don't-go-there look, and he returned his attention to his soup. Smart man.

"See, Drew agrees with me," Logan said, and it earned Drew another glare from Claire. "I'm gonna fight Town Hall. Me and the guys aren't going to let Mrs. Kingston ruin winter for us."

"Your winter isn't ruined." Claire reached for her glass again, but the look on her face said she wanted something stronger.

"What are kids supposed to do for fun? You grown-ups always say to get off video games and go outside. Well, outside we throw snowballs when there's snow. Sure, maybe Billy shouldn't have thrown the snowball at Mrs. Kingston, but we all shouldn't be punished."

"He makes a compelling argument," Hope said, earning her a glower from her sister. Lucky for her, she was immune to the look, seeing as it was their mother's signature expression to convey her displeasure with her daughters. She was proud of her nephew's newfound activism. Who knew where it could lead him?

Becca's head swung up and she looked at Ethan. "What's a com . . . compel . . ."

"Compelling argument. I'll explain later," Ethan said.

Becca's head bobbed up and down, and she went back to eating her soup.

"I guess it could be worse. My son could be trying to solve a mystery." Claire leveled her gaze on her sister. "I know you went to see Donna today."

"To find out more about the scholarship fund she wants to start. I volunteered to help," Hope said.

"It's a nice idea. I'm going to write a piece about it for the *Gazette*." Drew tilted his bowl to spoon out the last of the soup.

"Sounds like you had a busy afternoon. You also went to Oliver's place." Ethan wiped Becca's face with her napkin and then returned it to her lap. French onion soup was messy for a four-year-old.

"Not so busy." Hope returned to eating her soup and avoiding the subject.

"The scholarship article will appear in the next edition. Speaking of which, I thrilled my editor with my write-up of the accident, which means Norrie was unhappy." Drew's smile stretched from ear to ear.

"Cool," Logan said.

"Yeah, way cool," Drew agreed.

"You didn't discuss the accident or Joyce's disappearance with Donna?" Claire's tone was suspicious. She refilled her water glass and waited for Hope to answer.

"Well, those topics came up. Donna told me something surprising about Joyce." Hope paused. She suspected the girls were too young to understand, but Logan was at the age when he understood too many things. "But it's not important. Let's finish our soups. Then we'll have the salad while the steaks cook." Hope caught a look from Ethan, that all-too-familiar one that revealed his displeasure with her sleuthing.

After Hope and Claire cleared the soup bowls, salad was served while Hope prepared the steaks. The girls were more interested in dessert and were ecstatic when she told them she'd baked an apple pie. Though it confused Becca because it didn't look like the pie her mother bought at the store. Hope tried to explain what a rustic pie was but realized the simplest explanation was the best: her pie had only one crust.

"It's silly-looking." Becca giggled before eating a forkful of pie.

Drew said his goodbyes after dessert. He had an early morning and wanted to get his beauty sleep. Before he left, he asked Logan for an interview about his plan to fight Town Hall if Maretta's proposal to ban snowball throwing went through. Logan jumped at the chance, while his mother didn't look pleased.

Logan seemed to be walking on air for the rest of the evening, his resistance to the mayor bolstered by the interview request. On the way out the door, Claire pulled Hope aside. "I think Drew has created a little monster," she whispered. "He'll pay for this."

Hope's first instinct was to warn Drew. On second thought, letting it play out could be entertaining. She said good night to her sister and kissed her nephew on the head as he raced past her. He was eager to get home and prepare for the interview.

Yes, it would be very entertaining in the coming days.

Hope finished cleaning up while Ethan tucked the girls in for the night upstairs in their bedroom. During dinner, snow began coming down faster and the temperature dropped. Usually, Ethan wouldn't have given driving home on slick roads a second thought, but he had the girls with him, and they'd begged for a sleepover. They were excited about feeding the chickens in the morning if they got to stay the night.

Hope had set up two twin beds in a spare bedroom. With input from the girls, she'd purchased a lilac-colored set with a butterfly design for Molly and a princess themed set for Becca.

"A penny for your thought?" Ethan tightened his hold on Hope, and she snuggled closer against his solid chest on the sofa. They were finally alone.

"I was thinking about Logan. He's so grown-up." She craned her head to face Ethan. "When did that happen?"

Ethan laughed. "It happens fast. Right before your eyes. I can't believe how the past six years have flown by with the girls."

Hope re-snuggled and got comfortable. "I remember when they were babies. You and Heather . . ." Her words trailed off. She didn't like talking about Ethan's ex. Just like she didn't enjoy talking about her own ex.

"Yeah, I know." He gave her a squeeze and a kiss on the top of her head. "Have the girls told you how much they love their bed sets?" Ethan raised the remote and scrolled through the guide.

"They have. I have some paint chips for them to choose from and I saw the cutest pair of bedside lamps."

Ethan stopped scrolling. "Don't get carried away." He clicked on a show about knife forging.

"There are only two beds up there. They need a dresser and end tables and lighting. They're little girls. Not boys camping."

"They're good."

Hope got the message. The room upstairs wasn't theirs. Their bedrooms were at his and at Heather's house. It was too early in her relationship with Ethan to move the girls into her home. Heck, it was too early to move him in. She sighed and turned her attention to the television show.

She tried to understand the interest in making knives and putting them through rigorous tests to see who had made the better knife. But she couldn't. Ethan, on the other hand, was mesmerized by the three final contestants and their sharp blades.

"I'm looking forward to our ski trip." She craned her

neck again to get a look at Ethan, his eyes fixated on the television.

"Uh-ha."

On second thought, maybe it wasn't too early in their relationship for him to move in, because they were acting like an old married couple. She was talking, and he was ignoring her.

With the confirmation that the honeymoon phase of their romance was over, Hope stretched out her hand and grabbed her cell phone from the end table.

She checked her messages and found a new one. Gail needed help with her assignment. Hope took a quick look at her calendar and then replied. She could meet in the morning if Gail wanted to come over.

"How's Elaine doing? Is she all settled into her new house?" Hope had been meaning to talk to him about his house call ever since Elaine had gushed over how wonderful he was to do so. She'd like to say they hadn't had the right time for the talk. It would be partially correct. But mostly she'd feared what he'd say. Scared she'd hear an admission of betrayal . . . again. And she hated herself for it, because Ethan Cahill wasn't that type of guy.

He tore his gaze from the television. "What?"

Hope had his attention now. She shifted and sat up.

"Oh, yeah. After she came in to file the paperwork, she called me."

Hope didn't say a word.

"Oh, come on. Are you really jealous?"

"Not so much jealous." Totally a lie. "More like curious about why you didn't tell me, but Elaine did when she came to class the other night."

"She's in your class?" he asked with a chuckle.

"Not funny. You know how she is, and I felt blind-sided. Why didn't you tell me?"

"Because it was no big deal. Elaine can bat her eye-lashes all she wants and twerk all—"

"She twerked!"

"You are jealous." He grinned. "Babe, I'm not the least bit interested in her. She asked for help, and I helped her. End of story. Now, let's talk about what you've been up to. What didn't you want to say about Joyce in front of the kids?"

"You're a good man, and I'm happy you helped Elaine. Underneath the surface, she must be lonely and scared."

"I think you're right. But enough about her. It's your turn to share now."

"Right. Donna told me Joyce flirted all the time, right in front of her husband. Even Maretta mentioned something similar."

"That's it?" His tone was flat, and he seemed unimpressed by the newly discovered information.

"Come on, it's a motive for murder. A jealous husband, a spurned lover, or a jealous wife. Take your pick."

"We don't know she's dead."

"She's been missing for twenty years and no one I've talked to, *ever*, has believed she walked out on her family." Hope's cell phone chimed. Gail replied she'd come by tomorrow.

Hope set down her phone.

Ethan pulled her back to him, and he wrapped his arms around her. "I know a cold case is intriguing, but just on the off chance Devon's death is related to her mother's disappearance—and I'm not saying it is—I don't want you involved. It's too dangerous."

Hope opened her mouth to object, but before she could say a word, he covered her lips with his and her protest flittered away. She relaxed into his embrace and happily kissed him back. Her thoughts about Devon's death, the snow pelting her house, and her overbooked calendar all vanished. Until Bigelow lumbered over to the sofa and barked before dropping his head onto her lap.

"Somebody has to go out," Ethan said.

Hope untangled from his hold and gave her pup the stink eye. "We have to work on your timing."

Hope woke the next morning to a text from Josie, who'd decided to work from home. She looked out the window and understood why. Last night's snowfall wasn't epic, but it had turned to sleet and freezing rain, leaving tree branches sheathed in ice, and Hope expected the roads were also covered with slick spots.

Ethan's text an hour later confirmed roads had been dicey, but the town trucks were out working their magic to keep everyone safe. He'd dropped the girls off at their mother's house and then headed to the PD.

Iva managed to get her beat-up old car over to Hope's house before sunrise. Her work ethic continually surprised Hope. Though the bracelet was still missing, and Hope was still avoiding a conversation about it.

Pouring a second cup of coffee, Hope admitted to herself that the way she was dealing with the bracelet situation wasn't the best strategy.

The doorbell rang, giving her an excuse not to think about the piece of jewelry or Iva. She set her mug on the counter and headed to the front door, where Bigelow joined her. He hadn't sprinted for the door at the sound of the bell. Instead, he walked from the living room and waited patiently.

Before she opened the door, she swooped down and gave her pup a kiss on his snout and praised his good behavior.

The doorbell rang again, prompting Hope to straighten and open the door. She welcomed Gail inside and then hung her coat in the hall closet. Gail gave Bigelow a quick pat on the head before following Hope into the kitchen.

"How are the roads?" Hope walked to the island where she had a box of assorted teas set out. Meanwhile, Bigelow trotted to a spot in front of the wall of windows that overlooked the backyard. He lay down and kept a watch for squirrels or any other critters. "Would you like coffee or tea?"

"Tea, please. The roads are a little slippery. But they could be worse. There was a thick layer of ice on my dad's work truck when I left." Gail dropped her purse on the island and perused the varieties of tea while Hope set the kettle on the stovetop. "I love what you've done to this old farmhouse. It was such an eyesore before."

While the water heated, they chatted about the various projects Hope had completed and the ones she planned on tackling next. The kettle whistled, and Hope filled a mug for her guest.

Princess strolled into the kitchen from the hall. She never failed to impress Hope with her beauty. Long, white fur, sparkling, big eyes, and a lovable air of superiority only a cat could pull off.

"She's gorgeous." Gail squatted down and extended

her hand while making a gentle noise to encourage the cat to approach. Princess blinked before sauntering away. "And a little bit of a diva."

"She's a sweet girl. When she wants to be." With her coffee, Hope walked to the table. "Show me what's going on."

"I guess I won't take it personally." Gail dropped a tea bag in her mug and followed to the table. Her oversize plaid shirt hid her curves. She never did girly with her clothing, not even back in high school. She preferred jeans, T-shirts, and those hideous biker boots she loved. Hope snuck a glance at Gail's footwear. Not the same pair from high school, but still biker boots. Some things didn't change.

Gail sat, placing her mug down and resting her bag on her lap. She pulled out a notebook, a pen, and her leather-cased cell phone.

"I brainstormed ten ideas and outlined two in detail. I'm confused by the categories. I'm also wondering, do I need sub-headlines?"

"You need categories regardless of what you're blogging about. It keeps everything organized for you and your reader. Now, subheadings are used to break up text in your post, and with all the information coming at your readers, it's tempting for them to skim or skip reading a big block of text. On my food blog, I have the advantage of using photos to break up text."

"My blog won't be as photo-rich as yours. At least not at the beginning. I see your point about the subheadings. I guess I'll have to become proficient in writing snappy ones."

"It'll get easier with practice, I promise." Hope sipped her coffee and then was about to rattle off a shortlist of category ideas for Gail when her cell phone rang. It was Claire's ringtone. She excused herself to go grab it from the island.

"Hey, what's up?" Hope went back to the table and sat. "Gail is here with me."

"Felice is upstairs in the apartment to pick out an outfit for Devon," Claire said.

"I'm putting you on Speaker. Is Felice by herself?" Hope tapped the speaker button.

"Yes. She parked on the street and then went upstairs. I wanted to stay with her, but I have a client on the way. Can you come over? She's all alone."

"Of course. Gail, do you want to come too?"

"Yes. Why didn't she call me and let me know?" Gail closed her notebook and shoved it into her bag.

"We'll be right over." Hope ended the call. She stood and took both mugs to the sink.

"I'll follow you." Gail stood with her bag slung over her shoulder.

Hope walked Gail to the front door to get her coat. "I'm going out the back to the garage. Meet you at Claire's shop." She said goodbye and closed the door.

Hurrying to the mudroom, she passed Bigelow, who must have realized there was more activity inside now than outside and looked hopeful he would be going out. Hope paused for a moment and apologized. "Not this time. I'll be back soon. Then we'll . . ." She hesitated. She didn't want to say the word "walk" because he understood that word. "Never mind. Just be lucky you're a dog."

Minutes later, Hope and Gail arrived at the shop and parked. Inside, they climbed the staircase to the apartment. When they reached the landing, Hope knocked on the door.

The door opened and Felice appeared. Her eyes were bloodshot and swollen. The tip of her slender nose was red and irritated, and her full lips were dry and chapped.

Yesterday, Hope had heard the grief in Felice's voice and seen traces of it on her face. Now, it was tenfold. Anguish consumed Felice, and she looked frail in her baggy sweater over skinny jeans. Hope guessed the numbness had finally worn off.

"Oh, honey. You shouldn't be here alone." Gail swept in, brushing Hope's side as she ushered Felice farther back into the apartment. "Why didn't you call me? I would have come with you."

Felice shook her head, and her gaze darted between Hope and Gail. She seemed overwhelmed. "I don't know. I wasn't planning on coming here. Then the funeral parlor director called and said Devon needed an outfit." She wrapped her arms around herself and lowered her head.

Gail pulled Felice in for a hug. A hug Felice didn't reciprocate.

"This is too much for you to handle by yourself. Where's Patrick?" Gail drew back so she was eye to eye with Felice. "He should be here for you." Her tone was harsh, almost judgmental.

"We're here now. How can we help?" Hope closed the door. Gail and Felice had been close friends since high school, and she figured Gail would get a pass for her tone, especially because it was coming from a place of love and concern.

"Patrick is working." Felice wiggled free of Gail's hold.

Hope stepped farther into the apartment and dropped her purse on the table. It was bare except for the bulletin board, exactly like the last time she was in the apartment.

"What about your aunt? She's here now, isn't she?" Gail asked.

"Yes. She's helping plan for other family members to get here for the funeral." Felice propped her hands on her hips. "I've looked through Devon's closet, and it looks like she didn't bring anything I could dress her in for her funeral."

Hope wasn't surprised Devon hadn't packed an outfit to be buried in. Who would?

"As Hope asked, how can we help?" Gail closed the gap between her and Felice and stroked her friend's arm. Her voice was quieter and more sympathetic.

Felice patted Gail's hand. "Could you go to the mall and buy a dress and a pair of shoes for Devon? It would be a great help to me."

"Of course I can. Anything for you," Gail said.

"Could you go now? I told the funeral parlor I'd drop off the outfit at lunchtime. I'll text you her sizes."

Gail offered another weak smile. "Sure. I'll go now and drop the things off at the funeral parlor."

"Thank you." Felice eased Gail's hand from her arm and led her friend to the door. "I'll write you a check this afternoon."

Gail murmured not to worry about the money before she left the apartment.

Felice closed the door and turned to Hope.

"Now we can talk." Felice shoved her hands into her jeans' pockets and moved to the sofa. "Being here with her things, knowing how we left off the last time we spoke . . . do you know what's harder than having your sister die?"

Hope had no clue and she never wanted to find out.

"The answer is not knowing why she died. Was it an accident, or did someone make it look like an accident?" She dropped down onto the sofa, grabbed a decorative pillow, and wrapped her arms around it.

Felice had gone from numb to anguished to full-on suspicious in a matter of twenty-four hours. The emotional roller coaster she was riding was understandable and to be expected. Hope needed to keep a clear head for both of them.

"The more I've been thinking about Devon's accident and the reason she came back home, the more convinced I am that it's connected to our mother."

"I spoke with Donna yesterday." Hope sat next to Felice. She wanted to do something to help ease her friend's pain, but what could she do? She couldn't bring Devon back.

Felice nodded. "She wants to start a scholarship fund in Devon's name. I honestly don't know how much I can help her right now."

The stabbing pain in Hope's heart returned. Luckily, the rumble of a truck passing by outside drew her attention to the front window. It was a nice reprieve for a moment. But as the rumbling faded away, she was back with her thoughts about Devon's death.

"I'm sure Donna understands, and I'm certain she's willing to take on most of the responsibility for the scholarship fund-raiser. I've offered to help her do whatever I can."

"She was a tremendous support for us after Mom disappeared. She even came down from Boston to take me shopping for my prom dress."

"She did say a few things about your mom." Hope kept

her gaze on Felice's reaction. At any moment, she could fall apart. Any word or memory could trigger an onslaught of sorrow.

"What did she say? I need to know everything my sister knew." Felice squared her shoulders and straightened her back. She looked like she was bracing herself against unpleasant news.

"Okay. If you're certain." Hope continued when Felice nodded. "Donna said she witnessed your mother more than once flirting with other men, and your father wasn't pleased by the behavior."

Hope caught a flicker in Felice's eyes. She knew about her mother's flirting.

"This isn't news to you, is it?" Hope asked, relieved she hadn't hurt Felice any more than she already was.

"No, it's not. I saw it once. At a graduation party. Us kids hung out by the pool, and there was a volleyball court set up. Of course, Devon stayed by the pool, and I joined in on a volleyball game."

In high school, Felice ran track and got a college scholarship because of it. So Hope could easily see her on the volleyball court. Whereas Devon preferred nonathletic activities like sunbathing.

"I was having a good game, until I got hit on my nose by the ball. Talk about bad timing. I had my first date with Ronnie Taylor the next night. Remember him?"

Hope did. He played football. He also had a smile that melted nearly every girl's heart.

"So, I didn't want to have a swollen nose. It would have been disastrous."

"You'd been trying to get him to ask you out for months, if I remember correctly."

"You do! No way I was going with a big fat nose. I went inside to get some ice, but I needed a towel or something, so I looked for my mom. I spotted her in the living room, and my dad was in there too, with some other adults." Felice turned her head slightly and stared ahead at the bare beige wall. "My dad was standing by the window, staring out to the street. While my mom was standing next to a man I didn't know. Her hand was on his chest, and she tossed her head back, and her long hair bounced. And she giggled. But it wasn't a giggle I'd heard before." She looked back at Hope. "It was almost sultry. She was flirting with that man right in front of my dad."

"I'm sorry you had to see it."

"I wonder how many times she did it in front of my dad. Anyway, I eased away from the doorway and went back outside. After that, I didn't care about my nose, or Ronnie." Felice's chin quivered. "Why would she do that?"

"I don't know why." Hope knew Felice wasn't looking for an answer from her about her mother's conduct. Only Joyce could have answered the question. But she was gone.

"I need to know what happened to Mom, and I don't care how much it could hurt me. I need to know the truth. And I need to know if Devon died because of what happened to our family twenty years ago." She reached out and squeezed Hope's hands. "I can't wait for the police to determine what happened with Devon. We've wasted twenty years already. I need your help."

It was déjà vu for Hope. Just a few nights ago, she'd sat there on the sofa and been asked the same question. Two days later, Devon was dead. The last thing she wanted was for Felice to face the same fate. "I know I'm asking a lot. If there is a connection between what happened to my mother and Devon, I know we'll both be in danger."

"It's not like I haven't put myself in the path of a killer before." In fact, Hope had done that too many times in the past year. The sensible thing would be to let the police handle the matter. But how could she say no to Felice?

"I'm not a detective. I don't know how much help I can be."

"You're underestimating yourself."

"No, no, I'm not." There was no modesty at play there. She'd let her inquisitiveness get the better of her, and it had landed Hope face-to-face with a murderer. "I'll help with whatever I can do. I just don't think it will be a lot."

"I appreciate anything you can do. Thank you." The smallest of smiles touched Felice's lips. Nothing Hope or the police could do would bring Devon back. But maybe Felice would find some peace, some comfort in knowing the truth.

Hope raised her palm. "However, I want to clarify that whatever I learn, I will tell the police. I'm not going to keep any secrets to protect anyone."

Felice leaned forward and hugged Hope. "I understand. I wouldn't want you to." She released Hope and jumped to her feet.

Hope stood with less eagerness.

"I wish we had Devon's research notes. But I should be able to find the articles she got from the library and online. It's a place to start."

Hope offered to stay and help Felice pack up what little there was of Devon's clothing and the few personal items she brought with her to Jefferson. Thirty minutes later, they emerged from the building, going in separate directions.

Hope glanced in the window of Claire's shop and saw her talking to a client. She wanted to update her sister but didn't want to interrupt. Maybe she wanted to prolong not having to tell Claire what transpired upstairs. That she'd promised to help Felice, which meant she would be digging into the Markham family's past.

All families had their secrets.

An uneasiness bubbled in her stomach.

What would she find?

The woman Claire was talking with turned and walked toward the round table where Claire had her consultations, and her sister would see her at the window when she turned away from the counter to follow her customer.

Hope scooted out of view. She scolded herself for being a chicken. But she didn't want to have the discussion right there and then.

She pulled out her phone to send Claire a text with a promise to call later to give her a full update. Before she could send the message, she noticed a voice mail from Donna.

She accessed the call and listened.

"Hope, I . . . I . . . need to talk to you. I . . . I . . ." Donna's words faded and then boomed back, only to ebb out again in a bout of sobbing. "Can't . . . believe I forgot . . . work truck . . . saw driving by Joyce's . . . house." The message ended.

She tapped on the phone to redial Donna's number and was sent to voice mail.

Why wasn't she answering her phone?

Donna's words had been difficult to understand, but it

sounded like she'd remembered something from the day Joyce disappeared. Something upsetting enough to leave her crying.

Hope turned and hurried to her Explorer. She tossed her purse onto the front passenger seat and climbed in. What could Donna have remembered? Would it be enough to finally find out what happened to Joyce?

Or would it only be a false lead like so many of them twenty years ago?

Chapter Eleven

The cryptic voice mail had Hope ditching her planned return home for a quick drive over to Donna's house. Maybe Devon's podcast and arrival back in Jefferson had led to a break in her mother's case after all.

When she arrived at her destination, she parked in the driveway. Before exiting her Explorer, she grabbed her cell phone from her purse. There was a sensible explanation for the mysterious message, she told herself as she made her way to the home's entry.

Halfway, she stopped in her tracks and wondered what was the explanation for the open front door.

Her grip on her phone tightened as she recalled two other similar scenarios.

First, Joyce's door had been found open by her daughters the day she was reported missing. Then Devon's door had been found open when she had gone missing.

Hope gulped. Was Donna the next woman to go missing?

There was only one way to find out. Then again, there could be another reasonable explanation for why, in the middle of February, Donna chose to leave her door wide open. As Hope stepped forward and entered the house, she willed her mind to come up with some ideas.

"Donna," she called out. There was no reply.

She looked into the living room. Empty. She glanced down the hall that led to the bedrooms but decided to check the kitchen first. Maybe Donna had slipped and fallen. It happened all the time. Wasn't falling the leading cause of deaths in homes? She shook away the morbid fact as she made her way through the house.

She rushed to the kitchen, but Donna was nowhere to be found.

A half-filled coffee mug and a cell phone sat on the peninsula. On the table, she spied a piece of paper.

I'm so sorry. I can't live with this guilt any longer.
Donna.

What guilt? Before she could try to figure out what the note meant, her ears perked up at the sound of a low rumble.

She turned toward the garage door. Thank goodness. Donna hadn't left yet. There was time to stop her from doing something stupid. Hope hurried to the door and yanked it open.

A cloud of exhaust fumes overwhelmed her, and she coughed. She raised her hand to cover her mouth and nose, all the while doubting what she was seeing.

Donna's body slumped over the steering wheel in her sedan.

The shock of the scene hit her like a punch to the stomach. The blow nearly crippled her, but she couldn't give in. Donna needed help. She started to step down to the concrete floor, but the fumes were too much.

Her coughing turned into jagged fits as her lungs filled with fumes and through her tearing eyes, still she pushed forward, clumsily looking for the automatic door opener.

She found it and slammed her palm on it. As the door rolled up, she hurried to the car and yanked open the driver's side door. Every fiber in her body screamed to get out as a wave of light-headedness rolled through her, forcing her to grip the doorframe to steady herself. Once she had her footing, she reached into the car and shook Donna.

"Please wake up."

There was no response. She was too late.

A deep cough rose through her chest, followed by another one, and the wooziness made her sway. Her grip on the doorframe began to loosen. She had to get out of there. She had to leave Donna.

Hope pulled back and staggered out of the garage. She gulped in fresh air as she punched in 9-1-1.

"I've found Donna Wilcox dead in her car." While she gave the emergency operator all the pertinent information, she couldn't help but think about what Donna had remembered about her friend's disappearance and that now no one would ever know.

"You heard Donna's message. Clearly, she remembered something about Joyce's disappearance," Hope said, tucking the phone back into her pocket, then wrapping the thermal blanket around herself. She'd refused the EMT's offer of a gurney, and the oxygen had cleared her head. The responding officer who'd found her still struggling to breathe on the driveway, had handed her off to Detective Reid, who now nodded in a noncommittal fashion to Hope's observation.

"You spoke to her yesterday about the scholarship fund. Is that all you discussed?" Detective Reid asked.

Hope lowered the oxygen mask. "No. She told me she was here in Jefferson the day Joyce disappeared. They were supposed to meet for brunch, but Joyce never showed. After Donna left the diner, she drove to the Markham house. She didn't see Joyce's car there."

Hope took a deep breath from the oxygen mask.

"You really should go to the emergency room."

She shook her head defiantly. She wasn't about to continue her streak of being a regular visitor to the local ER. Just a little more oxygen and she'd be fine. And maybe another blanket.

"I will review Mrs. Markham's case files."

Reid didn't look cold. His dark gray wool coat added bulk to his lanky frame, and black leather gloves covered his slender hands. His tall and lean physique made him a standout next to the other officers, but his strengths were a sharp eye for details and an internal lie detector that zeroed in on inconsistencies and half-truths. She'd dare say they made a good team, but she kept that thought to herself so he didn't toss her in a jail cell.

"She must have remembered seeing the truck at Joyce's house. What truck could it have been?"

"We'll look into it, Ms. Early. Could you tell me what

type of mood Ms. Wilcox was in when you left her on Sunday?"

"I wonder if it was Oliver Marchant's truck." Hope set down the oxygen mask on the ambulance's tailgate.

Reid stopped writing. "Ms. Early—"

"Wait. Hear me out," she said. He needed to take what she said seriously. A woman just died, probably murdered because of something she knew about Joyce's disappearance. "Devon told me Oliver mowed the grass for her parents back around the time Joyce disappeared. Her mom said he made her feel uncomfortable, and when I asked him about working for them, he got nervous."

Reid clicked his pen. "When did you speak to Oliver about working for the Markhams?"

"Yesterday. I also ran into Maretta earlier and she suggested Joyce's flirtatious behavior caused her to run off."

"Sounds like you had a busy day," he said dryly. "I thought we had an understanding you wouldn't involve yourself with official police business."

"We do. And I'm abiding by it. I was only talking to people. I ran into Maretta at the store, Jane suggested I help Donna with the fund-raising, and I had to pay Oliver for plowing my property. The subjects of Joyce's disappearance and Devon's car accident just came up."

"Of course they did." No doubt his internal lie detector was registering off the charts at Hope's half-truth.

"Are you going to talk to Oliver?"

Reid shoved his notepad and pen into his coat's interior breast pocket. "You may be dating the chief of police, but you're not entitled to know my every move."

"I didn't think I was." Her relationship with Ethan

seemed to irritate Reid, and she didn't know why. Whatever the reason, it was his problem, not hers.

Ethan. Oh, boy. She had to explain this whole mess to him.

She glanced at her phone. There was a new message from him.

Car vs. truck accident. On scene. Will meet you at home. Love, E

She smiled. He didn't seem angry with her.

A small sedan pulled up to the curb behind the ambulance and the driver's door flew open.

"Detective!" Maretta emerged from the vehicle with her trademark scowl.

Reid looked over his shoulder and sighed. "If you'll excuse me, I have to update the mayor. I'll have Officer Roberts drive you home. There's nothing you can do here now. Please, let me know if you remember anything else."

He might have been ready to dismiss her, but she wasn't finished.

She jumped off the tailgate. "Donna wouldn't have killed herself. If she did, why did she call me? And why didn't she share in the note what she felt guilty about? And what about the handwriting?"

"What about it?"

"It was barely legible, messy. Donna took pride in her handwriting. She taught calligraphy classes for goodness' sake."

"Given the state of mind people are in when they decide to end their lives, it's not surprising a handwritten note might be messy."

Hope was about to protest when Maretta interrupted again.

"I'm waiting, Detective Reid!" Maretta stood beyond the crime scene tape with her hands on her hips.

Reid's lips flattened. Hope was pretty sure he found Maretta more irritating than her.

"I know she was a friend. The truth is, we never know what people are capable of. If you'll excuse me, the mayor is waiting. Go home." He turned and walked away.

Hope didn't envy his position. Nor did she believe Donna's death was self-inflicted. Or that she wrote the note. Somebody was determined to keep whatever happened twenty years ago buried.

Chapter Twelve

Waking up the morning after discovering Donna's body, Hope needed some big-time comfort. So, it was no wonder she tied on an apron first thing and pulled out her container of flour.

There was nothing more soothing than baking.

She measured out the dry ingredients for her Sunshine Corn muffins recipe. A sprinkle of grated orange zest gave the traditional corn muffins a little spark of brightness, which was why they were one of her favorite muffins.

She cracked two eggs and added the milk and oil she'd already measured out. After a quick whisk, she dropped in the tablespoon of orange zest. The tiny flecks of orange and the scent of fresh citrus made her happy.

A little happiness was welcome. Throughout the night,

she had been plagued with nightmares, each one increasing in terrifying intensity from the one before. The last one had her bolting upright, startling Ethan and Bigelow. It was a mash-up of Devon's car accident and Shirley's lifeless body in her vehicle. She had settled back down, cocooned in Ethan's embrace, and managed to fall back asleep for a couple more hours.

The oven beeped, signaling it was ready for the muffins to go in. She picked up her pace, and within minutes the batter was combined and divided among the muffin cups. She set the filled muffin trays into the oven and set the timer.

With a quick cleanup of the countertop done, she refilled her coffee cup and then settled at the table and opened her composition notebook.

Over her first cup of coffee, she jotted down notes about the gruesome scene she'd discovered yesterday. Not exactly the journaling her mother did daily.

She sipped her fresh coffee and made a notation about Donna's alleged suicide note. Heavy footfalls from the hall drew her away from her writing. Ethan was coming downstairs. She didn't want him to see her notebook. She quickly closed the book and looked around for where to stash it as the footsteps got closer.

Shoot.

Her tote. It was on the sideboard. She jumped up and dashed to the bag and shoved the notebook inside. That was when she felt a swipe to her hand.

Princess was sitting on the sideboard, peering at her.

"Where did you come from? You were in the living room." The cat sat, her pose regal. "You're like a ninja."

Princess blinked.

"Don't judge me."

Meowwww.

"Yes, it looks like I'm hiding this from Ethan, but I'm not really."

Meowwww.

"Why am I explaining myself to you?"

Princess rose onto all fours and walked along the edge of the sideboard, flicking her tail and swatting Hope in the face. She then jumped down and pranced out of the room as Ethan entered.

"Hey, I thought you might sleep in." He looked refreshed and well-rested in his JPD T-shirt under a flannel shirt and black work pants. He had arrived after his shift with a pizza and a shoulder to cry on. Hope had appreciated his concern and not having to make dinner. She hadn't had much of an appetite but managed to eat a slice before going to bed.

Hope moved back to the coffee maker and filled a travel mug for him. "I couldn't sleep."

"You're baking?" His nose wiggled. "Corn muffins?"

"Yes." She handed him the travel mug. "How about breakfast? I can whip up scrambled eggs."

He leaned forward and kissed her. "Thanks. But I can't."

"You know, I meant what I said yesterday. I don't believe Donna killed herself. I think someone murdered her."

"Hope, not every death results from murder. Let us do our job. Besides, you're busy with yours right now."

"I am?"

"The muffins." He nodded toward the oven. "You're baking them for the blog or a video, right?"

Hope glanced over her shoulder at the oven so she wouldn't be looking at Ethan when she answered.

"Right. My blog."

As she looked back to face him, he pulled her close to him for another kiss. "Love you. Call me if you need to talk. Okay?"

"I will." She watched him disappear out to the mud-room and, a few moments later, the back door opened and closed.

Meowwwww.

Princess's sudden vocalization startled Hope. "Where the . . ." Her voice trailed off when she realized the cat was sitting on the island. "I thought we had this discussion about where you can and cannot jump up on to. The countertops are off-limits." She scooped up the cat and set her on the floor.

Princess stared up at Hope.

"Don't look at me like that. I didn't lie to him. Well, not exactly. I'll use the recipe for my blog."

Princess's ears flicked back and gave Hope a doubtful look.

"Fine, I fibbed. And I hid my notes."

The cat turned and slinked away, leaving Hope to wrestle with her decision to be less than forthcoming with Ethan. But first she had to clean the countertop.

Fifteen minutes later, the timer dinged and she pulled the muffins from the oven. She was immediately hit with a waft of pure joy. Freshly baked muffins. There was nothing better on a cold, bleak morning. As she closed the oven door, she found Bigelow had finally joined her in the kitchen.s

"What took you so long?" She chuckled, setting the

muffin tins on cooling racks. "You already had your breakfast, and it's too soon for a snack. Besides, these are not for you." She patted the pup on the head.

She'd baked for two reasons. The first one was to have something to feed to Iva as they discussed the missing charm bracelet. The second was that she wanted to take them with her when she visited Alfred Kingston.

She'd heard what Maretta had to say about Joyce and now she wanted to listen to what her husband had to say. Alfred had a weakness for baked goods. They'd sit and chat while he enjoyed a snack.

The mudroom door opened, and Iva entered the kitchen. She wore a puffer vest over a denim shirt, jeans, and insulated work boots.

"Smells good in here." Her hair was pulled back into a ponytail and tucked under a wool cap.

"Sunshine Corn Muffins hot out of the oven." Hope gestured to the muffin tins. "Coffee?" She pulled out another cup from an upper cabinet.

"Love some." Iva walked toward Hope, and the floor squeaked. She glanced downward. "Need to fix that."

"I don't think so. It's a part of the flooring's charm."

"Charm?" Iva gave Hope a skeptical look.

The two women didn't share the same appreciation for old things. While Iva would help tackle some of the projects in the house, she definitely wouldn't be *fixing* the lovingly salvaged pumpkin pine floor anytime soon.

Hope handed Iva a full cup of coffee and then turned out the muffins onto another cooling rack. She plated a muffin and carried it to the table.

"If I don't say so myself, these are delicious. You have to try one."

Iva followed. "Thank you. I am a little hungry."

"How's your mom doing?" Hope refilled her cup and grabbed a muffin before joining Iva at the table. Bigelow followed. No doubt he was hoping for a few fallen crumbs.

"Every day is different. Yesterday it was rough. It's hard seeing her suffer. Then again, it's good to have her around." Iva sipped her coffee. She liked it black and strong.

"I love the paint job you did in the living room." Hope bit into her muffin. From experience, she'd learned to give Iva some positive feedback before broaching the subject of the missing bracelet.

"Thanks. The paint was superb. Most people go cheap with paint, but they regret it later." Iva broke off a piece of the muffin and chewed. The hard edges of her face softened, and her eyes brightened. "You're right, this is delicious."

Hope smiled. Hearing compliments never got old and having someone enjoy what she'd baked warmed her inside. Yeah, she was that corny sometimes.

"Thank you. I'm glad you like the muffin. How are my chickens doing? Is Helga still giving you a rough time?" The hen was notorious for pecking at people. She'd mellowed out since Hope got her, but she was still spirited.

Iva shrugged. "She's like my mom; she has good days and bad days." She broke off another piece of muffin and ate it. There were plenty of muffins, and Hope would send her home with a few.

"It's good everything is working out well. There is something I want to talk to you about." Hope lowered her gaze as her finger traced the rim of her coffee cup.

"Is there something wrong?" Iva asked.

Hope lifted her gaze and was about to launch into the dreaded conversation when Iva's cell phone rang. Hope knew the ringtone. Iva's mother was calling.

"Sorry, I gotta take this." Iva pulled her phone out of her jeans' pocket. She tapped on the phone and took the call. "What is it, Ma?"

Hope stood and walked to the island to give Iva privacy. She boxed up the muffins, dividing the big batch in half.

"Okay, no problem. I'm on my way now. Go back to bed." Iva disconnected the call and stood. "Sorry, I gotta go to the pharmacy for my mother. She forgot to tell me she needed a refill last night. Thanks for the coffee and muffin."

Hope grabbed one box. "Here, take these."

Iva smiled. "Thanks, Hope." She headed to the mudroom door. "Hey, we can talk about whatever it was you wanted to talk about later, okay?"

"Absolutely. Go take care of your mom." Hope watched Iva disappear out to the mudroom and then heard the back door open and close. She let out a whoosh of relieved breath, though their conversation was only postponed. She'd still have to discuss the missing bracelet with Iva. But that was for another day. Now, she needed to finish getting ready and head out to Alfred's office.

Hope's trek from her Explorer to the entry of the Jefferson Town Real Estate office was brisk, much like the weather. She juggled the box of muffins in one hand as the other opened the door.

Inside, a toasty warmth greeted her and so did Amy Phelan, the agency's full-time secretary. The young blonde pointed to the headset she wore and nodded.

"Yes, I'll let him know. Thank you for calling and have a great day!" Amy pressed a button on the telephone and removed the headset.

"Good morning." Hope wiped her boots on the mat before stepping forward. She lifted the box's lid, flashing a glimpse of the freshly baked muffins.

"Corn? My favorite." Amy leaned forward and plucked one out of the box, along with a napkin that Hope had tucked into the corner.

"Enjoy." Hope closed the lid.

"You know I'm on a diet, right?" Amy always seemed to be trying to lean out her curvy figure.

"Sorry." Hope flashed an apologetic smile. She never intentionally wanted to sabotage anyone's diet, but she couldn't imagine a life in which you couldn't indulge in a muffin.

Amy nibbled at the still-warm treat.

"No, you're not. I'm so glad you're not sorry. This is delicious." She wiped her mouth with the napkin. "I have to tell you, my mom is super excited about the blogging class. It's all she's been talking about since she registered."

"She's a great student. Her homework assignment was top-notch. I think she'll enjoy blogging."

Amy leaned forward and lowered her voice. "Too bad what happened to Devon. It's really dampened my mom's enthusiasm. She and Devon's mom were close friends. It breaks her heart to have to console Felice. Again."

"Devon's death was a shock to everyone."

"I remember Mom crying after Joyce disappeared. I

asked her why she was crying, and she told me she wished things had turned out differently with Joyce." Amy bit into the muffin.

"What did she mean by that?" Hope's curiosity was piqued.

Amy motioned that she'd answer in a moment, after she swallowed her bite. "Don't know. She wouldn't say. But I guessed it was like Violet Neville and me. Remember her? We were besties until she told a guy I liked that I had mono. I still can't believe she was so mean. Anyway, we weren't besties after that incident."

Hope didn't remember Violet Neville, but Amy was a few years behind Hope in school, so they hadn't traveled in the same circles.

"And my mom was so upset the day they found Devon's car. And now Donna's death. Was it really a suicide?"

Before Hope could reply, approaching footsteps drew her attention to the staircase.

"Hope?" What brings you by?" Alfred's gaze landed on the pastry box, and his usual smile broadened. Alfred was good-natured, mild-mannered, and amiable. A striking contrast to his wife, Maretta.

"Good morning. I baked muffins." Hope walked toward him. She lifted the top of the box, and Alfred got a whiff of the citrus aroma.

"I wondered with Claire gone if you would be dropping by with treats for me . . . I mean us."

Hope lowered the top of the box. "Of course I will. Claire striking out on her own doesn't mean I'll stop sharing my baking."

"Well, because you're here and I'm between appointments, why don't you come up to my office? We can have a chat and catch up."

Exactly what Hope was hoping for.

Alfred turned and ascended the staircase and Hope followed. They walked the long, narrow hallway, passing several offices. Would one of those have been Joyce's if she hadn't disappeared?

"Come, sit." Alfred gestured to one of the two chairs in front of his neat and organized desk as he sat in his leather chair.

There was nothing in the room that boasted how successful he was in his business. He'd started his career with a national real estate agency and quickly excelled as a salesman, eventually branching out on his own. Even with his success, he wasn't a flashy kind of guy. He drove an affordable car and lived in the same house he'd purchased decades ago. Though he did have a priceless view of Main Street through a bank of nine-over-nine windows. The snow-covered Congregational Church bell tower was off in the distance.

Hope set the box of muffins on the desk. She unzipped her jacket and loosened the scarf around her neck before sitting.

"How's Claire doing? Too bad about the tenant over her shop. We probably won't get a new one until spring." Alfred took a bite of the muffin.

"Devon's death is tragic. First her mother's disappearance and now the fatal car accident. Joyce worked here as a secretary, didn't she?"

"Hope, this muffin is amazing. So moist and flavorful. How do you do it?" He took another bite and shook his head in a good way. "I'll have to have Maretta try baking these too. The recipe is on your blog, right?"

Hope's mouth fell open. Maretta made her recipes? Well, wonders never ceased.

"Yes, it will be soon."

"Good. Good." Alfred continued eating the muffin and then must have had a moment of self-awareness. "Oh, please forgive me. Where are my manners? Do you want one? Or maybe coffee?"

"No, thank you. I would like to talk to you about Joyce, though."

"Ahh." Alfred set down the uneaten half of his muffin on another napkin and wiped any crumbs off his hands. "You're doing it again, aren't you?"

"Doing what?"

"Investigating. Sleuthing. Whatever you and Jane call it. I caught the two of you with your heads together in The Coffee Clique the other morning. You think someone murdered Devon, don't you? And that it's connected to Joyce's disappearance?" He leaned back and clasped his hands together over his rounded midsection. Over the years Alfred had filled out his lean figure, and he wore sweater vests as an attempt to disguise what her grandma used to call a jellybelly.

Today, he wore a blue vest over a plaid shirt. The disguise wasn't working.

"I admit, I'm curious about what happened to Devon. I'm even more curious about her mother."

"I'm not surprised you are. I'm learning that where there's a mystery, Hope Early is probably nearby." He flashed a good-natured smile.

Alfred's statement, which was so matter-of-fact, took

her by surprise. She wanted to deny it, but it was true. At least lately.

"Let me see what I can remember. It was a long time ago. Joyce handled our clients well, always had a smile for them, and she interacted with the agents professionally. She was an asset to our office."

"Devon told me she had ambitions of being an agent."

"She did. I think she had the personality to do well. But she seemed hesitant. Maybe it was a confidence thing. The studying and the exam can be daunting."

Hope nodded. "I remember when Claire was going for her license."

"Then you know how strenuous it can be. But I knew she had potential and so did Kent. He encouraged her to enroll in the class and helped her with the course material. He was like a mentor to her."

"He was?" Hope never thought of Kent Wilder as the mentoring type. No, he was more a slick salesman than a nurturer. When she moved back to Jefferson, he'd almost had Hope purchasing a house one code violation away from demolition. He'd called her and convinced her to look at the house. Claire had been out of town that day at a closing, so Hope went to see the house on her own with Kent. Luckily, Claire intervened before Hope signed any papers; otherwise Hope would now be the proud owner of a never-ending money pit. He'd played on Hope's emotions all too well.

"They were close?" she asked.

"I'd say so. He took her to a few open houses and closings to give her a feel for the whole process."

"At the time, he must have been working very hard to establish his own business. It's wonderful he wanted to pay it forward so early in his career."

"We've always been like a family here," Alfred said proudly.

Hope tried to figure out a way to delicately ask the next question. Who was she kidding? There was no delicate way to ask the question.

"Alfred, I don't mean to sound indelicate or speak badly of someone who isn't able to defend herself." Hope shifted on her seat. "Is there any possibility Joyce and Kent were having an affair?"

Alfred drew back, and his eyes bulged. "Absolutely not! Kent has never mixed business with pleasure. Never."

Hope couldn't argue Alfred's point. Even though her sister was Kent's colleague, he still tried to sell Hope a lemon of a house that would have bankrupted her.

"If not Kent, could she have been seeing someone else who worked here?"

"I do admire your spunk and determination to get to the truth. Sometimes, you've been so headstrong that it almost got you killed. But I have to say, you're way off base here. From what I remember, Joyce was a loyal and loving wife to her husband. The woman I knew back then wouldn't have stepped outside her marriage."

Hope couldn't recall the last time someone called her spunky. Elaine Whitcomb had called her a busybody not too long ago. In fact, she'd threatened to start a #busybody with Hope's name attached to it.

Alfred's desk phone buzzed. "Excuse me." He lifted the receiver. "Yes, I'll take the call." He covered the speaker with a hand. "I have to take this. Thanks for the muffins. I'm sure everyone in the office will love them."

Hope stood. "You're welcome. Have a nice day." She walked to the door and pulled it closed behind her as she stepped out into the hall. She continued to the staircase and stopped at another closed office door. It was Kent's.

Joyce might not have been having an affair with Kent or anyone else at the agency, but Alfred might not have known everything about her.

On her way out of the building, she stopped by Amy's desk to say goodbye and to find out where Kent was. Luckily for her, Amy didn't hold the fact she'd gone off her diet against Hope and told her Kent was at his newest listing. With the address in hand, Hope left, determined to learn more about Kent's involvement with Joyce's professional ambitions—or more.

Chapter Thirteen

Outside, she braved the wind as it swept down, jostling storefront banners and threatening to sweep away anything that wasn't nailed down. The cold pricked Hope's cheeks, making her tug up her scarf to cover her chin. February could be a fiercely cold month, and this year it wasn't disappointing. As she speed-walked to her vehicle, she kept reminding herself the weather was perfect for her upcoming ski getaway with Ethan.

With her car started, she punched the address Amy had given her into her navigation system and took off.

The narrow roads were even more harrowing with piles of snow on both sides and spotty ice patches. Her telephone rang, and she answered it.

"I was about to give up getting hold of you. This phone

tag is bananas." Corey's nasal voice came through the car speaker, loud and clear.

"Sorry. Things have been . . . hectic here." Hope took a curve on Old Chester Road slowly. Good thing she did, because she had to come to a sudden stop to let a deer cross the road.

"Yeah, yeah, I can imagine how busy things are up in Mayfield."

"Jefferson," she corrected and ignored his sarcastic tone. She eased off the brake and pressed down the accelerator after the deer made it across the road.

"Whatever. Look, I wanted to update you on Mama Mia. The contracts are being drawn up as we speak. This is big, Hope."

Yes, it is.

"I can't believe I'll be working with them. Do you know how long I've been cooking their pasta?"

"Yeah, yeah, I know. I pitched it to them, remember? Lifelong Mama Mia Pasta eater. Your mom cooked it every Friday night."

Sentimentality wasn't Corey's thing. But it didn't matter. He got Hope the deal.

"Also, I got the details from Frye-Lily about their partnership with Allied Home Centers and what posts they'd want from you. I just emailed it to you. Looks good. Let's make this deal happen too."

"I'll review it later." Up ahead, she caught a glimpse of something shiny, like ice, and eased off the gas. "Look, Corey, I can't talk. I'm driving."

"Yeah, well, I'm walking and talking." The sounds of Midtown traffic spilled over into their conversation. Corey always seemed to be out of the office. Come to think of it, she didn't know if he had an office or worked from a Starbucks.

"It's not the same thing. We're having a bad winter and the roads are slick." Why was she explaining this to him?

"That's what you get for moving up to Mayfield."

Hope sighed. Corey was a born and bred New Yorker who ventured out of the city only as far as the meticulously maintained hamlet of Greenwich, Connecticut.

"Jefferson. I'll call you later to go over the details and dates. Bye." She disconnected the call.

She probably could have continued talking with Corey, but she was too excited about the Mama Mia deal to focus on conversation and driving at the same time. Being connected with a national brand that had been a staple in millions of kitchens for generations was huge for her career. And the exposure working with Allied Home Centers would bring made her feel like she would burst. All her long hours and seven-day workweeks were finally paying off.

Minutes later, Hope's navigation system announced her arrival at her destination. She pulled off the road and traveled along the rutty driveway surrounded by dense forest on either side. Approaching a clearing, she spotted a sleek Mercedes parked on the large gravel pad.

She parked her car next to the Mercedes, just in time to see Kent pulling the front door closed behind him.

The midcentury home reminded Hope of the *Brady Bunch* house, with its sharp angles and floor-to-ceiling windows.

Out of her Explorer, she walked toward the entry of the house.

"Good morning." Kent's booming voice filled the quiet morning air as he crossed the bridge. "What brings you by? I know you're not interested in making an offer. This isn't your style."

No, her style was more run-down with Pinterest potential.

"It's not, but it's striking. It's an unusual style for this area."

"During the 1940s and '50s, there was a group of architects known as the Harvard Five. They settled in New Canaan and built close to one hundred homes. One of their former employees who broke out on his own designed this house."

Kent had an encyclopedic knowledge of architecture, and Hope suspected that was an asset he used to lure and entice potential owners. Who wouldn't want to own a piece of an architectural movement? His ability to romance the history of a home and his smooth selling style allowed him to rise through the ranks of a junior real estate agent to megaseller over the past twenty years. He was dressed in a tan wool coat and a Burberry scarf tucked into the neckline. His dark hair was thick and shiny. There wasn't a hint of balding or gray. In his gloved hands, he held a portfolio and a cell phone.

"I've never heard of them."

"Not surprising. But back then, those visionaries caused quite a stir." Kent pointed to the house. "This type of architecture wasn't welcome in the very Norman Rockwell town, with endless white picket fences, saltbox homes dating back to the Colonial period, and churches over a hundred years old."

"I can understand why. It's a masterpiece, but not very quaint."

Three oversize white orb pendants hung from the

porch, which stretched the length of the house. It didn't have the same warmth as Hope's wraparound porch and no furniture for a quick respite on a warm spring afternoon.

"Buyers for this type of house aren't looking for quaint." He turned halfway, looking back at the house. "The outside has held up well after all these years. The inside needs a little freshening up. I just got off the phone with Claire."

"You're keeping her busy these days."

"Speaking of busy . . ." Kent gestured to his car. "I have an appointment to get to."

"Of course. I don't want to keep you."

"But you're going to, aren't you?"

"I want to talk to you about Joyce Markham. It won't take long. I promise."

Kent flashed his toothy smile. "You never cease to amaze me. Her daughter dies in a car accident and you suspect foul play."

"What makes you say that?"

"You're here asking about her mother. Somehow those events are connected in your mind." Great. Now he was sounding like Alfred. "Look, I don't have time to indulge your inner Miss Marple or Jessica Fletcher or whatever was the name of Jane Merrifield's detective." Kent's long stride quickly took him to the driver's side door of his Mercedes, forcing Hope to chase after him.

"I'm not indulging anything. I'm simply curious why you took an interest in Joyce's career. I heard you mentored her and encouraged her to pursue a real estate license."

Kent opened the car door and tossed in his portfolio and phone. "I did. She was a nice lady who had ambition.

I like that in people. At the time, I was building my team, and I thought she'd be more of an asset to me as an agent rather than a secretary. Then she disappeared, and like everyone, I was shocked. And now her daughter. The family must be cursed or something."

Hope didn't believe in curses or in coincidences.

"I also heard she liked to flirt."

"You hear a lot of things, don't you?"

"I do."

Kent grinned. He seemed to appreciate Hope's honesty.

"You heard correctly. Though I never got the feeling she would have followed through. She wasn't that type of woman."

"You two never . . ."

"Had an affair?" Kent asked, finishing Hope's sentence. "No. Never."

"Did you know about her tattoo?"

Kent's eyebrow arched, and he looked sincerely confused. "What tattoo?"

"Never mind."

"Hope, why do you always suspect me of murder?"

"I don't. Not always." Though it did seem like she did. In her defense, he had had motives in two previous murders.

Kent laughed, but it wasn't a funny laugh. "Yes, you do. To be honest, I'm tired of it."

"You're not a suspect. You're someone who knew her at the time she disappeared."

Kent rested his hand on the car door's frame. "We worked together. We had a professional relationship. What I knew about her personal life, I told the detective investigating her disappearance."

"What was that?"

He blew out an irritated breath. "You're not going to give up, are you?"

She tilted her head to the side and gave him a look. A look that said she wasn't leaving until he told her.

"She loved her daughters and her husband, and I didn't believe she would up and leave them. I still don't believe it. Her husband . . . Greg . . . yeah, Greg, wasn't supportive of her being an agent. Her girls were caught up in their own teenage dramas, and Joyce liked to flirt with good-looking guys."

"It sounds like she was two different people."

"We humans are complicated." He glanced at his gold watch, and Hope noted that it was the real deal. "I need to get going. Am I off your suspect list?"

Nobody was off her suspect list.

"Remember what happened last time you were too curious." Kent's tone had darkened, sending a chill that wasn't from the weather down Hope's spine.

Now there was something she'd never forget. Almost dying in her own home. No, this time she was being more careful. But a quick glance around gave her pause.

She'd tracked Kent down to a secluded location to ask him about the disappearance of a former coworker. If he had been responsible, she'd just put herself in grave danger. So much for being careful.

"I appreciate you talking to me. Thank you." She turned and walked back to her car while Kent got into his and drove away.

Kent had the right idea. It was time to go. Walking toward her vehicle, she wondered what type of staging job Claire would do for this midcentury house. A ding from her cell phone interrupted her decorating thoughts. She pulled the phone from her jacket pocket. The new message was from Corey.

The man could be such a nag.

She replied, assuring him that she'd review the contract as soon as she got home.

The chugging of a truck alerted her someone was approaching. Why hadn't she left when Kent did? Now she was alone at an empty house, and no one knew she was there.

Well, except for Kent and Amy.

The vehicle came into view. It was Oliver's plow truck, and it came to a hard stop. The driver's side door swung open. He leaped out and marched toward her, his gait determined, and his gazed locked on hers. Gone was the friendly look she'd gotten only days ago when she gave him Double Chocolate Oatmeal cookies.

"What do you think you're doing?" He jabbed his finger in the air toward Hope, and his nostrils flared. His voice was thick with anger.

Hope froze as if rooted to the spot. Her heartbeat kicked into overdrive, creating a rhythm that frightened her as much as Oliver did.

"Calm down. We can discuss whatever has you so upset."

"Don't tell me to calm down!" He jabbed his finger again as he closed the gap between them.

"Stay back! Or I'll call the police." She raised the phone to show Oliver.

"Go ahead." He advanced, forcing Hope to step back, away from her car. Her only means of escape. "What are you up to?"

"Nothing." She glanced around. Yep, she was all on her own.

"You didn't come by just to pay your bill." He pulled his cell phone from his jacket pocket. After tapping the phone, he held it up so Hope could see the video playing.

"You were there to snoop. You peeped into the window of my home and garage! I knew something was up with you and Drew. What were you looking for?"

Hope swallowed. Where did he have the surveillance cameras located? She hadn't seen them.

"You're blowing this way out of proportion."

"No! I don't think so. You came to ask me about Joyce Markham. And now the police want to know where I was when Devon and Donna died. They want a freakin' alibi! And it's because of you!"

"Well, following me isn't going to make you look innocent."

Oliver barked out a laugh. "I'm not following you. I'm here to finish plowing."

She looked around again. She hadn't realized only the parking pad was cleared of snow. The three-car garage still had a half-foot of snow blocking it.

"Mind. Your. Business. Or mark my words, you'll be sorry." He swung around and marched back to his truck. He climbed into the driver's seat, slamming his door shut and starting the engine.

Hope forced herself to slow down her breathing. She took a deep inhale and slowly exhaled to steady her nerves and every other part of her body. Her legs quaked, her knees weakened, threatening to give way any second, and her hands shook. The pit of her stomach felt like a hard rock, and suddenly, she was so hot she was about to rip off her jacket.

But she couldn't stay, not with Oliver still there. She willed her feet to move, and move fast, toward her car. Inside, she wasted no time in starting the ignition and making a U-turn, then she tore out of the driveway as fast as she could, kicking up loose gravel. She didn't care. She wanted to put as much distance between her and Oliver as quickly as possible.

Hope didn't stop driving until she spotted her favorite consignment shop and pulled into the parking lot. Before turning off the ignition, she called Ethan and told him what had happened with Oliver. She was able to avoid going into detail about her reason for being at Kent's listing, because Ethan was more concerned about Oliver's threat.

At some point, she'd have to tell him the whole story.

She assured him that she was safe and would head home after she browsed around Zach's shop. Ethan protested, but she held firm. She didn't need him to come to pick her up, and she didn't need a police escort home. He accepted her decision, but insisted she call him when she left the shop.

After promising to keep him updated on her whereabouts, she headed to the shop's main entrance. Over the years, she'd found several items for her home and for photography props while digging around in there. The one-story, flat-roofed building needed a paint job. Though Zach didn't seem interested in doing any cosmetic updates. What mattered to him was inside.

Her nose twitched at the muskiness hanging in the air when she entered the building. The layout of the store was choppy, making it appear smaller than it was. Zach's haphazard way of merchandising was unique to him, and it seemed to appeal to his customers. There were a handful of them browsing.

"Good to see you, Hope. What brings you by today?"

Zach smiled. He stood beside a curio cabinet with a dust-cloth in hand.

Hope resisted the urge to share her need to decompress with the shop owner. No, she was a big girl and could handle her own problems.

"I thought I'd look around." And the curio cabinet had her interest. The price seemed too good to pass up. Though she really didn't need the piece of furniture. There had to be something else she could purchase on an impulse and not cost her a chunk of her savings account.

"You've come on the right day. Look at what we just got in." Zach crooked his forefinger and then turned on his tattered loafers. He lumbered to the back of the shop. "I was hoping you'd stop in."

She followed, passing a group of upholstered chairs in a garish print, but they were intricately carved and would be a perfect DIY project. Next was a base cabinet, distressed and weathered; it would also be a great project. Maybe attach a sink bowl on top? She could use it for her work with Allied Home Centers. Though she'd have to negotiate a lower price.

"What do you think?" Zach gestured to a five-foot vertical sign.

What did she think? As soon as she set eyes on it, she loved it. Though due diligence needed to be done. She approached for a closer look.

The word "bakery" was painted in a deep blue against a white background, and a lighter blue paint edged the sign. She inspected it from top to bottom. Other than fading in spots, because of years outdoors, advertising the bakery, and chipped edges, the sign appeared to be in good condition.

"Where did it come from?" Hope ran her fingers over

the rough wood. It would be a nice gift to herself for land-ing the Mama Mia deal.

"Someone's barn. A long-deceased relative owned a bakery and must have stored the sign when the place closed."

"I could put it in my mudroom." She'd stand it next to the door into the kitchen.

"Sounds like the perfect spot." Zach ran his hand over his bald head. His face grew somber, as did his tone. "There's something else."

"You're not closing the shop, are you?" she asked. He'd mentioned it every now and again. She couldn't blame him if he decided to sell. He wasn't a young man anymore, and business wasn't always that good.

"No. No, nothing like that. It's nothing to do with the shop. Well, not really."

"What's wrong?" Hope closed the small gap between them.

"I heard about Devon's car accident. I can't believe she's dead."

"You knew her?"

Zach nodded. "She came in here with her mother. Joyce loved the hunt. You know what I mean?"

Hope knew all too well what the adrenaline rush searching for hidden treasures to repurpose and give new life to felt like. It was addictive.

"Anyway, Joyce bought and sold here." He pivoted and walked to the front of the store. Hope followed again. "Before she disappeared, she came in to consign these earrings." Behind the sales counter, he bent over. When he reappeared, he held a small jewelry box. "She said they were a gift, but not her style." He opened the box, re-vealing a pair of tarnished, filigree earrings.

"They're pretty. They'd be even prettier if they were polished." Hope reached out and took the box from Zach. "Why do you still have them after all these years?"

Zach shrugged. "I remember there was something about her the day she consigned the earrings." He gripped the edge of the counter with his hands as his eyes took on a faraway look, like he was trying to access a memory. When he finally came back to Hope, he offered a weak smile.

"It didn't feel like the other times she brought in merchandise. I'm sorry, I can't explain it. Just a feeling she'd change her mind. That sometimes happens, especially with jewelry. I thought if they had a sentimental meaning, she'd regret selling them."

Hope looked at the earrings. Were they a gift from her husband? Or someone else?

"That was very nice of you."

His cheeks reddened at the compliment. "A few weeks after she left them here, we had the fire in the storeroom, and things got all moved around. I've never been good with recordkeeping, so I lost track of the earrings."

"Until now?"

"I came across them a few years ago, when my sister was helping with the shop. Big mistake there. We fought all the time, and then she quit. I hadn't seen the earrings since then. Sometimes my memory isn't what it used to be."

Hope couldn't disagree with him there.

"Anyway, I found them again. Somehow, it doesn't feel right to keep the earrings," Zach said.

"Would you like me to give them to Felice?" Hope closed the box.

"Would you?" He looked relieved.

"I'd be happy to." She slipped the box into her purse. "Do you remember anything else?

Maybe something Joyce said when she came in to sell these, or maybe on another day, that seemed out of character?"

"No, can't say I do. Sorry, Hope."

"Don't be. It was a long time ago. Let me pay for the sign." Hope slipped her purse from her shoulder. "Will you have it delivered?"

"For my favorite customer, of course." He shuffled over to the cash register. "How's Iva working out? My niece has a few rough patches, but she's a hard worker."

"Yes, she is. She's helped me tremendously. Does she ever consign things here?" *Like a charm bracelet?* Hope instantly regretted asking the question, but she couldn't help herself. She wanted to know.

"No. She has nothing worth consigning."

Hope cringed. That was harsh. Then again, Zach was family, and family could be brutally honest.

"Credit card or cash?" he asked.

Hope pulled out her wallet, but before she handed him the card, she made a counteroffer on the price. After a little back and forth, they settled on a number.

With her purchase paid for, she was back in her vehicle and texting Ethan that she was headed home. There were a few things to do before the blogging class. Then she had to deliver the earrings to Felice at some point. Perhaps she would recognize them and might know the story behind the jewelry.

Chapter Fourteen

The lower-level door slammed shut, startling Hope as she entered the library. She'd been jumpy since her encounter with Oliver earlier in the day. She scolded herself for the hundredth time. There was nothing to be nervous about. Oliver had to have known she'd tell Ethan what happened, and he'd be foolish to confront her again.

No, there was nothing to worry about.

She walked along the hallway to the elevator. The path was lit, but eerily quiet after hours. Her footsteps were the only sound as she passed by the children's reading room and the locked storage room.

She arrived at the elevator and pressed the Up button. While she waited, she diverted her worrisome thoughts to one a little more pleasant.

On her drive over to the library, Elaine had called her to

tell her she wouldn't be attending class because something better came up—a date. She'd gushed about Mr. Money Manager and his summer house on Martha's Vineyard. It looked like the widow wasn't wasting time in finding husband number five. Hope had done her best to hide the fact that she wasn't disappointed her last-minute student would be absent. But it was harder to keep irritation in check when Elaine said they'd have to get together and go over the lessons, so she didn't miss out on anything. Then it was "Toodles," and she was gone.

Hope wasn't going to lie. It felt like a weight had been lifted from her shoulders.

The elevator dinged, and the door slid open. The sound and door action snapped Hope out of her thoughts about her unpleasant run-in with Oliver and the earrings Zach had given her at the shop. She'd been distracted, so she was surprised to see someone in the elevator. That weight she felt earlier pressing on her shoulders was back, tenfold.

"Good evening, Maretta." Hope stepped aside to allow the mayor to exit into the hall.

"Hardly." Maretta exited with her perpetual scowl firmly in place. "I suppose you're here for your blogging class."

"Yes, it starts in fifteen minutes." Hope entered the elevator. "Well, have a good night."

"Easier said than done."

Oh, boy.

"There is something I'd like you to do," Maretta said.

"There is?" It was a question Hope dreaded an answer to, but she had to ask. Hope held the elevator door from closing.

"Tell your sister to control her son. He's circulating a

petition against my proposal to ban snowball throwing. It's unsuitable for a child to get involved in adult matters."

"For what it's worth, I think it's ludicrous to ban something like throwing snowballs. It seems to me Logan is acting more mature than you." Hope pressed the lobby button.

Maretta was about to say something, but Hope cut her off as the door slid shut. "Toodles," she said, giving a little wave.

Hope leaned back against the wall. Who knew channeling Elaine would feel so good?

She opened her eyes as the elevator stopped and the door slid open to the silent hall. The meeting room was a short walk past the new display of spring gardening books. Her mind drifted briefly to warmer days and shorter nights and blooming garden beds. When she entered the room and flicked on the lights, she had been in a dreamy mood. That ended abruptly.

Her mouth gaped open at the sight in front of her.

She inched into the room, closer to the whiteboard, to get a better look at the message written across it.

Coldness lodged in her belly, and her gaze darted around the room.

There was no one else there.

Only her and the warning.

Stay out of the past.

Hope had done her best to push past the distraction of the menacing message so she could continue with the class. Luckily, the topic for the evening was promotion and marketing. She easily lost herself in talking about likes, follows, reach, and content marketing. Before she knew it, class was over and she was headed home.

But now, in her quiet house, with no distractions, her mind churned with questions despite her best efforts to squelch them. The top question she continued to ruminate over was whether Oliver had sneaked into the library and written the message, or had Maretta? Oliver had motive, but Maretta had opportunity.

She had opted not to call Ethan to tell him about the warning on the whiteboard. What could he have possibly done other than delay the class and tell her to be careful?

But she had to tell him. And she would.

By the time she climbed into bed, it was well after midnight and she believed she was tired enough to fall asleep. She was wrong. All she could think about snuggled under her down comforter was Devon's podcast and where she had been before the car accident.

Devon had visited the retired detective who handled her mother's case twenty years ago. Lying in bed, staring up at the ceiling, Hope made the decision to retrace Devon's last known activity and that meant a trip to Milford to talk to the retired cop.

The next morning, Hope woke groggy from yet another poor night's sleep. She resisted the temptation to pull the covers over her head and go back to sleep. But Bigelow would have no part in that. He nudged her to get up.

It never failed. As soon as he heard her alarm clock go off, he moved from the foot of the bed where he slept to her pillows so he'd be the first thing she saw when she woke.

"You know you're pushy, right?" She patted the dog on

the head and got a good morning kiss before she tossed off her covers. She yawned and stretched while Bigelow jumped off the bed. "Go on, I'll be down in a minute."

Bigelow seemed to understand and trotted out of the room, his toenails clicking on the hardwood floor. Traditional oak flooring ran throughout the second floor. And just like downstairs, it all needed to be refinished. A massive project for another day.

One more big stretch and then Hope stood. She slipped into her fuzzy slippers and wrapped herself in a fleece robe on her way into the bathroom. There was a lot on her to-do list for the day. She liked to set no more than three priorities. It was her way of making sure the most important things got done.

The number one priority for the day was to tell Ethan what happened last night at the library and of her plans to visit Detective Voight. Well, it was second to stopping at The Coffee Clique.

An hour later, she had a large black coffee in hand and was making her way to the police department. There she was quickly reminded that hindsight was twenty-twenty. Perhaps she should have called him last. Her gift of coffee was welcome until Ethan found out the reason for the unexpected visit.

"I can't believe you didn't call me last night. Actually, I can believe it." Ethan broke eye contact over the brim of his coffee cup to take a long drink. "What were you thinking?"

Hope was thinking she didn't want to get into the conversation they were having now last night. Though she was pretty confident that wasn't the answer he wanted to hear. She thought reporting the threat on the whiteboard would go easier with coffee. Now, she wasn't so sure. Caf-feinating him may not have been the best thing to do.

"There was nothing you could do. Besides, everyone showed up for class." Except Elaine. Considering what happened, she was even more grateful for the no-show student. The message had unnerved her and she'd had difficulty concentrating for the class. Having Elaine there would have added to her stress.

Ethan set the cup on his desk and lifted her cell phone. He stared at the photo of the message. "Was there anyone in the building when you arrived?"

"I ran into Maretta. She was leaving."

"What was she doing there?"

"I don't know. I didn't ask. Though she asked me to do something."

"I'm almost afraid to ask."

"She wants me to tell Claire to rein Logan in. Maretta's not happy he's circulating a petition against her."

Ethan grinned. "I'm sure she's not. Did you see anyone else?"

She shook her head. "There wasn't anyone near the meeting room when I arrived. Do you think it was Maretta?"

He cocked an eyebrow. "I think it's more her style to say what she means to your face."

"True." Hope stood and walked around to Ethan. She took back her phone and leaned against the edge of the desk. "I'm sorry I didn't call you last night."

"Whoever wrote that on the board could have been waiting for you after class." His tone softened, and con-cern clouded his eyes. "Look, I know you're a big girl and you've been taking care of yourself your whole life, but that doesn't mean I'm not going to worry about you."

She reached out her hand and caressed his cheek. "I know. And I appreciate it. If it makes you feel any better, I made sure to leave with Gail and Phillip Rafferty."

"Phil's in your class? He wants to blog?"

Hope nodded and laughed. "He's an amateur photographer."

"What's so funny?"

"When Elaine showed up, he went all googly-eyed. Come to think of it, he reminds me of Alec Graves. Do you remember him? Gail's brother?"

Ethan nodded slowly, as if he had to recall the memory. "Kind of. He was a little off back then. I remember my sister saying he was a little creepy."

"Really? I don't think he was creepy. I think he wore his heart on his sleeve."

"Mr. Sensitivity?"

"Exactly. So much has changed since high school."

"Well, you're still as curious as you were back then. And your instincts are still spot-on."

"They are? What are my instincts right about?"

"I can't say too much, but what I can tell you is, Devon's death has been ruled a homicide due to the injuries she sustained that weren't the result of the car crash."

"What injuries?"

"Sorry, I can't comment any further."

She groaned. The man could be so frustrating with all his by-the-book procedures. He was going to leave her hanging with just a snippet of information that he had to know would make her even more curious.

"Now, tell me. Is there anything I can say to change your mind about going to Milford?"

"No. I'm not breaking any laws by talking to Voight." She'd told him of her plan to drive to the shoreline city to visit the retired detective. Because all of Devon's research was missing, she didn't know what the detective had told her when she talked to him before she was murdered. Of course, Hope was certain Reid had already spoken to Voight as a part of the investigation. But she'd get nothing from Reid, so she decided to do her own interview.

"I didn't say you were."

"But Reid might."

"True. And he'd be wrong. You're well within your rights to talk to the retired detective. Even though I don't think you should."

She leaned forward and kissed Ethan. She intended it to be a quick kiss and off she'd go, but he had other ideas. The kiss lingered, and when Hope finally pulled back, her lips were still buzzing. He cleared his throat and regained his professional composure. Good thing his office door was closed.

"I should get going." It was a weak effort, but it was all she could summon up. She'd much rather stay and kiss him some more.

"What do you hope to find out by talking to Voight?" Ethan held on to her wrist. He wasn't letting her go just yet.

"I don't know. I guess I want to know how someone not too different from me can be here one day and vanish the next."

"Babe, he's not going to give you an answer."

She nodded. "Probably not. You need to get back to work. I promise I'll keep you updated on where I am. So, don't worry."

*   *   *

Hope doubted Ethan wouldn't worry about her and, given the fact that she'd once again stuck her nose into a murder investigation, he probably had good reason to. But she was on her way to visit a retired police detective. Surely she'd be safe.

She looked over her shoulder as she merged onto the highway. In less than ninety minutes, she'd be in Milford, where Jim Voight had retired to ten years ago.

Her cell phone rang. It was Drew.

"What's up?" she asked.

"Don't forget about what we discussed."

"Drew, we talked an hour ago." She merged into the middle lane.

"I know, but this isn't like talking to one of your nosy neighbors. The guy is an ex-cop. He'll be guarded and measured in what he says to you."

"Like Detective Reid?"

"Right."

Well, then, I got this.

She wasn't sure if Jim Voight would tell her anything about Joyce's cold case. She wasn't a family member. She was simply a friend of Devon's. So, she had little hope he would talk to her. He'd probably view her as a busybody—there was that word again—who should be snapping photographs of her lunch, not digging around a cold case she had no stake in.

He'd be wrong.

She did have a stake in it. She felt called to accomplish the goal Devon didn't get to achieve: solving the mystery of her mother's disappearance.

"Be sure to call me when you leave his place. I want all the details." Drew had wanted to come along with

Hope, but a fire out at the Travis Dairy Farm had him occupied.

"I will." Hope disconnected the call and focused on her driving.

The navigation system came back up with the real-time map, and the voice command directed her off onto another route, getting closer to the shoreline city. It'd been years since she'd been in this part of the state.

Jim Voight's house was located on a narrow street within walking distance of the beach. She had trouble finding a parking space, but finally found one half a block from the two-story blue Colonial.

His small patch of lawn was secured by a fence, and she unlatched the gate and walked along the brick path to the front door. Hope pressed the doorbell and waited.

She heard a yapping and a holler to be quiet before the door swung open.

A slight man, much like Detective Reid but older, appeared. He had a receding hairline, small eyes, and a guarded look on his weathered face.

"Can I help you?" He peered out, looking around. She guessed he wanted to make sure she was alone. Once a cop, always a cop.

"If you're retired Detective Jim Voight, you can."

"I am. Who are you?"

She extended her hand. "I'm Hope Early."

His grip was firm and his expression still curious. "What can I do for you?"

"I'd like to talk to you about Devon Markham. I know she came to see you before her death."

"Are you family?" He let go of Hope's hand.

"No. I'm a friend. I promise, I won't take up much of your time. It's important."

He nodded and welcomed her inside his home.

She wiped her boots on the welcome mat before entering the white-and-black-tiled foyer. From where she stood, she could see straight through the living area to a snow-covered deck just outside a glass slider. She imagined in the summer it was a lovely spot to sit and enjoy a lazy day.

"Let me take your coat." He hung the coat on a peg-board next to a bulky gray parka and led her into the living room.

A small brown dog came racing toward her and slid to a stop at Hope's feet.

"Her name is Mabel." Jim scooped up the dog, who had to be no more than six pounds. Standing there holding his dog and dressed in a tan sweater with corduroys, he looked relaxed. Hopefully, he would remain that way for the rest of her visit. "She talks a lot but doesn't bite." He continued to the black leather chair kitty-corner in the room. It had a view of the fifty-two-inch television and the deck. "Have a seat." He released Mabel, who immediately ran to Hope.

Hope sat on the sofa and stroked the little dog's head.

"What is it you want to know?" He leaned back into the supple leather and kept his gaze trained on her. Maybe he thought he would make her uncomfortable, squirm a little, but she'd had Detective Reid do the exact same thing to her. She hated to disappoint the retired cop, but she wouldn't be squirming any time soon.

"Devon asked me for help with researching her mother's case for the podcast and I'm continuing to do that." Was it exactly what Devon had said? No. Hope didn't know what Voight would tell her, but she was confident if she told him

Devon had asked for her help to find her mother's killer, he would toss her out.

"Ms. Markham didn't mention a partner." His appraising look ratcheted up a notch. Was he detecting Hope's fib?

"She probably didn't see the need to at the time. Unfortunately, I don't have her notes from her meeting with you."

"Ms. Markham didn't write any notes. She used her phone to record our conversation. You're not doing either."

Darn.

"I have a good memory." She shifted to the edge of her seat. "I'm here to find out what happened to Joyce and Devon. You can ask me to leave and I will. But I hope you don't, because I really need to find out the truth. Devon was a friend. Her mom was a nice lady who baked the softest sugar cookies." If that wasn't the lamest thing she'd ever said, she didn't know what was.

His face brightened. "Those are my favorite."

"They are?" Okay, maybe not so lame.

"At Easter, I bake them in all sorts of shapes for my grandkids. Though I can't seem to get them as soft as I want them. And they spread. They're cookies; it shouldn't be so hard."

"It took me years to replicate Joyce's recipe, but I did it. It's one of the most popular recipes on my blog."

"You're a food blogger?"

Hope nodded. "I do. It's called *Hope at Home*."

"Get out! That's why you look familiar to me. I gotta find the recipe on your blog."

"Or I could show you now. That is, if you have the time."

"I'm retired. I always have time." He jumped up and led Hope into his galley kitchen. While he pulled out all the ingredients and Hope preheated the oven, he told her about his late wife and their three kids and nine grandchildren. By the time Hope rolled out the dough, she had his complete life story. This wasn't what she had expected, but her visit couldn't have been going any better.

Jim grabbed three different cookie cutters and a container of sanding sugar.

"I remember the case quite well. There are a few cases that haunt a cop. Joyce's case was one of those for me."

Hope slipped three bunny cookies onto the prepared baking sheet, along with the duck-shaped cookies.

"Because it was unsolved?"

Jim sprinkled sugar on the cookies. "Yes. There's always a gnawing at you that you missed something. Otherwise, you would have been able to solve the case."

"I heard Joyce liked to flirt with men. Sometimes she even did so in front of her husband."

Jim lifted the baking sheet and slid it into the oven, then set a timer.

"I was aware of the behavior. From what I found through my investigation, she didn't have a lover. From my experience, it seemed she was looking for attention from her husband and not those other men."

Hope collected the bowls and utensils and set them into the sink, which she filled with soapy water.

"Do you think her husband killed her?"

Jim shrugged. "I never crossed him off my list of persons of interest. Though I didn't find any evidence he was involved. All his financials checked out."

"You were looking to see if he hired someone?"

"Wouldn't be the first time a husband did."

A shiver ran through Hope at the thought. How could a man pay someone to murder his wife? The mother of his children? But it happened far too often. Compared to those situations, she was grateful her divorce was somewhat amicable.

Hope leaned against the counter. "When Devon spoke to you, did she have any information that you didn't have twenty years ago?"

Jim stiffened.

"I don't mean to imply you didn't do your job, but maybe twenty years ago someone kept something a secret."

"I knew what you meant. It's not uncommon for witnesses to come forward years later. That's how many cold cases are finally broken open. She did tell me that she had information about an affair her father was having prior to her mother's disappearance."

Hope wished she'd had a chance to read through Devon's notes. She was certain those notes were shredded or burned now. Whoever staged the car accident wouldn't chance those papers or recordings being discovered.

The timer dinged, and Jim grabbed a pot holder and pulled out the baking sheet.

"Let them set for a minute and then we can transfer them to the cooling rack."

"I'll put on the kettle for tea." He set down the pot holder and filled the kettle at the sink.

The cookies cooled while the tea was prepared, and they settled at the table beside the large window overlooking the fenced yard. It was long and narrow, but enough room for his grandkids to play in nice weather.

"It's a shame, what happened to Devon. She struck me

as someone determined to get answers." Jim reached for a cookie while Mabel lay beside his foot.

"We'd lost touch after high school graduation. Even back then, she was like a dog with a bone. She hadn't changed much." Hope sipped her tea. She waited for his review of the cookie.

"These are delicious." He smiled and finished eating the cookie. He then helped himself to another one.

Hope let out the breath she was holding. "Thank you." She reached for a cookie and took a bite. Tender and lightly sweet.

"My grandkids are going to love these." He finished eating his second cookie. "Thanks so much for the recipe."

"It's the least I could do."

He shrugged. "I wasn't much help."

"You didn't throw me out." She laughed.

He chuckled also. "Devon was lucky to have a friend like you."

"I wish I could have done more sooner." She glanced at her watch. "I should be heading back to Jefferson. I want to get back before the storm hits." Another snowstorm was heading for Connecticut and the last thing she wanted was to get stuck on the road as it barreled into the state.

"How's the new chief working out?" Jim stood and walked her to the door.

Ethan was hardly the new chief. He'd been in the position for nearly six years.

"Good. Well, I may be a little biased. I've known him since high school." Hope shrugged into her coat and put on her gloves.

"I retired soon after he joined Jefferson PD. He seemed like an all right guy."

"Your instincts are spot-on. Thank you again." Hope reached for the doorknob.

"The knife!" He snapped his fingers. "Of course. The knife."

Hope looked over her shoulder. "What knife?"

"I can't believe I'm just now remembering." Jim ran his hand over his head. "There was a knife missing from the knife block in the Markham kitchen. There wasn't any evidence of a struggle in the home."

Of course. That was what had seemed off to her and Devon. Why hadn't she seen it earlier, when she'd looked at the photo of the Markhams' kitchen that Devon had pinned to the bulletin board? The knife block had an empty slot. Such a small detail. Could it really be significant?

"But the knife could have been a murder weapon."

"Or it could have been tossed out by accident. It's not uncommon. My son never paid attention to what he dropped in the trash can. We never determined whether Joyce willingly left her family or not. Until there's more evidence, we won't know for sure."

Hope opened the door and stepped outside. "Thank you for talking to me. I appreciate it."

"You're welcome. And thanks for the recipe. Be sure to keep me informed, or call if you have any questions."

Hope nodded and then hurried back to her Explorer. Making her way back to the highway, she went over the visit. What had she accomplished?

Not much. It also seemed Devon hadn't learned much either.

Or Jim could have been withholding information from Hope.

* * *

Hope arrived home before the snow started to fall. The updated forecast she heard on the drive back to Jefferson called for heavy snow within a couple of hours. That scenario was never a good one because road crews had a hard time keeping the roads safe with several inches of snow falling in a short period of time. She entered the mudroom and was greeted by Bigelow. She let him out to do his business while she got out of her coat and boots.

In the kitchen, she was greeted by Princess. The cat slinked by her legs with her tail high and flicking in the air. Hope dashed out back to the mudroom to allow Bigelow back inside.

Shaking off the cold, Hope returned to the kitchen and then checked her phone. She'd heard a text come in while she was hanging up her coat.

It was from Ethan. Because of the storm, he wanted to stay at the PD. It looked like she'd be eating alone tonight.

She made a quick dinner of lasagna rolls. There was enough to drop off to Ethan tomorrow for lunch. After filling the dishwasher, Hope wiped down the countertops, then fed Bigelow and Princess.

Hope then did a quick tidy-up of the family room before grabbing her notebook and settling on the sofa to listen to another episode of Devon's podcast. Bigelow jumped up and made himself comfy on the other end of the sofa. She hadn't the heart to make him scoot off, especially when Princess had commandeered his bed in the corner of the room.

She tapped on her phone and the podcast began, and she was ready to make notes.

"The morning after we realized my mother had disappeared was cold and dreary. I remember

opening my eyes, convinced the day before was a nightmare. My mom would come into my room any moment and tell me to get up and greet the new day. She always said that to us. I waited and waited. My bedroom door never opened.

"I finally got out of bed and went to the window. It had rained the night before. I could see what snow was left had been washed away. I still had hope she'd open my bedroom door and walk in.

"The door opened. My breath caught as I looked over my shoulder. Mom was home. I was about to run to her when I realized it was my sister, Felice. All the hope I had whooshed out of me in one hard breath. Felice's eyes were red and swollen and she held a damp tissue in her hand.

" 'It wasn't a dream, was it?' I asked her. She shook her head and rushed to me. I stood and hugged her and we cried. Our mother hadn't returned home." Devon's voice cracked. *"She was gone. I knew right there and then, my mother wasn't going to come back. Something terrible had happened to her, even if the detective who was assigned to her case didn't believe that. My mother wouldn't have up and left us. She wasn't that kind of woman. Someone took her from us."*

A *bing* drew Hope's attention from her notebook to her phone.

A message appeared from an unknown number.

Leave the past in the past or you'll have no future.

Hope dropped her pen and grabbed her phone. Her heart raced. She stared at the message. She shot up from her chair and rushed to the windows that overlooked her property.

All she saw was a dark and snowy night.

Was the person out there watching her house? A lump caught in her throat. She tapped on the app for her smart doorbell. The video included with the doorbell gave her a fairly good view in the front of her house and at the back of her house, where the second doorbell was located. She didn't see anyone in the area.

Irritated by the anonymous threats and by feeling like a victim, she took the bold, but probably not a smart move and texted back.

Who is this?

She waited for a reply.

Someone who is giving you one more chance. Choose wisely.

Bigelow stirred and snuffled. She looked over to the sofa. At face value, he didn't look much like a guard dog, but he'd saved her life not too long ago. She peeled herself away from the window and walked back to the sofa, sitting next to her best buddy. He lifted his head and then rested it on her lap. She chewed on her lip and stared down at her phone.

Who had sent the text? What did he or she think Hope knew?

Chapter Fifteen

After her alarm woke her, Hope reached for her phone and checked for new messages. None. She pressed the phone against her chest and breathed as she tried to decide whether she was relieved or disappointed. She was thankful the unknown texter hadn't continued to toy with her, yet she was dismayed that she didn't have another chance to try to find out the identity of the person behind the threats. Though unless he or she revealed a name, she had no idea of how she'd track down the identity on her own.

She'd set the alarm for her regular time and now regretted it. She'd barely slept again last night. During the night, she'd drifted from dream to dream. Most of them had Devon's voice narrating what was happening. There were flashes of the threatening text messages, and every time they appeared, they got bigger and bigger and bigger. As if that weren't enough, the message played through her car radio while she was driving.

What had her bolting upright at four thirty was Devon's crash scene and, as the first responders carried Devon's body to the ambulance, she'd suddenly sat up and asked Hope, "Why didn't you help me?"

That nightmare had Hope's heart racing and her brow sweaty. Bigelow nearly leaped out of the bed. She thought she may have kicked him by mistake. It took almost an hour for her to fall back to sleep. She was scared she'd *see* Devon again, and have to answer the question.

She lifted the phone off her chest and checked online for the weather. As expected, the northwest section of the state had been walloped with snow. She texted Iva and told her not to worry about coming over; she'd take care of the chickens. By the time Hope was in the bathroom, splashing water on her face, Iva texted back. She appreciated the morning off and would be there tomorrow.

When Hope emerged from the bathroom, Bigelow was stretching. It seemed the dog liked to ease into his mornings. She hated to admit it, but she was jealous of her dog. She called him and he eagerly jumped off the bed to follow her downstairs.

Dressed in jeans and a fleece top, she was ready to go out to the barn.

It took longer than usual to feed and water the chickens thanks to the pile of fresh snow and frigid temperatures. The birds didn't seem eager to venture out beyond their enclosed pen. Even Poppy preferred to stay in her nesting box, while Helga followed Hope around the barn, overseeing the chores so they were done properly. With the chores completed and the chickens fed, Hope headed back to her house.

She peeled off her outerwear while Bigelow did his little dance for breakfast. His toenails tapped the floor and even gave a yowl in hopes of speeding up the process. Hope knew she shouldn't have, but she served his meal before hers. With him fed, she was able to make a pot of coffee in peace. As she gathered the ingredients for her breakfast, she scanned the family room for Princess. She was nowhere in sight.

With a couple of eggs cracked and whisked, she added them to a pan along with two heaping handfuls of spinach for a quick scramble. After she set a lid on the pan, she dropped a slice of her homemade honey wheat bread into the toaster.

A chime from her doorbell's app alerted her that someone was at the back door. She grabbed her phone and saw Claire unlocking the door. A moment later, the mudroom door opened.

"Remind me when the first day of spring is." Claire unbuttoned her full-length coat and set her purse on the island.

"Not soon enough. How are the roads?" Hope poured a cup of coffee and handed it to her sister. Then she filled a cup for herself.

"Not great. But I'm not here to talk about the roads. I'm here to discuss Kent."

"He told you about my visit to see him?" Hope lifted the lid from her sauté pan and checked her eggs. Almost done. It looked like her breakfast was coming with a lecture. Lucky her.

Claire nodded as she shifted her stance.

"Do you want breakfast? I can make you egg whites and spinach."

"I've already eaten. Now, back to Kent. I don't need you alienating one of my clients."

"I did no such thing."

"Are you sure? He was pretty steamed when he called me. Why were you asking him questions about Joyce Markham?"

"Because he mentored her. Before she disappeared, she was planning on becoming a real estate agent, and he took her under his wing, so to speak."

"Wait. How do you know that?"

"Alfred told me."

"You talked to Alfred?" Claire's voice had ratcheted up, and she sighed.

"Yes. Speaking of the Kingstons, you should know Maretta came looking for me before class. She's upset about Logan's petition." Hope removed the pan from the stovetop and slid the eggs onto a plate. By the time she set the pan in the sink, her toast popped up and she glided a pat of butter over the slice. "She wants you to get control of your kid."

"What? How dare she!"

Hope dipped her head as she walked to the table with her plate and coffee to hide her smirk. She'd successfully shifted Claire's anger to someone else.

"Who does she think she is? She actually told you to tell me to get control of my son?"

"I think she's the last person to be doling out parenting advice." Hope took a mouthful of her egg and spinach and chewed.

Claire marched to the table and set down her cup. She shrugged out of her coat and draped it over another chair before sitting. She crossed her arms over her chest and set her lips in a firm, thin line. She studied Hope with narrowed eyes.

"Wait a minute. I know what you're trying to do. It's not going to work. I'll deal with Maretta later. I'm here to deal with you!"

The distraction almost worked. Hope ate a forkful of egg before answering. "All I did was talk to Kent."

"There's the problem. In your head, you heard a conversation, while Kent felt like he was being interrogated."

"Nonsense. It was a conversation. And I believe he had nothing to do with Joyce's disappearance."

"Do you hear yourself?"

"I'm sorry I upset him. And I'm sorry he's angry with you. If it helps, I'll apologize."

"Thank you." Claire unfolded her arms and reached for her cup. "You're awfully accommodating today."

Hope swallowed a bite of toast and then took another. She hadn't realized how hungry she was. "What do you want from me? I offered to apologize and now you're suspicious?"

"I most certainly am." Claire leaned back and crossed her legs.

"All right. The truth is, I'm not up for a fight. I had a bad night. I'm exhausted and a little freaked out."

"Why? What happened?"

Hope pulled up the text messages from last night and showed the phone to her sister.

Claire's eyes bulged as she read the messages. "Oh. My. Goodness. Am I reading this right? You texted back? Are you crazy?"

"I was trying to find out who the person was." Hope set the phone on the table.

"Let the police figure it out. Have you shown this to Ethan yet?"

"Not yet."

"The man must really love you." Claire took another drink of her coffee.

"Why do you say that?"

"You're obviously doing something that's making someone very nervous. You know darn well Ethan doesn't want you investigating because it's dangerous, yet you continue to do so. Though I'm sure he'll forgive you like he's done in the past."

"Right. Just like he's always done."

Claire set her cup down and leaned forward. "Have you thought about how much damage your sleuthing is doing to your relationship?"

"I'm only asking questions. How can it possibly damage what Ethan and I have?"

"By eroding his trust. Hope, you keep things from him and only tell him about them when you absolutely have to. How does that make for a good relationship? He's a good man. He's good for you. I blame Tim for the breakup of marriage number one. If you keep doing what you're doing, and Ethan breaks up with you because he can't trust you, this time it's on you."

Stunned, Hope pulled back from her breakfast, absorbing her sister's words.

Claire stood and put on her coat. She grabbed her purse and then patted her sister on the shoulder.

"You need to tell him everything. And then you need to back off. You've gotten lucky the past few times you got yourself involved in police matters. Luck has a way of running out at some point." She disappeared out the mudroom door.

The door closed, and Hope leaned forward, propping her elbows on the table and rested her head in her hands. Her sister was right. She hadn't been up front with Ethan since the night she met with Devon, and it was a mistake. A big fat mistake.

She'd been so worried about not repeating past behavior, she hadn't realized her quest for answers was jeopardizing what she had with Ethan. Why hadn't she seen it?

She lifted her head. Okay. She now knew what she had to do.

She'd come clean with everything going forward. No more keeping things from him. She'd deal with whatever his reaction was, good or bad. And it started now. She stood and did a fast cleanup of the kitchen. When she was done, it was time to head out to the police department to show Ethan the messages.

While her car warmed up, she texted Ethan to let him know she was on her way to see him. By the time she arrived in the parking lot of the PD, he hadn't replied.

Inside the main entrance, she was greeted by Freddie, the dispatcher. He told her to have a seat. A moment later, the door to the back offices opened, and she frowned. Detective Reid. He gestured for her to follow him.

In his office, he gestured to a chair as he made his way around his desk to sit. The surface was clutter- and memento-free. Not even a framed photograph. Clearly, the detective had a well-defined separation between work and his personal life. Maybe he didn't have a personal life. Maybe his whole world revolved around his work. Come to think of it, she didn't know if he was married or not. Did he have kids? Did he have a pet?

"Chief Cahill is out at the moment. So, Miss Early, what brings you by?" He'd forgone his usual dark blazer in favor of a sporty, half-zip top over a pale-blue T-shirt and chinos.

"Last night I received this text message." She showed him her phone.

Reid leaned forward and took the device. After he read the text exchange, he asked, "Any idea who sent this?"

"No. I wish I did. I think it's the same person who left the warning in the library for me."

Reid gave the phone back to Hope and reached for a pad of paper and pen. "Start from the beginning."

"The beginning? Well, it was when Devon came into Claire's shop and said 'hi' and asked if we could talk."

"Keep going." Reid's voice was dry, no hint of emotion.

Hope continued recounting her activities since her meeting with Devon the night after her first class. To his credit, he remained silent and just took notes.

"We have no evidence Mrs. Markham was murdered." Reid stopped writing when Hope suggested what had happened two decades before was related to Devon's death.

"There's no evidence she wasn't . . . well, except for the missing knife from the Markham house."

His lips twitched. "How do you know about that detail?"

"Jim Voight told me yesterday. He said one of the kitchen knives was missing from the block on the counter. No one in the house knew what happened to it. What if it was used to kill Joyce?"

"There wasn't any blood or signs of a struggle in the house."

"Maybe the person cleaned up. Twenty years ago, the police didn't have the technology they do now to find minute traces of blood or DNA."

Reid cocked an eyebrow.

"Devon's podcast was very thorough in discussing not only her mother's cold case but others."

"It is all but impossible to remove all DNA evidence from a crime scene," he acquiesced.

"So, there could have been some trace evidence left behind. I guess it's too late now to reexamine the Markham house, especially the kitchen. Then again, maybe the person used the knife to force Joyce to go with him or her."

"Or the knife was misplaced or even accidently tossed in the trash, and Mrs. Markham left on her own."

"Why would a woman with two daughters walk out on them?" She'd heard too many times over the years that Joyce may have left on purpose. Even as a teenager, Hope hadn't been able to wrap her mind around that theory. Who would do that?

"You'd be surprised by what some people will do."

Hope shrugged. Reid had a point. She'd been surprised recently by people she'd known, people she never thought capable of murder. So maybe running away from home wasn't so implausible.

"Devon believed her father had been having an affair at the time of her mother's disappearance. She told Jim that. Maybe she'd finally found out who the other woman was. Maybe the woman wants to keep it a secret at any cost."

Reid jotted down some more notes. When he stopped writing, he set down his pen and leveled his gaze on Hope. His scrutiny was uncomfortable. She braced herself for the "speech."

"Ms. Early . . . Hope . . . I understand your need to find an answer to why Devon's car crashed, killing her. I also understand the lure of an unsolved mystery like her mother's case. What I need you to understand is, as of now, we have no evidence of a connection between what happened to Devon and her mother's case. However, these messages left for you lead me to consider a possible connection, because someone wants you to stop asking questions."

Hope blinked. He hadn't threatened to toss her into a cell. He hadn't told her to mind her own business. He'd just said there might be a connection between Devon's death and her mother's cold case. She wanted to make sure she heard him correctly.

"What are you saying, Detective Reid?"

"I'm saying I want you to be careful going forward, and I will look into Mrs. Markham's case personally."

"Really? Will you speak to Oliver again? Maybe he thought warning me in person wasn't enough. Can the text message be traced?"

Reid raised his palm. "Hope, I've got this. Remember what I said. Be. Careful."

"I will. Thank you." She stood and walked out of the office. Wow! He didn't lecture her and he didn't tell her to stop her own investigative pursuit, just to be careful. And he'd called her Hope. Now was the time to leave, before their relationship regressed. She picked up her pace and got out of there before he changed his mind.

Instead of heading home right away, Hope decided to go to the library. When she arrived, she found a space in the parking lot and dashed into the building. Two middle-aged women smiled as they passed by with armfuls of books. Beyond the lobby, Hope saw a dozen or so of Jefferson's residents browsing through the stacks, seated at tables reading periodicals, and Angela at the circulation desk, helping a patron. She then spotted Sally pushing a book cart toward the elevator. She followed the hall toward the staircase. The archive room was in the lower level. There she could search through newspapers.

She started with the *Gazette*. Devon had had numerous articles from the newspaper and Hope wanted to find them. She began looking for articles on the Markham family. It was possible someone close to them was responsible for Joyce vanishing. Maybe she'd get lucky and find a photograph of her with someone giving her a dark look and then Hope would have a new potential lead.

Could she get that lucky?

By what seemed like her one hundredth article, she hadn't gotten lucky.

Scrolling through old articles was tedious, but it also was a trip down memory lane she hadn't expected.

She came across the article on her high school graduating class. She lingered on the article and enjoyed the flood of memories.

They were all smiles in the class photograph. They had new adventures ahead of them: college, jobs, travel, love. Then there was Devon. She'd graduated with a profound sadness. Hope enlarged Devon's face. While her fellow classmates were all toothy, Devon's lips were pressed together in a straight line. Hope couldn't remember seeing Devon smile after her mother disappeared. She remembered her friend's slumped shoulders, heavy steps, and lack of interest in anything. Devon had gone from a thriving A student to barely passing, with a C average.

Hope leaned back into the chair and tried to remember who'd been friends with whom.

Claire was friends with Felice, but she didn't get along with Gail. There had been a fight over a boy they both liked. Gail had a small circle of friends. It included Felice and another girl Hope couldn't remember the name of. Hope was friendly with Alec, Gail's brother. She scanned more photos looking for him and found him tucked between two beefy guys with exaggerated grins on their faces.

Alec was tall, lanky, and awkward. He stumbled over his words, blushed around girls, and spent too much time in the computer lab. She studied his acne-prone face and wondered what had happened to him. After high school, he'd disappeared, and no one really talked about him. She'd have to ask Gail for an update on her younger brother.

Hope continued going through the articles and came to one about Gail's family. Back in the day, Gail's father owned the best auto body shop in Jefferson; Ernie's Auto Body was celebrating its tenth anniversary with a big celebration, complete with balloons and a hotdog truck. Featured in the article was a photo of Ernie and his two children. Alec was smiling. It was sweet and genuine. If only he hadn't been so awkward around girls. But that didn't stop him from falling for all the pretty girls in school. She chuckled. It wasn't just her classmates. He'd been starry-eyed for their new English teacher. Miss . . . Miss Engel. That's right. Alec was probably the first hopeless romantic Hope ever knew.

Another article popped up about Oliver's lawn services. The photo featured him leaning against his truck. She skimmed the article, which was all about how he started his business while still in high school. She studied the photo. Back in the day, he'd been quite handsome. Why hadn't he married? Maybe he thought Joyce was the woman for him, but she had no intention of leaving her husband. Hope shook her head and chided herself. Total conjecture, nothing solid. She moved onto the next article and the next. And thirty minutes later she declared her visit a bust.

She had learned nothing new. Not even a clue. So much for her sleuthing skills.

Bundled up in her jacket, Hope headed for the back exit, so she didn't have to walk around the outside of the building.

Hope made the turn into the corridor leading to the back exit and saw Shirley entering the building with a stack of books in her arms. Shirley lumbered forward with hunched shoulders and a troubled look on her face. Hope wondered what was wrong.

"Good afternoon, Shirley." Hope stopped and waited for a reply. Based on the past few days, she wasn't sure what type of greeting she'd receive.

"I've got to return these books." Shirley gave Hope a passing glance, revealing wet eyes as she tried to sidestep around Hope.

"Is everything all right?" Hope asked. She'd never seen Shirley this upset. The whole situation with Devon's return and then her death had rattled everyone, but it seemed to upset Shirley the most.

"No. No. Everything isn't all right. Far from it." Shirley shook her head. She exhaled a deep breath. "Everything is a mess."

"Come sit. Let's talk. What's going on?" Hope guided Shirley to the bench. When they were seated, she took the books from Shirley and set them on the floor.

Shirley didn't make eye contact with Hope. Her gaze went over Hope's shoulder. "I've done something awful. I hurt a friend. And I prayed that no one would find out."

Hope reached out and patted Shirley's knee. "We all do things we regret. Things we're not proud of."

"Oh, boy, do I regret it." Shirley's gaze locked on Hope's. "It was a long time ago. I was so lonely back then. And he was . . . he was so kind to me."

Hope chewed on her lower lip. She had a sinking feeling in the bottom of her stomach about what Shirley was about to reveal. *Please, please don't let it be about Joyce.*

"I made the foolish mistake of letting another man comfort me." Shirley dropped her head. "I should have known better."

The pieces were now starting to fall into place. Shirley's shift in demeanor and her insistence that the past be left right where it was—in the past. Could she have been behind the threatening messages? And the two recent deaths? No, Hope discarded that thought immediately because she couldn't believe Shirley was capable of such a thing.

"It was Greg Markham. You were the woman he was seeing when Joyce disappeared."

Shirley nodded. Her hand covered Hope's. "I didn't mean for it to happen. My late husband and I were having problems."

Oh, boy. Hope really didn't want to hear the sordid details.

"You don't have to explain. Really, you don't."

"Isn't this what you wanted? The truth? Well, let me tell you something, the truth isn't always pretty."

Hope stared at Shirley. Her secret was the reason why she was against opening Joyce's cold case. The first time around, Jim Voight had missed the affair. But Devon wouldn't. She hadn't. She just hadn't uncovered who the woman was before her death.

"Don't look at me like that. It wasn't like I was a

home-wrecker. The last thing I wanted was to break up their marriage. She was my friend. And I betrayed her. But we did break it off, right before she disappeared. We both realized it was a mistake. A terrible, terrible mistake."

"Do you know if he told Joyce about your affair?"

Shirley thought for a moment. "He said he wouldn't, and I promised I wouldn't. Why hurt Joyce when we both agreed never to do it again? Now that you know, would you please not tell anyone?" With the back of her hand, Shirley wiped her face dry. She did her best to compose herself given the situation.

Hope's shoulders tensed. She wanted to keep Shirley's confession private. She had zero interest in broadcasting the indiscretion. She'd never want to hurt Shirley in that way, but the police should know. They should have known twenty years ago. If Greg had deep feelings for her and believed if he were single, they could have been together, that gave him a motive for murder.

"I'm sorry, I don't think it's possible to keep this a secret any longer. You have to tell Detective Reid."

"No!" Shirley recoiled. "I will not do any such thing. This is *my* private matter. And I expect you to keep your mouth closed about it."

"I'm sorry, Shirley, I can't make that promise."

Shirley's face contorted into a mixture of anger, hurt, and fear. She scooped up her books and shot up. She gave Hope one final look before she spun around and hurried off, eventually disappearing around a corner.

Hope sucked in a deep breath. The last thing she wanted to do was hurt Shirley. Would revealing the affair really help solve Joyce's case? She shrugged. Perhaps not. Did she think Shirley was the one sending her anonymous threats? Not really.

She pulled herself up and headed to the exit. As the door closed, she looked over her shoulder. Who said going to the library was boring?

A gust of wind smacked her and, being no match for her opponent, she hurried to her vehicle. With the ignition started, she was about to pull out of the parking space when her phone rang. It was Gail.

"Hey, Hope. Sorry to keep bothering you, but I'm stuck again," Gail said, her voice edgy.

Any other time, Hope might have been irritated at yet another call for assistance—after all, she wasn't a helpline—but she was relieved to be focused on anything but Shirley's bomb of a secret.

"What happened?"

"I ran into some trouble in the back end of the blog. I was trying to create a menu, and now it looks like I messed up the whole website."

Hope felt her friend's pain. When she'd started her blog, she couldn't afford a designer, so she had to roll up her sleeves, dive headfirst, and figure out all the parts of blog design. She had been up to her eyeballs in coding, plug-ins, and widgets. She took in a deep, hopefully cleansing breath, before speaking.

"It's probably not as bad as you think. I'm just leaving the library, so I'll be there in a few minutes."

After a grateful sigh, Gail thanked Hope. With the call ended, Hope backed out of her space and pulled out of the parking lot, heading to the house Gail shared with her father, Ernie.

* * *

"Well, hello, Hope!" Ernie Graves opened the door of his house and flashed a grin, revealing yellowed teeth from too many years of smoking. His brown eyes were hooded with thick brows and his forehead was deeply creased.

"Good morning." Hope wiped her boots on the welcome mat before entering the small foyer. The space opened to formal rooms on either side, and just ahead was a staircase leading to the second floor. An area rug covered most of the hardwood floor and the smart use of organizational tools made Hope's inner organizer very happy. A coatrack hung on one side of the door with a bench that had built-in shoe storage beneath it, and on the opposite side was a three-drawer cabinet that housed a mail station and a charging station, with all its ports being used. Hope had a similar one for her phone and tablet.

"Gail will be right down. Come on into the living room. She's set up her computer in there." After Ernie hung up Hope's coat, he led her into the other room.

He hadn't changed much from the photos Hope had seen while researching Joyce's disappearance. Still short and paunchy, his gray hair was thinning and creating a bald spot at the top of his head. He slipped his hands into the pockets of his black pants.

The living room was bright and airy thanks to the white, slipcovered furniture and whitewashed fireplace wall. On the coffee table was a seventeen-inch laptop. The computer was sleek and thin; it looked new.

Ernie must have noticed her interest in the computer. "Yeah, got that for her when she told me she wanted to start a blog. Made sure it was top-of-the-line. Take a load off." He dropped onto an armchair.

Hope murmured a thank-you and sat on the sofa. "You made a good choice with this model." Hope was happy Ernie was supportive of his daughter. In the past, he always seemed angry whenever Hope saw him. Now, he seemed like a different person. Maybe age had mellowed him out.

"You've known my girl for a long time." Ernie leaned forward, resting his forearms on his thighs and clasping his hands. "You know Devon's death has rattled her. I'm not sure how much you remember from when Devon's mom disappeared, but let me tell you, everyone was scared because we didn't know if it was an isolated incident or if there was a lunatic looking to harm random women. We all wondered who'd be next. Terrible thing to think about."

"Yes, it is."

"The one good thing was, because Gail's mom had already passed, God rest her soul, she didn't have to worry about going through what Devon and Felice did."

"You've done a good job raising both Gail and Alec on your own. Gail is very ambitious. And I hope Alec is doing well."

"Yeah, my girl has big dreams. Always had. Though it hasn't been easy for me or the kids. I worked too much."

"You had a family to provide for. You did what you needed to do."

"I guess you don't go through life without any regrets. I always told my kids that." He shook his head. "Like how I warned Gail not to smoke, drink, or get a tattoo, but you know how teenage girls are. Full of rebellion." He chuckled.

"Dad!" Gail hurried into the room. "I never did any of those things."

Ernie continued laughing. He seemed to enjoy his daughter's embarrassment. "Well, I know for sure you didn't get a tattoo. The other stuff?"

Gail's cheeks flushed. "Every one of my friends wanted one. I wanted a little heart on my ankle."

"Teenage girls are rebellious by nature. You tell them not to do something and they have to do it. It's in their DNA. Guess that's why grown women get those things too. It might be a flower, but it's still a tattoo." He wagged a finger at his daughter. "I got lucky, though. You were always a good kid."

Gail blushed again. "Hope doesn't want to hear about my antics when I was in high school. Besides, she probably knows about most of them." She joined Hope on the sofa.

Ernie shrugged. "Probably right."

"I am right. Don't you have your coffee meetup with the guys?" Gail's nudge for her dad to leave wasn't subtle.

"Right. Right. Don't want to keep the boys waiting. Good to see you, Hope." Ernie stood. "Oh, you left your phone in my vehicle the other day." He pointed to the coffee table and then turned to leave the room. Moments later, Hope heard the front door open and close.

"He gets together a couple of times a week with the guys who used to hang out at the auto body shop. It keeps him active." Gail reached for her white phone and slipped it into her jeans' back pocket. "Now, to the mess I've created." Gail's shoulders sagged.

"I'm sure it's not too bad." Hope inched to the edge of

the cushion while Gail brought up the dashboard on her website. Each blog theme had its own default navigation menu, but a blogger could create a custom one. Though it could be tricky the first time.

Hope reworked the menu. Gail watched on in awe and asked a dozen questions while Hope clicked the mouse and arranged the menu structure the way Gail had wanted it. She heaved a big sigh of relief when Hope finished.

"You made it look so easy. I finally have the drop-down tabs!"

Hope smiled. She knew exactly how her friend felt. There had been many times over the years when she was tempted to toss her computer out the window because she was so frustrated. Thankfully, she never did. Instead, she managed to develop some skill level in website design.

"The more you do this work, the easier it will be."

Gail gave Hope a sideways look. "If you say so. Now my menu is fixed, do you want some coffee?"

Hope checked her watch. "Thanks, but I need to get going." She stood. Her stops at the police department and the library had put her behind schedule.

"Right. Sorry if I interrupted your work." Gail stood and escorted Hope to the front door.

"I'm happy I was able to help. You're doing a great job with the blog. Nice design, by the way." Hope recognized the theme Gail had chosen for her blog. It was a free one that came with her website hosting and she was starting to make it her own by selecting a color palette and purchasing a font plug-in.

"I appreciate your encouragement." Gail handed Hope her coat.

"It seems your dad is very supportive of your venture." Hope shrugged into her coat and zipped it.

"Yeah, he is. He's been my rock. The divorce wasn't easy for me."

"It rarely is." Since returning to Jefferson, Hope had tried not to dwell on her own failed marriage. Some days it was easier than others. "How's your brother doing?"

"Oh, Alec is doing good. He's living in Ohio now, working in customer service for an auto supply company. It's the perfect job for him."

"Sounds like it. Nice to hear he's doing well. See you in class?"

Gail laughed. "I still can't believe you're my teacher. See you in class."

Hope left and walked to her car. Inside, while she waited for the seats to warm, she wanted to satisfy her curiosity about Alec. So many of her classmates had taken off for college and not returned to Jefferson, like Devon. She wondered what happened to them all. While she couldn't search social media for all of them, she did find Alec's social profile, with no security settings.

She scrolled through his posts and pieced together that he'd recently married for the second time and gotten a promotion at work. Good for him. She continued to scroll and found a bunch of photos of old cars. No surprise there; he grew up around cars at his dad's shop. There was a link to an article in a local newspaper about a car Alec restored and showed. She tapped on the link and navigated away from the social profile to the newspaper's website. The short article was about his prized Mustang. She guessed you had to be a car enthusiast to appreciate the story.

While on the website, she searched Alec's name out of curiosity and came up with another article, and this one wasn't about an old car.

The second article recounted Alec's arrest for stalking a former neighbor. The unidentified thirty-three-year-old woman had contacted the police after several unwanted visits, phone calls, and a physical altercation.

Had the starry-eyed romantic Hope had known back in high school morphed into a stalker?

Chapter Sixteen

She really needed to clean out her purse more often, Hope thought as she turned the bag upside down and all its contents rained down onto the countertop. She sifted through her pens, keys, crumpled receipts, bookmarks, a pressed powder compact, hand wipes, too many lipsticks, and the tube of concealer gifted to her by Elaine. But no mascara.

She'd somehow misplaced the fifty-dollar mascara. She'd hoped it had made its way from her bathroom to her purse.

It hadn't.

She rested a hand on her hip and scanned the kitchen. She'd searched the drawers, hoping it had been stashed away during a frenzied cleanup session after filming a video. She usually had her lipstick, mascara, and pressed powder handy for quick touch-ups between takes.

Fifty bucks was a lot to pay for the mascara, but it did lengthen and thicken her lashes.

There was one more spot she hadn't checked. *Please. Please. Please.* It had to be there.

At one end of her island were cubbies for storage, and in the middle cubby was a basket. With any luck, the mascara had fallen into the basket. As with her purse, she emptied the basket on the island. A quick look at the items, mostly pens, sticky notes, and eyeshadow quads. No mascara.

Darn.

Her phone chimed with an alert that someone had opened the back door, and a moment later, Ethan walked into the kitchen.

"Hey," he said, closing the door. His eyebrows drew together, and his forehead crinkled. "Looking for something?"

"What do you think?" Hope tossed the items back into the basket. "Sorry, I didn't mean to snap. Yes, I'm looking for my mascara. I have no idea where it is."

Ethan surveyed the messy island. "You always know where everything is."

"I know! It's driving me crazy." After setting the basket back in the cubby, she returned the items from her purse to the bag.

"Just buy another mascara." He walked to the refrigerator and opened the door. He stood there for a moment before pulling out a container of fried chicken. She'd been working on a new recipe and had fried enough chicken to feed an army. He opened the container and took out a drumstick.

"I'd love to, but at fifty dollars a tube, I don't have the budget. I need to find it."

Ethan swallowed his bite of chicken. "Fifty dollars?"

Oops. Hope forgot guys didn't understand the cost of beauty or, in her case, the saving of time the mascara gave her because she didn't have to fuss with false lashes.

"Never mind. Eat your chicken." She patted him on the arm and went to get a plate from a cabinet.

"I'd rather talk about your recent text exchange with a possible killer."

"Maybe I shouldn't have engaged, but I couldn't help myself. I thought I could possibly reveal his or her identity. It didn't go as planned. We don't know who it was." She set the plate on the counter and took out a few pieces of chicken from the container. "I have some potato salad."

Ethan nodded. "Yes, please."

Hope retrieved the bowl from the refrigerator and added two heaping spoonfuls to the plate. She grabbed a fork from the flatware drawer and gestured to the table as she handed Ethan his lunch. She poured two glasses of water and joined him.

"We don't know the identity, but we were able to find out the text messages came from Devon's phone."

Hope's mouth gaped open. "Her phone?"

"You said you didn't recognize the number."

"The number came up as unknown. Devon never gave me her phone number. The few times we talked, it was in person. So, all this time the killer has kept her phone? Wait, can you find the phone by tracking it?"

"No luck there. It's probably turned off or destroyed by now."

"You haven't found her purse yet, have you?"

Ethan shook his head as he ate a forkful of potato salad. "I don't like the cat-and-mouse game this person is playing with you."

"Me neither. The thing is, I don't know anything. Well, I know in my core that Donna didn't commit suicide. It wasn't her handwriting on the note I found." Hope sipped her water.

Ethan didn't look up; he kept his gaze on his plate of food.

"I'm right, aren't I?"

He wiped his mouth with his napkin. "Her case is still open, so I'm limited in what I can share. However, it does appear, based on some other writing samples, the handwriting does not match up."

The temptation to say "I told you so" was a hard one to let pass. Hope knew Donna wouldn't have killed herself, and if she had, her final note to the world would have been far more eloquent and beautiful. Not some chicken scratch on a sheet of paper.

"Again, your instincts were right." Ethan pushed away his plate and reached out for Hope's hand. "The thing is, your instincts can get you into trouble. Serious trouble."

"I know. Earlier, I was at the library and I ran into Shirley. She told me something you should know." She noticed Ethan's gaze held steady on her. He wasn't going to interrupt. "She admitted to having an affair with Greg prior to Joyce's disappearance."

"She just came out and told you about the affair?"

"Sort of. I saw she looked upset and I asked her what was wrong, and she blurted it out. I think she wanted to tell someone. Get it off her chest. And I was there."

"How convenient."

Hope sighed. "I've known Shirley for years. I don't think she had anything to do with Joyce's disappearance."

"Reid will still want to talk to her." He glanced at his watch. "I'd better get going. Look, I want you to be careful. Extra-careful. I need you in one piece for our ski trip."

Hope's shoulders slumped. With everything going on, all thoughts about the getaway had been shoved to the back burner. How could she have forgotten?

"Nothing is going to keep me away from our trip. Four glorious days of just the two of us skiing all day and cozying up by a roaring fire every night."

"Maybe we should start a little early. How about tonight?" He stood.

Hope smiled. "Sounds good. See you later."

Ethan kissed her on the top of her head and walked out of the kitchen. A moment later, her cell phone chimed, indicating he'd exited out the back door. She sipped her water and leaned back. She was a hundred percent certain she had no idea who was behind the murders and the threats made against her. Though Donna must have had an inkling. She remembered something about the day Joyce disappeared. If only Hope had taken the call.

In Donna's message, she'd mentioned a work truck. She could have seen Oliver's truck at Joyce's house. No. Something didn't feel right about the theory. She'd never heard any whisper of Oliver being inappropriate with his female clients. Surely in a small town like Jefferson, there would have been gossip, warnings not to hire him. Though he was angry with her for sharing what Devon told her with the police, and for snooping around his property. In all fairness to him, a person didn't have to be guilty of a crime to feel violated by someone invading his privacy or sending the police in his direction regarding a crime.

She took another sip of water and played out different scenarios. Had Greg, finally fed up with his wife's behavior, confronted her, and things got out of hand? Or had someone read more into Joyce's flirting and wanted to go further but was rejected?

Over the next hour, Hope wrote a blog post while Iva tackled painting the living room. She also wanted to use the time to muster the courage to finally talk to Iva about the missing bracelet, and now the missing mascara. First, she wanted to touch base with Drew. She texted him about Alec Graves, asking him to find out all he could about Gail's brother. She had a feeling there was more to his banishment from Jefferson after high school than Gail or their father had let on over the years. Especially because he'd been arrested for harassment and was on wife number two. She slipped her phone into her back pocket and entered the living room, where Iva was folding a drop cloth.

The paint job was complete. After countless paint swatches, Hope had finally found one she loved and now, looking around the room, she felt reassured it was the right choice. The shade was perfect. Not too dark, not too light or dull or shiny. Just perfect.

She glanced around the rest of the room. So much more work needed to be done, but it was mostly cosmetic. The floor had already been refinished, the fireplace mantel and windows had been stripped and stained. Now she needed to bring in furniture. She had some pieces stored in the garage.

"What do you think?" Iva held the drop cloth in her arms. A paint-smattered flannel shirt covered distressed jeans. She topped her hair with a black baseball cap.

"It looks amazing." Hope stepped farther into the room. "You did a great job."

"Yeah, well, I had to learn how to do a good paint job, because paint is the cheapest way to freshen up a room."

Iva set the drop cloth on the card table. The makeshift workstation held the paint cans and trays.

"Are you sure you don't want a cup of coffee?" No time like the present to discuss the missing items.

"I'm good. I'm gonna clean up and then head out."

"Sounds good. By the way, would you happen to know of a snowplow driver I could hire for the remainder of the season?" Considering her recent interactions with Oliver, she wouldn't be able to use his service any longer.

Iva placed her hand on her hip and gave Hope a hard stare. "Heard you and Oliver had a dustup the other day. Guess it serves you right for sticking your nose where it doesn't belong."

The fact that Hope was writing Iva a weekly paycheck didn't stop the woman from saying exactly what she was thinking.

"Devon was a friend."

"Don't matter. You don't have the right to go around accusing people of crimes."

"I didn't. I simply asked a few questions."

"Your questions are never simple. You should mind your own business and leave the investigating to the police." Iva glanced at her watch. "I need to go."

"Wait. There's one more thing we need to discuss." While her stomach was unsettled earlier at the thought of having this discussion, now, after Iva's unsolicited lecture, Hope wasn't feeling so apprehensive.

"Well, don't you sound all ominous. Wait, don't tell me, you want to question me about Joyce's disappearance and Devon's death."

"No, I don't. I want to talk to you about my missing charm bracelet and tube of mascara."

Iva drew back, visibly offended. "Why? You think I took them?"

"I don't know. All I know is that they are missing."

"You think I took them! Yeah, you and your sister are definitely alike. She thought I stole one of her bracelets. I may be poor and I definitely have my share of troubles, but I'm not a thief. Here I thought you understood that. My bad."

"I just want to find the bracelet and mascara. I don't want to cause any problems for you."

"Why, thank you, ma'am."

"Don't be like that, Iva."

A soft meow drew Hope's attention to the doorway. Princess moseyed in and rubbed Hope's leg as she passed by on her way to the sofa. There, she leaped up and settled on the back of the sofa to look out the window.

"I'm not a thief, but that cat could be!" Iva pointed to Princess.

"Are you serious? You're blaming my cat?" Hope couldn't help but sound incredulous.

Iva nodded. "Cats steal things all the time."

"I think you should go now." How someone could blame a cat for stealing items baffled Hope. She wanted Iva to leave before she said something she'd regret.

"Happy to." Iva stormed past Hope, and within a few moments, the app on Hope's phone chimed, signaling Iva had left the house.

Hope pulled her phone out of her back pocket and did an online search for videos of cats stealing things. All the while typing her search criteria, she hadn't expected to find any videos, so when a long list of videos came up she was shocked. She pressed Play on one of them and saw a cat snagging a sandwich, and then another cat sneaking off with a pen, and then another cat scurrying away with a pancake. She looked up at Princess.

"Are you the thief?"

Princess leveled a cool look at Hope.

"What am I thinking? You're a cat." Hope turned and walked back to the kitchen. She wondered how many more people she could alienate. Later, she had the blogging class, so there were more opportunities. And that reminded her: she had to prepare for class. Her cell phone chirped a notification.

She'd contacted Felice after getting the earrings from Zach and asked to meet her. In the text, Felice apologized for the delay and said she was on her way to the funeral parlor. She suggested they meet there, because the remainder of the day she'd be meeting with an attorney.

Hope replied back that she could meet at the funeral parlor and then headed to the mudroom to grab her purse and bundle up before heading out.

The funeral parlor receptionist opened the door to the interior office, where Felice was seated on the leather sofa. The black dress she wore seemed to swallow her up and her gray hair aged rather than flattered her. Hope's heart broke for her friend. Over her shoulder, Hope thanked the receptionist and stepped into the room. She heard the door close behind her.

"I can't believe this is happening. Detective Reid said they're now investigating Devon's case as a homicide." Felice's chin trembled, and she wiped her swollen, red eyes with a tissue. "I'm relieved they're investigating." Her eyes widened with terror. "Was Devon right about the person still being here in town?"

Hope joined Felice on the sofa. She'd left her coat out in the reception area but kept her purse. Inside was the jewelry box for Felice.

"What if I'm next? What if the killer thinks Devon told me something?" Felice's head dipped again and she sobbed.

Hope rubbed Felice's back to comfort her. What was she supposed to say? The fear was reasonable.

"Did she tell you anything? Her suspicions? Theories?"

Felice shook her head and then stood. She walked to the desk, an impressive antique that anchored the room. Behind the desk were two large, curtained windows looking out over a frozen pond. The funeral parlor was situated on a tranquil piece of property north of Main Street. Felice plucked a tissue out of its container. She wiped her face and blew her nose before tossing the tissue in the wastebasket.

"I need to pull myself together and stop thinking these crazy thoughts." Felice scrubbed her hands over her face.

"They're not crazy thoughts."

Felice gave a half smile. "I'm not surprised to hear you say that." She reached for her purse on the sofa.

Her tone seemed off, and it struck Hope as odd and had her squaring her shoulders. "What's that supposed to mean?"

"Hope, I know you want to help. I even asked for your help. Now, looking back, I shouldn't have. We need to let the police handle this. I want the person responsible for my sister's death to be held accountable, and the last thing I want is for something or someone to jeopardize that outcome."

"I completely understand. I'd never want that to happen."

"Good. Then please stay out of this matter and allow

the police to do their job. Maybe they can get it right this time."

The office door opened, and the receptionist poked her head in. "Felice, are you ready to continue with the planning?"

Felice nodded and then looked back to Hope. "Thank you for coming, and know I'm grateful for your help."

"I know you are. This may not be the right time to tell you this, but it's important."

"I'll be right there," Felice said to the receptionist. "What is it?" she asked, sounding irritated.

"Devon was right about your father having an affair at the time of your mother's disappearance. The other woman was Shirley Phelan. She told me earlier today."

Felice fidgeted with her necklace. "I can't believe it. She and my mother were good friends."

"I'm sorry I had to tell you now, but I've shared the information with Ethan and I don't know what will come of it. I didn't want you blindsided."

Felice shrugged. "I guess that explains why things got weird between Mom and Mrs. Phelan."

Hope had heard the same thing from Amy.

"My mom and Shirley spent so much time together, and then Shirley stopped spending time with her. Mom seemed upset by it. She didn't know why her friend didn't like her anymore. I guess we never outgrow that feeling."

"Probably not."

"I appreciate you telling me. I really need to go." Felice gave Hope a quick hug and then left the room.

Hope grabbed her purse and slung it over her shoulder. Shoot! She'd forgotten to give Felice the earrings. Now, thinking about it, maybe it would be better to give the jewelry to her after the funeral.

She walked out to the reception area, as nicely appointed as the interior office, only with a lighter feel, thanks to lighter wood tones and beautiful floral arrangements. Hope retrieved her coat from the closet and slipped into it. Felice was right to be worried about the case and skeptical about the police bringing the culprit to justice. The police had let her family down twenty years ago. But Hope had let Devon down now too by not being able to find answers that her friend had died trying to uncover.

She pulled open the heavy wood door and stepped outside. She accepted that the police were more equipped to investigate. They were the professionals. As Reid had told her on more than one occasion, she wasn't a detective.

She hurried to her vehicle and got in. She should honor Felice's request and step aside to let the police do their job. She should also let herself off the hook for Devon's death.

Easier said than done.

She glanced at the funeral parlor one last time before driving out of the parking lot. She needed to respect Felice's wishes. Especially because, so far, Hope had only managed to upset people rather than actually help the police.

No, it was time for her to shift her focus back to her blog, her class, and her upcoming ski trip with Ethan. It was only days before they'd be heading up north for four blissful days of skiing and snuggling by a fire with nobody else around. She turned on the radio and set it to her favorite news station.

"Get ready, you folks in the northwest corner of the state. We got another wallop of a storm heading our way." The forecaster's voice was far too cheerful about another snowstorm, one that sounded like it could derail her get-away with Ethan. "We might even be bracing for a blizzard."

On her way back home, Hope stopped at her sister's shop for a quick visit. She needed to arrange to pick up the ski clothing Claire said she'd loan her. She hadn't bargained on a lecture.

"Don't you have enough on your plate right now? The other day you mentioned actually creating the online blogging class." Claire was busy multitasking: rearranging a display of pricey crystal knickknacks and lecturing Hope. She didn't miss a beat on either task. "Then there's the Mama Mia Pasta deal. Don't you have some macaroni to cook?"

Hope chewed on her lower lip. Her sister had valid points that were hard to argue against. So why had she told Claire about her talk with Felice? Glutton for punishment?

"I have Josie now. Which means I have extra time." Ah-ha! Point for Hope.

Claire stopped fussing with the miniature crystal collectibles and propped a hand on her slim hip. "Extra time you should be devoting to your business. Do you see me running all over town trying to solve a murder? No! I'm right where I belong, running my business. And because I was where I was supposed to be, I met a new staging client. She came in to browse and we got to talking. I'm meeting with her next week."

Point for Claire. Hope sighed.

The front door swung open with force and Amy barged in, her sights set on Hope.

"How could you? She's my mother! She was in tears!" Amy jabbed a finger in the air toward Hope.

Claire stepped away from the display table and stood by Hope's side. "Amy, calm down. What's the matter?"

Amy's nostrils flared and she looked at Claire. "I'll tell you what's the matter. Your nosy sister made my mother divulge a secret she's been carrying for decades. Now she'll be a murder suspect."

Claire's shocked gaze landed heavy on her sister, and Hope felt her insides twist, leaving her speechless. But she had to say something to defend herself.

"I didn't force her to reveal anything. Actually, it seemed she wanted to unburden herself."

"What did you do now?" Claire asked.

"Do you have any idea how bad my mother feels about her stupid mistake? Do you know how embarrassing it was for her to have to tell me she had an affair with Mr. Markham? My friend's father? No. You. Don't."

"I'm sure it wasn't easy for her—"

"No! You don't get to defend yourself. What you did is indefensible. I bet you wasted no time in telling your boyfriend all the sordid details about my mother's lapse in judgment." Amy was crying. The flood of tears dragged her heavily applied mascara down her cheeks.

"The police need all the information that's pertinent to Joyce's disappearance and Devon's murder." Hope doubted the police wanted details of Donna's death revealed, so she kept quiet about that crime.

"Do you hear yourself? You think *my* mother had something to do with those two things? Wow. I thought we were friends. Looks like I was wrong." Amy pivoted and stormed out of the shop.

Claire followed Amy to the door. When the door shut,

she turned and faced Hope. "Whatever you think you're doing, I hope for your sake it's worth losing friends over." She marched past her sister and disappeared into her office.

Hope dropped onto the chair beside the round table. She reached out and moved one of the crystal figurines a smidge, and then moved the one behind it. She wanted to be angry with Amy for her outburst, for insinuating she'd interrogated her mother under a hot light for endless hours to get her to confess her sins, for not letting her speak, but she wasn't. Amy was in protective mode over her mom and Hope couldn't blame her for that. She would have done the same thing.

But Claire?

Hope eyed the doorway to her sister's office. Wasn't her sister supposed to stand by her? Defend her? Understand why finding whoever killed Devon and Donna was important to her?

The front door opened, and an older woman in a puffy coat entered, her gaze drifting around the shop.

"Hello," the woman said, smiling.

"Good afternoon." Hope stood and looked over her shoulder. "Claire, you have a customer," she called out before leaving the shop. Outside, she lingered and watched through the window as her sister approached the customer with a smile. She lowered her head and walked away. How badly had she messed things up?

Chapter Seventeen

All Hope wanted to do when she got home from Claire's shop was dive into her bed and pull the covers over her head. She'd made a mess of things, and now it looked like she'd lost a friend because of her snooping. She didn't even want to think about the rift between her and Claire.

A deep woof dragged Hope from her pity party of one at the kitchen table, where she had work spread out, yet she failed to do any of it because she couldn't focus.

Looking up from the grocery list she was attempting to write for her next video shoot, she found Bigelow seated beside her with his head tilted and his eyes eager. She knew the look, and her own eyes widened with alarm. Had it gotten that late already?

Bigelow barked again.

She reached out and stroked his head. "I'm sorry. I lost track of time."

A *bing* from her cell phone drew Hope's attention away from Bigelow to her emails. There was a new one from Corey.

He'd forwarded an invite to speak at the Southwestern Food Bloggers Conference in the fall. Maybe getting away from Jefferson for more than a few days would be a good idea. Though the date was far off. She could really use an escape now.

Maybe Elaine would want to return to Bali with her best friend.

Whoa! Hope's situation wasn't that bad. Surely she and Amy would make up once Shirley moved on from the embarrassment of a mistake she'd made twenty years ago.

A meow had her glancing to the spot in the kitchen where she fed Princess. It looked like her cat wanted a meal too.

Before she did anything, she replied to Corey with a firm yes to attending the conference. Another meow reminded her that she was slacking. Her pets wanted their dinners.

Where had the day gone?

She shook her head. She knew exactly where the day had gone, and it was all her fault. A paw on her knee prompted Hope to get her behind up off the chair and over to the island. As Hope dished out the food into two bowls, she considered making herself a light dinner. She hadn't eaten since breakfast because she'd been too busy sticking her nose where it hadn't belonged to stop for lunch.

After her pets were fed, Hope took Bigelow for a walk even though she barely had an ounce of energy left in her. When they returned home, Hope felt her mood brightening. Maybe it had been the fresh air or Bigelow's gusto. She shrugged. It really didn't matter. She was just glad she was feeling better.

Hope cleaned up the kitchen while both Bigelow and Princess curled up. Once she was done with tidying up, she packed her tote for class. It was the last night of class, and she had to dig deep within herself to summon up the smallest amount of enthusiasm between now and when class would begin. After the day she'd had, it was going to be a struggle to be upbeat.

Hope made it to the library with little time to spare before her students arrived. When they did, they were eager to participate in the last lesson, which was social media management.

Next was a thirty-minute block of time she'd set aside for everyone to talk about what their plans were. When she'd written up the curriculum, she'd thought a half hour would be enough time.

She was wrong. The library had a strict policy about closing time for after-hours events. There was a collective groan at the announcement, and that was when Laila's hand went up.

"Why don't we all go over to the diner for coffee and dessert to finish our discussion?" She looked expectantly at her classmates.

"Sounds like a good idea. I'm kinda hungry," Phil said.

Everyone's head nodded in agreement, except for Hope's. She wanted to go home and hide.

"Okay, let's do that." As much as Hope wanted to bail,

she couldn't. In a matter of minutes, all her students had gathered their belongings and headed out the door with her promise to catch up. She wanted to check her emails and social media, something she'd neglected to do earlier in the day.

Alone and seated at the table, she typed on her laptop's keyboard and waited for her email account to come up. Waiting, her gaze drifted over the top of the computer to the seats where her students had sat. Shirley's spot had been empty. No big surprise there.

She sighed.

The email account opened, and on top of the long list of new emails was one from Drew. She clicked on it and read what he'd sent. It was more information about Alec, who apparently had been busy being creepy. He'd had more than one arrest for harassment.

According to Drew's research, while in community college, Alec had stalked a female professor.

The college professor wasn't his first crush on an older woman. Hope remembered the incident with the English teacher back in high school. It seemed he was drawn to older women. Was it possible he'd had a crush on Joyce? A fatal crush?

He'd been friends with Devon, and it was possible he'd spent time at her house. Back then, they hung out wherever they could whenever they had the chance.

She shook her head and chided herself. She'd accused Drew of leaping to conclusions in the past and now she was doing the exact same thing. Just because Alec was arrested for stalking a professor didn't mean he'd harmed Joyce in any way.

She quickly typed a thank-you reply and then closed her email account. She checked the time on the computer.

She had better get a move on, because she was hungry. First, she called Ethan, but got his voice mail.

After telling him she'd be late, she rambled on about her theory of Alec possibly being involved with Joyce's disappearance. She gave him the highlights of Alec's run-ins with the law and ended with acknowledging she could be way off base. She set down her phone and was about to turn off the computer, but did a quick check of her social media first.

She had a scheduled post published and perused the comments. All positive. She smiled. Feeling a little better, she was about to navigate off the page when an ad popped up for a fashion website she'd visited online before. The model had a tattoo on her forearm.

Hope stared at the photograph. The tattoo was visible because it was on the model's forearm.

Joyce's tattoo hadn't been visible. At least, she didn't think so by the way Devon described it on the podcast. It sounded as if the black rose was situated on her lower back.

Wait.

What was Ernie's comment about tattoos?

Guess that's why grown women get those things too. It might be a flower, but it's still a tattoo.

A rose was a flower.

At the time, she hadn't given his comment much thought. Now, thinking back to it, his comment seemed odd.

She shook her head. Maybe his late wife had a flower tattoo. Besides, Joyce's tattoo would have only been visible to someone handling her body.

Sure, Ernie was rough around the edges, but he wasn't a killer.

It was time to pack up and head to the diner. She reached for her phone and it slipped from her grip. Thankfully she caught it before it landed on the floor. She really should get a case for it like Gail had on hers. A nice sturdy leather case . . . wait . . . Gail had a case on her phone.

The phones were different.

Hope saw Gail's phone when she invited her over to help with the homework. But the phone Ernie said Gail left in his truck was white . . . like Devon's phone. Though, she only saw it a moment at the apartment, but she was certain it was white.

Why hadn't she noticed when she was at Gail's house?

She could be wrong. There was only one way to find out. Hope quickly gathered her computer and papers and shoved them into her tote bag. As she stood, she swiped up her phone and grabbed her jacket. Bustling out of the room and heading to the parking lot exit, she checked social media to see if she could find out if Alec was back in Jefferson. Surely there'd be some clue, like a comment or photo. Everyone did that.

Nothing. He was smart.

He must have slipped back into town without anyone realizing. Though it was dangerous to have invited Hope to the Graves house if he were in town.

Did Ernie and Gail know? Maybe Alec was hiding out. No, if he was, how did Devon's phone end up in the Graves's house? Hope slowed her pace and her racing thoughts.

There was no proof the phone Ernie had given to Gail earlier had been Devon's phone. Though every fiber in her body was telling her it was Devon's phone.

The trek from upstairs through the corridor seemed to take forever. The narrow space had seemed bright and cheery earlier in the day, with its bulletin boards covered with flyers and narrow book tables showcasing novels perfect for wintery nights. But now, alone in the building with thoughts about murder, the space seemed eerily silent.

She reached out to open the door but froze when she spotted Oliver's truck outside. And it wasn't plowing. It was just idling.

Her heart thumped. Was she one hundred percent certain Alec was responsible for the murders?

No, she wasn't.

She spun around and headed back through the corridor. She'd go upstairs and call Ethan. Good. She had a plan.

Maybe calling Ethan now was a better idea. She paused and tapped on her phone to open up the contacts, and that was when she heard the back door open.

Her heart thumped again. This time the thump felt more like a slam knocking some wind out of her.

Footsteps sounded on the tiled floor. They were getting closer.

Thump. Thump. Thump.

"There you are. Everyone is waiting for you."

Hope wanted to feel a rush of relief that it wasn't Oliver, but seeing Gail standing there with a not-so-sincere smile made her tense. Warning signals flooded her body, threatening to overload her.

"Sorry, didn't mean to startle you."

Hope licked her lips and made the hopefully smart decision to play it cool.

"I'm just heading out now." She squeezed her tote closer to her body and glanced at the phone in her hand.

"Is everything okay?" Gail stepped forward, her pace measured and precise. "I'm thinking everything isn't okay.

How could it be, with you talking to so many people about Devon and her poor missing mom?" Her voice had changed to harsh and cold.

Gail's razor-edged voice raised alarm in Hope, which wasn't too hard to do, because she was already on the verge of a full-blown panic episode. But she couldn't indulge. She needed to stay calm, cool, collected. Oh, what a phony façade she was attempting to show.

"I saw Oliver outside. Maybe he'd like to join us at the diner." Yeah right. But the weird vibes coming from Gail had Hope feeling Oliver wasn't the threat she'd originally thought.

Gail glanced over her shoulder and gave Hope a nanosecond to tap the Record button on her phone.

"Nah, I talked to him. He was just driving through to see if he had any plowing to do. Looks like he did a good job the first time around."

Hope gulped. So, it was just her and Gail. "You're right. There are a lot of things wrong now. Devon's murder is one of the things that's wrong."

"It appears she talked to too many people too. Asked questions someone didn't want answered."

"You really can't blame her. She wanted to know what happened to her mother. I think all of us would want the same thing. Even Felice wants answers."

"Felice asked you to step away from the investigation. She told me that you both talked at the funeral parlor." Gail stepped forward. Her eyes had hardened, just like her voice.

"She did. I respect her wishes."

"Not enough to abide by them, though?"

"Come on, the rest of the class is waiting for us." Hope

forced a smile. She didn't want to let on she knew all about Alec's troubles, and that he could have been the one to have harmed Joyce and killed Devon and Donna.

"No. You have a theory of what happened to Joyce. I want to hear it."

Hope considered for a moment. It didn't seem she had a choice. She had to decide how much to say. She'd keep it general. There was no need to let on she considered Gail's brother a suspect.

"I believe Joyce was killed and her body disposed of somewhere."

"Everyone has that theory. You have an idea of who killed her." Gail advanced forward. "Come on, who do you think did it?"

"Alec." So much for keeping it general. Now there was no turning back for Hope. "He was impressionable in high school. We all knew how easily he fell in love. And so very hard when he did. Joyce had a flirtatious side that could easily be misinterpreted by someone. Especially someone younger. It's possible he made an advance and she rebuffed him and he accidentally killed her and your father helped dispose of the body."

Gail barked a laugh. "Wow. You're definitely creative. I can see how you could imagine my brother being involved. You're right, he was quite the hopeless romantic; still is."

Interesting spin on stalking.

"I'm curious about how you came up with my father being his accomplice?"

"It's only a theory. And having said it out loud, it's not much of one. The Alec I remember was too sweet to hurt anyone." Hope forced her mood to lighten and stretched her lips into a smile. "Come on, I'm starving. I could go for a slice of apple pie."

"Me too. And you're right about your theory not being a good one. My money is on Shirley Phelan. Now that her affair with Greg has become public, it gives her a motive for wanting Joyce out of the picture and wanting to keep Devon from discovering her secret. I bet once the police realize that, when they go and search her house, they'll find the knife used to kill Joyce. Shirley liked collecting things, so she probably kept it as a souvenir."

Hope's grasp on her tote bag tightened, and she saw the look of regret on Gail's face. Her former high school classmate realized she'd said too much.

"How do you know a knife was used? How do you know Joyce was murdered?"

Gail stiffened. "Because I was there. Are you happy now? I was there!"

Hope flinched at Gail's raised voice. "It wasn't Alec. It was you?"

"Why did you have to keep poking? Why? Killing Devon was easy. I never really liked her. But you? I've always liked you, Hope. And with these classes, you've taught me so much. Too bad I have to get rid of you too."

"What happened, Gail? Why did you kill Joyce?" Hope inched backward.

"Stop moving!"

"Okay. Okay." Hope lifted up her hands in surrender. She wanted to keep Gail as calm as possible. The longer they talked, the better the chance of Hope coming up with a plan to escape.

"Give me that!" Gail seized the phone from Hope's hand and threw it on the floor. She sucked in a deep breath and then expelled it with as much vigor. "I went to her house. I only wanted to talk to her. Get her to realize what she was doing could hurt Alec."

"What was she doing? Flirting?"

"Flirting. It sounds so harmless, doesn't it? A toss of the hair, a batting of her lashes and some breathy giggles. It's only harmless if the person being toyed with isn't an impressionable boy who had boundary issues. I was trying to keep him from getting into trouble, from ruining his life. We didn't have a mom, so I was the only person who looked out for Alec."

"What about your father?"

Gail rolled her eyes. "He was too busy with his business. Besides, he treated Alec so badly. If he found out that Alec had a crush on Joyce, I think he would have killed him. He almost did when Alec went all crazy in love with the English teacher. He took his belt and then his fist to Alec. He said he was knocking some sense into his boy. He hated feelings. He never understood Alec. Still doesn't."

"Alec has been arrested for harassment."

"You've been a busy little bee, haven't you? I know my brother has problems, but he's harmless. I figured if I could reason with Joyce. Tell her about my father and how he felt, and how Alec would be treated if our dad caught any whiff of the flirtation."

"She didn't see the problem, did she?"

"She laughed in my face!" Gail's face twisted as rage filled her eyes, and her step forward was determined.

"I hadn't realized how much she and Devon were alike. Alec thought Devon was his friend, but I saw what she was really like. She made fun of his inexperience around girls right in front of him, but you should have heard the things she said behind his back. I *did*. I tried to convince him to stop hanging around with her, but he didn't listen. Then I saw why he wanted to stay friends." Gail used air quotes around the word "friends." "I saw the way my brother looked at Joyce the night of the Winter Formal."

Hope hadn't thought about the annual dance in years. The name sounded far more sophisticated than the event was. Even so, Hope and Claire had enjoyed dressing up and dancing for hours that January night.

"I'd forgotten Joyce had been one of the chaperones. Did something happen between Alec and her?"

"No! I made sure of it." Gail took a deep breath, trying to control her rage. "Between Devon's cruel teasing and Joyce's need for attention, the Markham family was ruining my life. I had to protect my baby brother. At all costs."

Hope gulped.

How far had Gail gone twenty years ago?

Chapter Eighteen

"You killed Joyce?" Hope braced herself for the answer, but the detached look in Gail's eyes already told her.

"It was an accident. I swear it was. After she laughed at me, she told me she was a grown woman with no interest in a boy like Alec. He'd meant nothing to her. He had feelings, but she didn't care. How could she not care?"

Hope had never seen that side of Joyce. Then again, people were very clever in hiding things about themselves they didn't want others to see. Besides, at the time, Hope was a teenager and not interested in the private life of her mother's friend.

"You're right. She should have cared." Hope was stalling for time. The more Gail talked, the better chance there was of her calming down and realizing it was time to turn herself in to the police.

"She was too self-absorbed. She told me that she had to be somewhere, and I needed to leave. She talked to me like a was a five-year-old. I *wasn't* leaving until she agreed to end all contact with my brother. I didn't want him at her house anymore. Joyce refused to agree to anything. Then we both started yelling. I got so angry! I pushed her. She pushed back. Then we started fighting. At some point, I was thrust toward the counter, and that's when I grabbed a knife out of the block. I don't know what came over me. I saw red. Before I knew it, she was on the floor and I was holding a bloodied knife. I panicked."

Hearing the details of Joyce's murder sickened Hope. She pushed all that down, though, because she needed to keep Gail talking. "It was an accident. You hadn't meant to hurt Joyce."

"I didn't! It happened so fast." Gail's eyes took on an eerie look that made Hope wonder if the scene in Joyce's kitchen twenty years ago was playing out in Gail's head. "I couldn't breathe. I ran out of the house for air. Then I kept running all the way home."

"You left Joyce in her kitchen?" *To die?* Hope left the last part of her question unspoken.

"I didn't think she'd die! When I got home, I called my dad and told him what happened. He told me to stay put and he'd take care of it."

"What did he do?"

Gail shrugged. "All he said when he got back home was that he'd cleaned up the mess and I was never to speak about it to anyone."

"So he removed Joyce's body from the house and disposed of it somewhere in town? Or nearby?"

Gail gave a casual shrug. Like it wasn't a big deal.

"Just in case anyone asked any questions, I was to tell them I was home all day because I had a stomach bug."

"Did the police talk to you?"

"No. But we thought they might, because Dad said Donna's car drove past the house after he'd arrived to check on Joyce."

"He saw her?" Then the work truck Donna saw hadn't been Oliver's, but rather Ernie's truck. "You both were worried she'd mentioned that to the police?"

"Of course. How would Dad explain being at the Markham house?"

"Is that why you killed Donna? To make sure she didn't tell anyone about seeing your dad's truck that day?"

"When I went to Donna's house, I didn't intend to kill her. After all this time, I thought she'd forgotten the truck. Though how could someone forget something like that? But she was getting older, and she's had her own troubles over the years."

"She remembered, and you had to kill her."

"I had no choice. Just like I don't have a choice in killing you, Hope." Gail nodded and then pulled out a knife from her crossbody bag.

Hope's heart thumped. Sweat beaded at her temples. Gail had always been one to follow through on her plans, and it appeared she wasn't going to change now. Hope backed away.

"Donna was agitated when I arrived, and I immediately knew she'd remembered seeing my dad's truck. She told me so. She also told me she was going to tell the police. When she turned, I pushed her, and she fell. I dragged her out to the garage and staged her suicide."

"You wrote the suicide note?"

Gail nodded.

"What about Devon?"

"Well, she was going to be a big problem. She was smart, not like that detective who handled her mother's case. She already knew too much. I had to get rid of her. I lured her out to the old Miller farm by dangling a lead to finding her mother's body. There was no way I was going to let what happened twenty years ago ruin my life. My dad's life. You understand, don't you?"

"No, I don't. You've killed three people!"

"I'll do anything for my family."

"You won't get away with this."

"I think I will." Gail stepped forward. "Let's see . . . oh, I know. You're in an unfamiliar space, it's dark, and you're in a hurry to catch up with your students when you trip and fall down the stairs. And. Break. Your. Neck."

Chills skittered down Hope's spine. Gail had the whole scene planned out.

Gail lunged and grabbed Hope's arm.

Hope stretched her free arm, which held her bag, and swung it at Gail. The bag struck Gail's head and stunned her enough to lose the hold on the knife and it fell, landing with a clank on the floor. Hope darted around Gail and headed toward the exit.

She didn't get far. Gail recovered and was right behind her. She yanked Hope by her hair.

Hope elbowed Gail in the stomach and heard her groan.

With Gail feeling the strike, Hope stomped on her foot, forcing Gail to let go of her. As she turned to face Gail, she balled up her hand into a fist and swung at her attacker's face, striking her. Gail lost her balance and staggered sideways.

She had no idea where this was coming from, but she was in the fight of her life and she had no choice but to fight dirty, using everything she had.

Hope lifted her leg and kicked it into Gail's midsection, forcing the woman to stumble backward, cursing as she took the hit and fell to the floor.

Hope didn't care if Gail was hurt or what she was saying. She just needed to get out of the library. She spun around, ready to flee, when she saw Elaine walking down the corridor.

"There you are! I've been calling you!" Elaine stopped and propped a hand on her jutted-out hip. "What is going on?"

"Don't just stand there! Call 9-1-1!" Hope scrambled to grab her phone, not sure if it was damaged.

"Not until you tell me what's going on," Elaine said defiantly.

"She was going to kill me! Okay? Never mind." Hope had her phone in her hand, and aside from its cracked screen, it worked. "I'll call."

"Hope!" Ethan's voice bellowed from the entry, followed by rushed footsteps. "Hope! What happened?"

"That's what I asked and all I got was attitude," Elaine said, rolling her eyes.

"It was her! She's the killer!" Hope pointed to Gail, who was making a run for the knife when Ethan blew past Hope and Elaine to grab Gail. There was very little struggle on his part to get control over Gail and handcuff her.

"She's crazy! She attacked me!" Gail resisted Ethan's grip of her arm.

"What kind of class were you running?" Elaine asked, shaking her head.

Hope sucked in several deep breaths before she could think clearly. One of the first thoughts she was able to process was the one to ignore Elaine.

"You need to arrest her!" Gail demanded.

Hope shouldn't have been surprised by Gail's attempt, but she was still stunned by the audacity of the woman.

"Nice try." With her shaky hand, Hope held up her phone. "I recorded everything. I can send you a transcript," she said to Ethan after she tapped on the app to close it.

"Recording me without my consent is illegal! Isn't it?" Gail looked to Ethan.

"Tell it to your lawyer." Ethan read Gail her rights and then called in the incident on his radio. Minutes later, several officers rushed into the room. One took custody of Gail and escorted her out of the building.

While Gail was handed over to the officers, Hope settled on the bench in the corridor and dropped her head into her hands. Her whole body shook, and her mind raced with *what-ifs*: if if she'd left earlier, if she hadn't been able to fend Gail off, if Ethan hadn't arrived when he did, if Elaine hadn't strolled in.

Don't go there.

Hope steadied her breathing. Inhale. Exhale. Repeat.

"Hey, how are you doing?" Ethan asked as he squatted down to be at eye level with her.

She lifted her head from her hands and stared into his caring eyes, thankful he'd showed up. Heck, she was thankful Elaine showed up. Never in a million years would she ever have imagined that scenario

"Okay, I think."

"Do you need to go to the hospital?"

"No. I wasn't hurt. Is she gone?"

Ethan glanced over his shoulder. "Yes. She's going to

be processed and held until tomorrow morning for her hearing." He sat next to Hope. "You'll need to make a statement. But you're used to doing that." He offered a smile. His attempt to lighten the mood.

"Yes, I am. Was Gail right about not being able to use the recording I made?"

"Don't worry about that now. What happened?"

"I was getting ready to leave and she came in. I'd thought Alec had killed Joyce and Ernie had gotten rid of her body. Turns out I was half right."

"How did you figure it out?" He sat next to her.

"Something Ernie said. He made a comment about older women getting flower tattoos. Joyce had a rose tattoo. Also, he gave Gail her phone when I was there. It was different from the one I saw her with the other day. I bet it's Devon's. I had no idea Gail was the killer until she mentioned the knife."

"Guess you can only go for so long without slipping up."

"Twenty years." Hope rested her hand on Ethan's thigh. "Why did you come here? How did you know?"

Ethan caressed her cheek. "I was at the diner picking up dinner when I saw your class gathered waiting for you. Then I listened to your voice mail and thought I should check on you. Little did I know I'd find you confronting a killer. Again."

Hope covered his hand with hers and squeezed. "Well, I had no idea that's what I'd be doing tonight."

"Are you sure you're okay?"

Hope rested her head on Ethan's shoulder. "I will be." She stayed there for a little while longer and allowed her mind to stop churning over the incident. With a nudge from Ethan, she picked up her laptop bag from the floor and gathered her belongings. It was time to leave.

"I might have broken my computer tonight." She hitched the strap of her tote over her shoulder. If it was broken, it was a small price to pay to save her life.

"We'll worry about that tomorrow. Come on." Ethan slung his arm around Hope. She felt like he didn't want to let her out of his control. Not in a bad way, but she'd worried him again by putting herself in danger. If he was a little overprotective, so be it.

"I can't believe how close I came to almost being killed tonight," Elaine said in a breathy voice as she approached Hope and Ethan. She'd been questioned by another officer about what she'd seen and heard when she arrived at the library.

"Yes, it was a close call for you." While Hope didn't have the energy for Elaine's dramatics, she couldn't be irritated by her either. It definitely was a conundrum. "Why did you come? I thought you had a date tonight?"

Elaine sighed deeply. "I did. But it was over the first course that I found out he was married. Not divorced, like he led me to believe. I make it a rule not to date married men."

"Sounds like a good rule." Ethan's hold on Hope tightened.

Elaine's head swayed from side to side, as if she wasn't completely sure having morals was a good thing. Hope guessed the guy was really rich and walking out on him wasn't an easy thing for Elaine to do.

"We'll see." Elaine's hand covered her heart. "This near-death experience makes me grateful to be alive. And I don't think I want to be in stuffy classrooms learning geeky stuff. Thanks, Hope, but I won't be needing any private tutoring."

Hope bit her lip to keep from smiling. "Whatever will you do?"

Ethan squeezed her shoulder as a reminder to play nice.

"You know, I was thinking about becoming a real estate agent." Her shoulders shimmied. "Drive people around and show them houses. How hard can it be? I'm sure Claire will be more than happy to help me."

"I'm sure she will," Hope said.

Elaine nodded in agreement. "Well, I must get home. Toodles!" She pivoted and strutted out of the building, leaving the remaining officers to stop what they were doing to watch her leave.

"Are you sure you're okay?" Ethan asked, returning his attention to Hope.

"Yes, I am. I promise."

"Good. I need to get my officer's mouths up off the floor." He stood and headed for Jefferson's finest.

Hope leaned back and prepared for her next stop. The PD to give her statement. She was there for a couple of hours, giving her statement and then reviewing it before she signed it. The officer who took her statement made a comment: "Quite a night you had." Now, there was an understatement.

When she arrived home, Ethan let Bigelow out while Hope put the kettle on the stove and waited patiently for the water to boil. Normally, she busied herself with tidying up a counter or replying to an email while she waited, but not tonight. She stood there at the stovetop and stared at her blue kettle.

The shrieking whistle startled her. She'd drifted back to the moment Gail pulled out the knife.

Was it really the knife she'd used to kill Joyce? She shook off the dark thought and made her cup of tea.

A gentle purr drew her attention to Princess. She settled on the sofa with her tea and the cat. The white puff ball snuggled against her leg and allowed Hope to pet her long, white hair. Bigelow settled beside Hope's foot when he returned inside and chewed on a biscuit.

She blew on her tea to cool it and in a little while her cell phone chimed again with another text notification. She glanced at the phone. Word spread quickly through Jefferson about Gail and Ernie's arrests.

She stroked Princess and sipped her tea. All the texts would have to wait until tomorrow. Hope needed time to process what had just happened. She needed to find the answer to the question nagging her. How had someone she'd known since grade school managed to turn into a cold-blooded killer?

Chapter Nineteen

"Are you sure you don't want to stay while I record the podcast?" Hope asked as she inspected Devon's podcast equipment all set out on her kitchen table. Her nerves were still frayed from last night's encounter with Gail, and now her stomach quivered as she thought about recording the podcast.

When she'd called Felice earlier, it had seemed like a good idea. Now? She had her doubts.

"I'm sure." She dabbed her eyes with a tissue. She'd seemed relieved to hand over the equipment.

After Felice unpacked the box of equipment, Hope gave her the earrings Joyce had left at the antique shop all those years ago. Hope had planned on giving them to her friend at the funeral, but now, alone in the kitchen, she thought it was the right time to give Joyce's earrings to her daughter. Hope had cleaned the earrings before setting them in a small jewelry box.

Felice cried when Hope explained where the jewelry came from, and she quickly changed out her diamond studs for her mother's delicate earrings.

"I don't know how I can ever repay you for everything you've done. You almost got yourself killed." Felice's gratitude was eclipsed by her grief from her losses, almost exactly twenty years apart. She tucked her stud earrings into the box.

Hope didn't want anything in return for what she'd done. She was glad justice was finally being served. Even if it took twenty years.

"I thought Gail was my friend. I thought I knew her, but . . ." Felice's voice hitched. "But I knew nothing about her. How could I not have seen how evil she was?"

Hope reached out and rubbed Felice's arm. "People like her are very careful to let others only see certain things. I thought we were friends too."

The discovery of Gail's true colors chipped away at Hope's heart. Once again, she had to face the fact that people could be horrible and cruel. Fortunately, those individuals were few and far between.

Felice's chin trembled. "I don't know what it says about me, because I believed her lies all these years."

"Hey, we all did. There's nothing wrong with you or me. This is all on Gail and her father."

"I guess you're right. I also guess it'll take some time to come to terms with everything that has happened." Felice adjusted the purse strap on her shoulder. "I should get going. Thank you for recording the last episode of the podcast."

"It's my honor to do so. Call me, okay?"

Felice smiled and gave Hope a final hug before leaving the house. With the door closed and Felice heading toward her car, Hope let out a sigh of relief. Though she didn't say it out loud, she was thankful Felice opted not to stay and listen. She really didn't want an audience for the recording of the final episode of *Search for the Missing*.

While Hope had waited for Felice to arrive, she'd done an online search on how to operate the equipment. She'd never recorded a podcast before, but had been thinking about starting one for her blog. Now was her chance to take podcasting for a test drive.

Hope gathered up all the equipment and carried it to her office. The late morning sun streamed into the room, warming the space and reminding her that it was a good day for a good day. She first saw the saying years ago on a sign when shopping the Elephant's Trunk Flea Market in New Milford. She didn't get it then.

Now she did.

Last night, she'd come face-to-face with a killer and managed to escape unharmed.

Today was most certainly a good day for a good day.

She tucked her chair under her desk. Her stomach fluttered, creating a cold space threatening to overtake her. She inhaled a deep breath.

I can do this.

Set up on her desk was all of Devon's podcasting equipment. What Devon used wasn't fancy or expensive. It was functional and, lucky for Hope, it was easy to get set up quickly.

She was all ready to go. The coldness in her belly grew. It was her nerves, and she was second-guessing her decision. Was recording the episode the right thing to do? Felice had given her blessing. She believed it was a good idea to bring closure to Joyce's story and to tell Devon's listeners about the tragic ending of her life.

No pressure there.

Hope took in another deep breath, released it, and then pressed the Record button before she changed her mind. She leaned forward to the microphone.

"Welcome to the final installment of *Search for the Missing*." She heard her voice, too soft, too fast. She had to try it again. "Welcome to the final installment of *Search for the Missing*." Better. She continued. "I'm Hope Early, in for Devon Markham."

She paused and swallowed the lump in her throat.

"Devon began this podcast to work through her own emotions about her mother's disappearance twenty years ago and recently had begun her own investigation. She took you along with her as she dug into the case. Sadly, Devon is not here with us any longer to continue this podcast.

"I'm recording this episode because her quest to find out the truth about her mother's disappearance led to Devon's own death, which has been classified as a homicide. Gail Graves and her father, Ernie Graves, have been arrested for the murders of Joyce Markham, Devon Markham, and Donna Wilcox, a friend of Joyce's and my attempted murder.

"So as not to compromise the case that will be brought against Gail and her father, I'm not going to share the conversation I had with Gail last night, or describe what occurred before the police arrived. All of that will come out soon enough."

Her throat tightened as the struggle with Gail flashed in her mind.

Get it together, girl.

"What I want to tell you today is about the Devon I knew all those years ago. And I want to share with you her mother's sugar cookie recipe. Yes, I know this isn't a foodie podcast. Please, bear with me."

Along with the podcast equipment, Felice had dropped off her mother's cookie recipe, which she got from her aunt. It seemed fitting to share it with Devon's listeners.

"Devon wanted answers not only about her mother's case, but about the other cases she covered on this podcast. She wanted to make sure those women were not forgotten. I'd like to encourage all of you to consider making Joyce's cookies. While we can't always find justice, we can bake a little kindness and share it with those around us. Maybe we all can bake the world a nicer place to be, and podcasts like this won't be needed any longer."

Sharing her memories of Devon from high school helped Hope become more at ease in front of the microphone. She fell into a natural rhythm and even laughed at a few of the memories.

There were a few stories she'd long forgotten about, but they popped into her head as she continued to talk. There would be a lot of editing to do later, but maybe she'd just put it out there real and raw.

Hope turned off the recording and removed the headset. The session had run well over an hour. Too long for a podcast episode, in her opinion. Once she began talking, she couldn't stop, and that surprised her. She'd never thought she'd feel so at ease recording. She was one of those people who didn't like the sound of her own voice, and that made editing her videos challenging for her.

Now she needed to edit the session.

But first, she had a cake to bake.

Two hours later, with the podcast recorded and the kitchen cleaned up from her baking session, the timer dinged, signaling to Hope that her two-layers of marble cake were ready to come out of the oven. She savored the moment of opening the oven door and inhaling the heavenly scent of fresh-baked cake.

She wasn't the only one in the house intoxicated by the fragrance. Bigelow had come trotting in with his nose held high.

She eyed her dog. He'd never turn down food, but she wasn't about to offer him any of the cake. Leaving the layers to cool, she went for the container of his homemade treats. She gave him one and he chomped and swallowed. A quick lick to his lips and he was ready for another one.

"Okay. One more. But that's it." She handed over another peanut butter cookie and then fastened the lid and returned it to its spot on the countertop. The front doorbell rang, and she passed by Bigelow, patting him on the head.

At the front door, she peeped out the side window and then smiled.

She opened the door to her very much welcome visitor.

"Hi, Amy."

"Hey, Hope. Do you have a minute?"

"Of course. Come on in." By the time Hope closed the

door, Bigelow had joined them and was relishing the attention from their guest. "Let me take your coat."

"It's okay. I can't stay long. I know you must be busy." Amy unzipped her parka.

Hope nodded. She wasn't going to argue. She had to frost the cake, photograph it, and then take it over to Iva's house. A little peace offering, she hoped.

"Do I smell cake?"

"You do. It just came out of the oven. Come on." She led Amy into the kitchen. "It's a marble cake. Don't mind the mess." She was referring to the photography equipment set up around the table and the various serving pieces laid out for her to choose from after she frosted the cake.

Amy stopped at the island and looked at the two cooling cake pans. "The smell is intoxicating."

Hope retrieved a plate from an upper cabinet and turned out the first cake layer and rested it on the cooling rack. "It's taking all my strength not to dive into them." She turned out the second cake layer. "What brings you by?"

"I came to apologize for my behavior the other day. I was awful to you." Amy's gaze flicked downward, and her shoulders slumped.

Hope reached out and touched Amy's arm. "If it was my mother, I probably would have behaved the same way."

"No. You wouldn't have. I blew up and said things I'm so very sorry for."

"I accept your apology. How's your mom doing?"

Amy shrugged. "Right now, she's so upset about Donna. I can't believe Gail killed her. Or Devon and her mother. I thought we knew Gail."

"It seems like we don't really know people the way we think we do."

"I guess you're right." Amy glanced at her watch. "I'd better get going. Thank you for accepting my apology."

"I'm glad we're past the incident." Hope hugged Amy and then walked her to the door. "Be careful driving." A new round of snow had begun falling and the forecast wasn't good. The B-word was still being used. *Again*. Another blizzard was on the horizon. It looked as if her weekend getaway with Ethan wasn't going to happen.

A woof drew her attention toward the kitchen. Knowing her dog as well as she did, she wasn't surprised to find him seated beside the island with his snout in the air, sniffing the cake. But it was Princess who drew her interest. The cat slinked by with a tube of Hope's berry-flavored lip balm and trotted up the staircase.

"No. It couldn't be." *Or, could it*? Hope followed the fluffy feline up the stairs and down the hall to the bathroom. The door was ajar, and Princess slipped into the room. Hope pushed the door open and entered. Princess looked up at Hope, her eyes wide open, and inched slowly back with the tube of lip balm still in her mouth. "What are you doing, sweetie?" Hope kept her voice soft, and she peered around the door and found her bracelet and mascara.

Those two items were piled on top of a green washcloth and a pair of socks Hope had thought she'd misplaced a month ago. The little fur ball must have raided the laundry basket.

"You gotta be kidding me." Hope looked back at her cat. "You really are the thief. Iva was right." She expelled an aggravated breath. "You know what this means, don't you? I have to apologize to her. Good thing I baked the cake." She walked around to the other side of the door and retrieved her missing belongings and then took the lip balm tube out of Princess' mouth. "You can't keep stealing things." Princess blinked twice and then strolled out of the bathroom.

Clearly, the cat was having none of the lecture. Hope stood with her belongings cradled in her hands. She had to give it to the cat for finding a good hiding spot. Hope rarely came into the room because it was in dire need of a remodel. The tile floor was grimy and chipped. And then there was the tub and sink. Both were ancient, and the toilet looked unstable. The room definitely needed a makeover and she had big plans for it. All she needed was a big budget.

She carried her items out of the bathroom and dropped them off in her bedroom before returning to the kitchen to frost and photograph the cake.

Hope braved the wind on the front porch of Iva's rental house. She'd recently moved so she could have her mother stay with her. On the other side of the door, she heard footsteps approaching, and then the door opened.

"Didn't expect to see you here." Iva took a drag of her cigarette.

Not much of a greeting, but because it was Iva, Hope hadn't expected much more.

"I came to apologize to you." Hopefully, Iva would be as forgiving as Hope was earlier with Amy. "And I brought you a cake!" Hope lifted the cake box up higher and smiled.

"Cake, huh? You think you can make up for accusing me of stealing with a cake?"

Iva had no intention of making this easy for Hope. "It's a marble cake with chocolate frosting. I remember you saying it's your favorite cake."

Iva rolled her eyes. "All right, come on in."

Thank goodness. It was freezing out there. Hope dashed inside and followed Iva to the small but functional kitchen. Rental bland with no pops of color, it was all white, with well-used appliances.

"Set it on the table." Iva busied herself with gathering the plates, forks, and a cake knife. "There's coffee if you want some. Help yourself." She took a final drag of her cigarette and discarded it in an ashtray on the countertop.

Hope poured a cup of coffee and pulled out a milk carton from the refrigerator. "I'm sorry I suspected that you stole my bracelet and mascara." She sat at the table.

"Mascara? I'd never steal mascara from someone. That's unsanitary." Iva opened the box and pulled out the cake.

Good to know Iva had boundaries.

Iva cut two generous slices. "My mother will enjoy a slice of this later when she wakes up from her nap." She set a plate in front of Hope and then closed the lid of the box after sitting down with her plate. She took a forkful and chewed. "This is delicious."

"Thank you." Hope ate her bite and concurred with Iva's assessment. The cake was moist, and the flavors of the two layers and the frosting mingled together, creating a very happy moment for her taste buds.

"I'm guessing you found the missing items."

Hope swallowed her second bite of the cake. Now it was time to fess up about who the real thief was and brace for Iva's I-told-you-so speech.

"I did. It was Princess." She dipped her head and ate another piece of cake.

"Aha! I told you so! Cats are sneaky little creatures. Where'd you find her loot?"

"The upstairs hall bathroom."

"Sneaky and smart. She knows you don't go in there." Iva ate another bite of cake. "I accept your apology."

"You do?"

"Yeah. I understand why you thought it may have been me. There was a time in my life when I wasn't the most honest person. But I'm trying not to be that person anymore."

"I know you are."

"It's going to take time for me to rebuild trust with everyone."

"Rebuilding trust doesn't come quick, but I think it's worth it. I need to work on being less judgmental."

"We all got something we need to improve, don't we? I thought by now I'd have my whole life figured out."

"We did have big plans back in high school, didn't we?"

"We did. But I guess it's not too late to try to make them happen. I mean, it's the least we can do for Devon."

Iva's sentiment struck Hope hard. Devon had wanted to see justice done for her mother. She'd ended up giving her life for that justice.

"You're right. Look, we have our rocky history, but I'd like to be a part of your big plans. Will you come back to work for me?"

Iva took another forkful of cake and chewed it slowly. After she swallowed, she nodded. "Yeah, I'll come back."

"Wait, there's one more thing."

Iva tilted her head. "Really? After you accused me of stealing?"

"Do you know a snowplow guy I can hire? A blizzard is coming."

Iva burst out laughing. "I know a guy. But don't go and accuse him of murder."

Hope joined Iva and laughed. "I promise I won't. I'm done with this amateur sleuthing thing."

Chapter Twenty

Five days later and the weather forecast hadn't changed. It only became more distressing. The state had a big bull's-eye on it and a blizzard was indeed heading for Jefferson.

"You love a brisk walk, don't you?" Hope chuckled as she kept up with Bigelow. He was focused on his walk and greeting the few people who passed them on Main Street. Each one of them smiled at Hope and then acknowledged Bigelow, and he ate up the attention. Because she had him with her, a stop into The Coffee Clique wasn't in the cards. While the owners may have overlooked his species, she knew it was against health regulations, and it only took one disgruntled customer to cause all sorts of problems. It was for the best, really. She didn't need a cinnamon bun. Her deal with Mama Mia Pasta meant she had to develop six recipes using their various pastas. Later in the day, she'd be making a Triple Cheese Lasagna for dinner, and there were plenty of calories in even the smallest serving.

"Good morning, Hope!" Angela came to a halt on her way up the shoveled walkway to the library's main entrance. She bent over to pat Bigelow on the head. "He looks so dapper in his red plaid jacket. I can't believe another blizzard is coming our way. Is this winter ever going to end?"

Hope shared the sentiment. Snowflakes had begun falling as Hope and Bigelow set out on their walk. They were both bundled up in their coats, so she continued with their planned outing.

The blizzard meant Ethan couldn't get away for their trip to Vermont. To say she was disappointed would be a major understatement. She'd planned her wardrobe, borrowing ski clothes from Claire, and looked forward to drinking hot cocoa by the lodge's fireplace. She was looking forward not only to a long weekend of being alone with Ethan, but also to a few days of being disconnected from the rest of the world. No phone, no social media, no comments, no murderers.

It'd been almost a week since she was held at knifepoint by Gail in the library. Hope glanced at the stately brick building. So many wonderful things had happened in there over her lifetime; she'd discovered new authors, faraway places, and her love for reading. And she'd almost been killed in there too.

"I'm still getting so much positive feedback on the blogging class. Is there any chance you're open to doing another one?" Angela looked hopeful.

Hope's immediate reply was going to be a firm "no."

But she wasn't sure if the answer was coming from the fact of nearly being killed by a student or if she wanted to pursue creating an online course. The downside to producing the course would be the financial investment and the time it would take creating all the modules. The upside was that once she created the course, she wouldn't have to go out to the library or somewhere else to teach the course. That meant more time for herself and a nice passive income stream. Two things bloggers loved.

"I'll think about it. We'd better get going back home before the snow starts coming down harder." Hope tugged on Bigelow's leash, and Angela said her goodbyes to both of them. Hope picked up her pace and encouraged her pup to do the same. The snowflakes were bigger and coming down more fiercely. It was definitely a day to hunker down inside and cook.

When Hope and Bigelow returned home, she got to work on the lasagna. By the time Claire and the kids arrived, the main dish was in the oven cooking and the worse of the storm hadn't arrived yet. That gave Logan and Hannah time to play outside until supper was ready.

Hope pulled the mudroom door closed behind her as she stepped outside. She folded her arms across her chest and rubbed her arms. She should have layered up before venturing outside to get the kids. Hannah screamed and ducked when her brother threw a round of snowballs at her. Logan laughed loudly as he kept the snowballs flying.

She smiled at the sight of them fully engaged in a good, old-fashioned snowball fight. Maretta had backed down from her proposal to ban the activity, and Hope was certain kids across Jefferson were celebrating their victory today. Logan had gotten over a hundred signatures on his petition, which he'd walked into Town Hall and presented to Maretta. Hope wished she could have been there for the moment; according to Claire, it was a priceless moment. Maretta's demeanor was respectful, and she even thanked Logan for his activism. What Hope would have given to be a fly on the wall when Maretta returned to her office.

With all the publicity on the arrests of Gail and Ernie, Maretta had more important matters to tend to than pursuing a ban on snowball throwing. Good grief, what had she been thinking?

"Hey, you two! Dinner is almost ready!" She'd taken the three-cheese lasagna out of the oven and set it on a trivet to rest, while Claire tossed a salad and sliced the freshly baked loaf of bread Hope had made.

The kids stopped playing and brushed off the snow from their jackets as Drew drove into the driveway. He'd borrowed Hope's Explorer to pick up Sally and Jane, who were coming for an early supper before the roads were inevitably closed. The car doors opened, and the Merrifield sisters-in-laws stepped out, both wearing snow boots and their warmest coats. Drew dashed around the vehicle and guided them toward the house.

The driveway and path had been cleared by Hope's new plow guy, Iva's brother. With more than a foot of snow forecast, he'd definitely be back several more times before tomorrow morning.

"Isn't it lovely? The snow on the tree branches and endless stretches of snow-covered fields." Jane passed Hope and entered the house with Sally behind her.

"She wasn't the one trudging out to feed our rooster this morning," Sally quipped as she entered the house.

Hope pressed her lips together. She felt Sally's pain about

feeding the flock. She had ventured out in the dark, cold morning to feed her own chickens.

Helga griped as usual, while Poppy had flown up onto the workbench, where Hope had mixed together the supplements for their water. Poppy stayed long enough for Hope to stroke her feathers. She was pretty sure Poppy would enjoy living inside the house. Though Princess would have a big problem with that.

"The roads are clear for now." Drew held the door open for the kids and Hope. "Good thing we're eating early. Who knows what it'll be like later?"

Hope and Claire set out the food on the table. Hope's phone rang, and it was Ethan.

"Hey, are you coming? I made a three-cheese lasagna," she said, hoping to tempt him.

"Sorry, I can't. Look, about our weekend . . ."

"Don't worry about it. They said we could reschedule because of the weather. We'll just go another weekend." She sighed, leaning against the refrigerator.

"Are you sure?"

"I am. Drew will be driving Sally and Jane home, so I'll have him drop off some lasagna for you."

"I heard my name. What am I doing?" Drew asked from the table.

"It's amazing how his hearing can be so good at some times, while at others, not so much." Hope laughed. "Call me later."

"Will do. Love you."

"Love you too." She disconnected the call.

"Aww," the whole table said in unison.

"Ha ha. Very funny." Hope walked to the table and sat. She wanted to be irritated at them for eavesdropping, but their silly grins had her laughing instead. She reached for the salad bowl and added a heaping mound to her plate.

"This lasagna is delicious." Jane set down her fork. "We must get the recipe, right, Sally?"

"Of course. You've outdone yourself." Sally took another bite of her pasta dish.

"It'll be published soon." Hope worked the lasagna pan to cut a wedge and carefully transferred it to her plate.

"Speaking of published. I heard your podcast. It was very moving. Good job." Sally patted Hope's hand.

"Devon would have approved," Jane said.

"Thank you," Hope said. She broke off a piece of lasagna with her fork. As they ate their meal, they talked about anything but murder and the weather. Finally, rounds of laughter filled the room, as well as sibling bickering between Hannah and Logan. But there was a collective "oohing" when Hope presented a plate of whimsically decorated sugar cookies for dessert.

Claire carried the coffeepot to the table and set it on the trivet. "You're pretty pleased with yourself, aren't you?"

Hope looked at her sister, puzzled by the statement. "What are you talking about?"

"The podcast, getting a confession from Gail, and now these cookies." Claire reached for one and took a bite.

"How do they taste?" Hope asked. After reading Joyce's recipe, she'd realized her own cookie recipe was similar to it. So, when she began baking, she decided to follow Joyce's recipe. It only seemed right.

Claire swallowed her bite. "Delicious. Like Sally said, you've outdone yourself." She finished the rest of the cookie as Hope looked on with amazement. Pasta, bread, and now a cookie. Claire was playing loose and fast with carbs. "About what happened the other day with Amy about her mom . . . we're good, right?"

Hope smiled as she pulled her sister in for a hug. "Always and forever."

RECIPES

THREE-CHEESE LASAGNA
posted by Hope Early

When you add cheese to any recipe, you know you're going to have an amazing meal. Add three cheeses— well, technically four—and we're talking about off-the-charts yumminess. I love the comfort of a casserole meal whether I'm making it in the colder months or during the summer. Serving all those around my table from one dish and seeing the eyes light up as all the cheese pulls into gooey (yes, it's a culinary term) strings yumminess. I know, I've used that word twice so far, but it fits when writing about this recipe. You can make this recipe healthier if you choose, use whole wheat noodles, but I like to live on the edge, so I use regular boil noodles. Enjoy!

Ingredients
Olive oil, to coat the baking dish
9–12 lasagna noodles
1 cup full-fat ricotta cheese
1 egg
¼ cup grated Parmigiano Reggiano cheese
Zest of 1 lemon
½ teaspoon kosher salt, or to taste if you prefer
Ground pepper, to taste
6 ounces grated mozzarella
6 ounces grated sharp white cheddar
6 ounces grated fontina cheese
24 ounces marinara sauce

Directions
Preheat oven to 375 degrees. Coat a 2-quart baking dish with olive oil, then set aside to prepare lasagna.

Cook the lasagna noodles, according to the package directions, until al dente. Then rinse under cold water and lay the noodles flat while you prepare the filling.

In a medium bowl, combine the ricotta cheese, egg, Parmigiano Reggiano, lemon zest, salt, and pepper. Set aside.

In another bowl, combine the remaining three cheeses. Set aside.

Begin building the lasagna. Spread a light layer of the marinara sauce on the bottom of the baking dish. Lay 3–4 noodles lengthwise over the sauce.

Layer one-third of the remaining marinara sauce over the noodles. Then cover with half of the ricotta cheese and then spread one-third of the three-cheese mixture over the ricotta. Repeat the pattern of noodles, sauce, ricotta cheese, three-cheese mixture one more time.

Top with a final layer of noodles, then add remaining three-cheese mixture.

Bake lasagna for about 45 minutes or until the top cheese is melted and golden.

Remove from oven and allow to cool, between 10 to 15 minutes, before serving.

RUSTIC APPLE PIE
posted by Hope Early

Growing up, I knew fall was right around the corner when Mom took me and my sister, Claire, apple picking. We'd spend the afternoon filling bushels with all varieties of apples and tossing around ideas about what we'd bake. Of all the options we came up with, my favorite was and still is, apple pie. Any type of apple pie. Regular, deep dish, or single crust. As long as there's crust involved, I'm good. I love this recipe because it's fast and easy. One crust, a few apples* and cinnamon, and in no time, I'm scooping out vanilla ice cream and serving this dessert to my friends and family. It also makes a great late-night snack. No judging.

Ingredients

For the crust:
1½ cup all-purpose flour
½ teaspoon salt
2 tablespoons granulated sugar
1½ sticks unsalted butter, cold and cut into ½-inch
    pieces
¼ cup iced water

For the filling:
1¾ lbs. baking apples*
⅓ cup granulated sugar
1 teaspoon vanilla extract
1 teaspoon cinnamon
2 tablespoons unsalted butter, melted
⅛ teaspoon salt

To assemble and bake:

1 tablespoon all-purpose flour

1 egg, beaten

2 tablespoons granulated or turbinado sugar

1 tablespoon apricot jam for optional glaze

Directions:

To make the crust:

Line a baking sheet with parchment paper.

In a food processor fitted with a steel blade, combine flour, salt, and sugar. Pulse to combine. Add the cold butter and process until the butter is the size of peas.

Sprinkle the ice water into the mixture and process until moistened and crumbly.

Transfer dough onto a floured surface and knead until the dough comes together in a ball.

Pat the dough into a disk.

Flour the surface again and lightly dust the dough with flour. With a rolling pin, roll dough out into a circle of 8 to 10 inches in diameter, turning and adding more flour as necessary so the dough doesn't stick. Be careful not to use too much flour.

Transfer the dough to the parchment-lined baking sheet and refrigerate while you prepare the filling.

To make the filling:

Peel and core the apples and then cut them into ⅛-inch slices and place in a large bowl. Add in the sugar, vanilla, cinnamon, melted butter, and salt. Toss everything to combine.

Clean up your work surface.

Remove the dough from the refrigerator and slide the parchment paper onto the countertop. Keeping the dough on the parchment paper, roll the dough into a 14-inch circle and about ⅛-inch thick. The edges don't have to be perfect. Return the parchment and dough back to the baking sheet; the dough will hang over the edges of the pan.

To assemble the pie:

Sprinkle the tablespoon of flour over the dough. Arrange the apple slices, keeping them 3 inches from the edge of the dough. Overlap the slices to form concentric circles. Fold the edges of the dough over the apples in a free-form fashion, creating pleats as you go. Patch any tears by pinching a bit of dough from the edge. This doesn't have to look perfect. It's a rustic pie.

With a pastry brush, brush the pleated dough with the beaten egg. Then sprinkle with sugar over the top of the crust and half the fruit. Chill the pie in the refrigerator for 15 minutes.

Preheat the oven to 350 degrees and set a rack in the center of the oven.

To bake the pie:

Bake for 55 to 65 minutes, or until the apples are tender and the crust is golden and cooked through. Transfer the pan to a rack and let cool.

Meanwhile, make the optional glaze. In a microwave-safe bowl, mix the apricot jam with 1½ teaspoons water. Heat in microwave until bubbling, about 20 seconds. With a pastry brush, brush the apples with the syrup.

Carefully transfer the pie to a serving platter or cutting board. Slice and serve warm or at room temperature. This pie is best served on the day it's made, but no one has ever turned down a leftover slice.

ONE-BOWL BROWNIES
posted by Hope Early

One bowl, a few ingredients, and you'll have delicious chocolate brownies in no time. These are great to whip up for my nephew's softball games or my niece's sleepovers or for me and my sister when we're hanging out together. Yes, Claire will indulge in a brownie every now and again. I mean, how could she not? And you'll be finding yourself whipping up these brownies every chance you get. They're that good.

Ingredients
1 cup butter, melted and cooled
1 cup granulated sugar
1 cup brown sugar, packed
4 large eggs
1 tablespoon vanilla extract
1 cup all-purpose flour
1 cup Dutch-processed or unsweetened cocoa powder
1 teaspoon kosher salt
$1\frac{1}{4}$ cup chopped chocolate, divided

Directions
Preheat oven to 350 degrees. Spray a 9x13-inch baking dish. Line with parchment paper with an overhang on the sides and spray again. This extra step will make it easy to lift out the brownies when they are baked.

In a large mixing bowl, combine melted butter, granulated sugar, brown sugar, eggs, and vanilla extract and stir until smooth.

Sift in flour and cocoa to the mixture. Add in the salt. Don't overmix.

Fold in 1 cup of chopped chocolate.

Spread evenly into prepared dish and sprinkle the remaining ¼ cup chopped chocolate on top of brownies.

Bake for 25 to 50 minutes on the middle rack until brownies are set to touch. Don't overbake. They will set up as they cool. Remove from oven and set on cooling rack. Cool before cutting into squares.

How many servings you get will be decided upon how big your squares are.

You can store any leftover brownies for up to 4 days, but there usually are never any leftovers.

SUNSHINE CORN MUFFINS
posted by Hope Early

It happened on a whim. I had some leftover lemon juice from a recipe and was mixing together my corn muffins for a Sunday brunch for Ethan, his daughters, and Drew. I had the batter all mixed and decided at the last minute to drop in the lemon juice. What could it hurt? Well, the muffins turned out wonderful. Moist, full corn flavor and a zip of citrus. They were definitely muffins that got your attention first thing in the morning, so I named them Sunshine Corn Muffins. Now, you can decide how much *sunshine* flavor you want. I like two tablespoons of lemon juice in my muffins, but Ethan prefers when I use only one tablespoon. It's turned into something similar to our chocolate chip cookie debate. You can even add in fresh orange juice. It's up to you. Bake what makes you happy.

Ingredients
1 cup cornmeal
1 cup all-purpose flour
⅓ cup granulated sugar
2 teaspoons baking powder
½ teaspoon salt
1 egg, beaten
¼ cup canola oil
1 cup milk
1–2 tablespoons lemon (or orange) juice

Directions
Preheat oven to 400 degrees. Grease or line muffin pan with paper liners.

In a large bowl, mix together cornmeal, flour, sugar, baking powder, and salt.

To dry ingredients, add in egg, oil, milk, and lemon juice. Stir gently to combine.

Spoon batter into prepared muffin cups.

Bake at 400 degrees for 15 to 20 minutes.

Remove muffin pan from oven and set on cooling rack. These are best eaten fresh out of the oven with butter.

SUGAR COOKIES
posted by Hope Early

Sugar cookies at Christmas are magical. They're light, delicate, sweet, and decorated. They are the cookies I always left for Santa, and I know he enjoyed mine the best because he always left a thank-you note telling me he did. But sugar cookies aren't just for Christmas. I bake them for Easter, Fourth of July, and on any random day I'm craving a perfect sugar cookie. Let's get into the recipe.

Ingredients
1 cup unsalted butter, room temperature
1 cup granulated sugar
1 large egg, room temperature
1 teaspoon vanilla extract
½ teaspoon almond extract
2 teaspoons baking powder
3 cups all-purpose flour, sifted

Directions
Preheat oven to 350 degrees. Prepare baking sheets with parchment paper or silicone liners.

In bowl of your stand mixer, add butter and beat on medium-high until butter is smooth and lighter in color, about 1–2 minutes.

Turn down mixer speed to low and slowly add in sugar and then the egg.

Add in vanilla and almond extracts and combine fully.

Add in the baking powder and then the flour, adding a ½ cup at a time, until fully incorporated. Be careful not to overmix.

Drop dough onto a clean and floured work surface. Roll out into a flat disc, about ¼-inch thick.

Cut cookies into desired shapes and bake for 6 to 8 minutes. If you've cut out larger shapes, you may need to add an extra minute or so to the baking time.

Let cool on the cookie sheet until firm enough to transfer to a cooling rack.

A quick tip: After experimentation (aka a lot of sugar cookie baking fails), I've found chilling my cookie cutouts before I bake them helps to keep them from spreading while baking. It's an added step, but I think it's so worth it. What I do is place my cookie sheets with the cookies on them in the refrigerator for about 10 minutes before baking. When I'm doing a big cookie baking session, I'm rotating cookie sheets from fridge to oven.☺

DOUBLE CHOCOLATE
OATMEAL COOKIES
posted by Hope Early

There are times when I want all the cookies. I want the chocolate chip cookie, I want the oatmeal cookie, I want the chocolate walnut cookie. But eating three cookies—okay, I'd probably eat way more than just one of each—would be a little much and require me to up my daily running miles. So, what's a cookie lover do to? Well, if she's a food blogger, she figures out a way to have her cookies and eat them too. I give you my amazing Double Chocolate Oatmeal cookies. There's a lot in this cookie, and be forewarned: I advise using a heavy-duty stand mixer because there's a lot of dough. You'll also get a lot of cookies, depending how big you make your cookie mounds when you're shaping the dough. I typically freeze half the dough unless I'm baking these cookies for an event.

Ingredients
2 cups unsalted butter
2 cups granulated sugar
4 large eggs, beaten
2 teaspoons vanilla extract
4 cups all-purpose flour
2 teaspoons baking powder
2 teaspoons baking soda
1 teaspoon salt
5 cups old-fashioned rolled oats
24 ounces bittersweet chocolate chips, or chopped
8 ounces semisweet chocolate chips, or chopped
3 cups roughly chopped walnuts

Directions

Preheat oven to 375 degrees.

In stand mixer bowl, beat together butter and sugar until light in color and texture, about 3 minutes. Add eggs and vanilla and beat until combined.

In a medium bowl, whisk together the flour, baking powder, baking soda, and salt.

Add dry ingredients to the wet ingredients and mix together, careful not to overbeat.

Add oats to mixture and combine.

Then add in chocolate chips and nuts to mixture.

Form dough into golf-ball-size mounds. Place two inches apart on silicone baking sheets. Bake for 6 to 9 minutes, until tops are just golden and cookies are still soft.

Cool on baking racks.